Praise for *The Kill Club*

"An emotional rollercoaster ride...utterly genius."
—Carissa Ann Lynch, *USA TODAY* bestselling author
of *My Sister is Missing*

"AMAZING... One dark, addictive thrill ride of a book. It'll make you think about how far you would go to save someone you love...and make you a little paranoid about that stranger standing too close to you at Trader Joe's."
—Kathleen Barber, author of *Follow Me*

"The protagonist, Jazz, is dark, gritty, and determined, with a wicked sense of humor and an occasional tender side, but she certainly doesn't need anyone to save her... A knock-out thriller. Buckle up; you're in for one hell of a ride."
—Hannah Mary McKinnon, author of *Her Secret Son*

"A nonstop nail-biter...a must-read thriller."
—Diana Urban, author of *All Your Twisted Secrets*

"A breathless, chilling adventure...intricate and masterful plotting, surprises around every corner, and an ending that chilled me to the bone."
—Megan Collins, author of *The Winter Sister*

"Loved it! Intense, with multi-faceted characters, and twists that hit you over the head when you're least expecting it."
—Meghan O'Flynn, author of the Ash Park series

"An unputdownable thriller and a love letter to East LA."
—Halley Sutton, author of *The Lady Upstairs*

"Jazz is a char⬚⬚⬚⬚⬚⬚⬚⬚⬚⬚⬚⬚⬚⬚⬚⬚⬚⬚⬚⬚⬚⬚⬚⬚⬚⬚⬚. The
high-stakes te⬚⬚⬚⬚⬚⬚⬚⬚⬚⬚⬚⬚⬚⬚⬚⬚⬚⬚⬚⬚⬚t-wrenching
twist of *Black*⬚⬚⬚⬚⬚⬚⬚⬚⬚⬚⬚⬚⬚⬚⬚⬚⬚⬚⬚⬚⬚⬚⬚⬚⬚⬚

⬚⬚⬚⬚⬚ome and Get Me*

"This phenom⬚⬚⬚⬚⬚⬚⬚⬚⬚⬚⬚⬚⬚⬚⬚⬚⬚⬚⬚⬚⬚⬚⬚ial issues
without sacrific⬚⬚⬚ g a second of its action-movie pacing."
—Layne Fargo, author of *Temper*

Also by Wendy Heard

Hunting Annabelle

THE KILL CLUB

WENDY HEARD

mira

mira

ISBN-13: 978-0-7783-0903-1

The Kill Club

For questions and comments about the quality of this book, please contact us at CustomerService@Harlequin.com.

BookClubbish.com

Printed in U.S.A.

Recycling programs for this product may not exist in your area.

This is "riot city" after all.
—Luis J. Rodriguez

SATURDAY

1

JAZZ

SOMETHING IS ON fire. I can smell it.

I pull my truck up to the curb in front of Carol's little house. The street is quiet, the palm trees black against the charcoal night sky.

I roll down my window and inhale. Yeah. Fire. Somewhere east.

Joaquin is giggling wildly next to me. "A whole cup of coffee. He spilled it right on his teacher. I thought he was going to die. Literally. Die."

"Was the coffee hot?" I flick off my headlights.

Joaquin gasps. "Oh my God, what if it was hot?" A new round of hysterics seizes him. "And, Jazz, this kid is really shy. I felt so bad. It looked like the teacher peed her pants." His laughter rises an octave. He makes a weird squealing sound that sets me off, and now I'm laughing so hard I'm crying. Joaquin's told me about this math teacher, an authoritarian woman who carries a yardstick around like a nun from the eighteen hundreds.

I wipe my eyes. "Did he get in trouble?"

"Naw. She was actually kind of cool about it. Said it's what she gets for drinking too much coffee."

"That's good." I fix his long emo bangs, which have parted themselves dorkily straight down the middle. His hair is lighter than mine, more brown than black, like my biological mom.

"Stop," he protests and squirms away.

"Do you want to look like the nerd you are?" I grab him and force him to let me fix his hair.

The porch light goes on. Our faces snap toward it. My stomach sinks like I'm on an elevator. Carol. The name, even the thought of her, fills me with dread.

"The warden is watching," I say.

"She's so crazy right now, dude, she's back at that snake charmer church."

"No!" I groan. "Not again. I can't. I *can't*."

"She's speaking in tongues while she's making dinner and stuff. Abbadabba shrrramdabba hanna shackalacka…" He rolls his eyes back in his head and raises his hands. It's a perfect imitation of Carol. "She needs to pray to be a better cook. She burned the mac 'n' cheese yesterday, set the fire alarm off. How do you even burn mac 'n' cheese?"

I shake my head. "She's gonna try to make me go to church with her and repent for all my sins. Which is so tedious because, as you know, it is *quite* a list." I flip my visor down and examine my reflection, fixing my own bangs, which hang shaggy over my dark eyes. My eyeliner is a mess. I lick a finger and try to do damage control.

Joaquin gets his phone out and checks Snapchat. "She took my Miley Cyrus poster. Stole it while I was at school."

I shoot him a sideways look. "'Cause she knows you're jacking off to it, you little pervert."

He elbows me, which makes me jam my finger into my eye. I cry out in protest. He shoves me again. I raise a fist like I'm going to actually punch him, and he cowers dramatically. I return to my eyeliner and he returns to Snapchat. He sighs. "But yeah. She stole my precious Miley."

"In my day, we looked at the Victoria's Secret catalog like normal people."

He waves his phone at me. "Take some of the parental controls off this thing and I'll just look at other stuff on here."

"No way!"

"You know I've seen porn," he drawls in his most grown-up voice.

They don't prepare you for any of this. I turn toward him. "Just because you already saw it doesn't mean I want you to have access to the whole internet in your room all by yourself. There's some crazy shit out there."

"Worst sister," he grumbles.

"Best sister."

A corner of his mouth creases, mischievous. He has my crooked smile. "You're conservative because you're old."

"Shut up! You little shit." He knows I'm already feeling weird about turning thirty even though it's two years away.

The front door opens and Carol appears, a slim silhouette against the golden living room light. "Time's up," I say. "I hereby release you from my gay dungeon of sin and return you to your pristine temple of Jesus."

He grabs his backpack and pockets his phone. "Thanks for dinner."

I capture him in a tight hug and press my face into his sweatshirt, savoring the scents of school and deodorant and laundry detergent. "I love you, kid." He hugs me back, still sometimes cuddly despite the onset of puberty. I pull away and pat his cheek. "You're due for a refill on your insulin. Meet you after school Monday?"

"What about your show?" he asks.

"I don't have to be at the venue till nine. It's plenty of time." I grab his sleeve. "Are you taking care of yourself? Checking your blood sugar, tracking your carbs?"

"I'm fine. I'm being good." Unexpectedly, he leans over and kisses my cheek. His face is smooth and soft. I know he wishes he had facial hair, but I can't help being glad it hasn't come in yet. "Stop worrying," he says.

"But you're my little angel."

"Stop!" He crashes out of the truck onto the sidewalk.

"My baby!" I cry after him. He pulls his hood over his head and trots toward the house.

I get out, beep the alarm on my truck and follow him across the street. The neighbors' pit bulls hear our approach and erupt into barking. Through the chain-link fence, I see their shadows in the backyard as they strain against their chains. I feel sick with pity for their eternal captivity.

The spring air is cool on my skin. I rub my arms, run my fingers over the tattoos that cover them from shoulder to wrist, and trot up the three concrete porch steps. In the middle of the dead lawn, Joaquin's old play structure looks injured, as though it's been frozen midlimp in a quest to run away. Carol's old Ford Taurus cowers behind the ancient Chevy that's been rusting in the driveway since I lived here. This used to feel like home, but now it feels like returning to the scene of a crime.

Joaquin brushes past Carol with a muttered "Hey" and heads straight for his room. I get a rush of spiteful satisfaction at how much he obviously loves me more than her. It's stupid; of course he loves me more. She's the worst. But still.

Carol watches me approach. Her dishwater-blond hair falls lankly to her shoulders, her weathered face drawn into a frown. Her eyes drift down over my Trader Joe's T-shirt.

"How ya doing?" I ask in a tight voice I never recognize.

"You had him out too late," she says in her old-school smoker voice.

My hackles rise. "It's only eight o'clock."

She grips the doorknob. "While you're here, I may as well tell you. We're going to be skipping Sunday dinners for a while."

"What? Why?"

"I don't have time to get into this with you right now, Jasmine."

I hold a hand out, but the door pushes forward. "That's not our deal. If you're going to cut Sundays, you have to give me a different—"

The door clicks shut.

I want to bang on it, bash it in and take Joaquin away from her. But I can't. I have to just stand here staring at the door like a little bitch while she gloats over another in her endless chain of victories.

2
DEVIN

ON THE SOFT sand below the Santa Monica Pier, with the lights of the Ferris wheel sparkling in the waves, kids in sopping T-shirts screech like seagulls as they chase each other with bits of seaweed stolen from the sea. Devin rests his forearms on the splintery wooden railing and pretends to watch them from above. He's really got his eyes on Amber.

A middle-aged woman leans on the railing nearby. He catches her checking him out, and he shudders. Like he'd ever be interested in this soccer mom–looking cougar. He returns his attention to Amber.

Careful in her heels on the boardwalk, Amber weaves through the groups of tourists. She's beautiful tonight, but then, she's always beautiful. Her fluffy blond hair flutters in the salty breeze, her smooth, round cheeks and lips cherubic in the colorful light that shines from the stores and restaurants. She's still wearing the black dress she wore to work, but it looks like she freshened up her makeup. Her lips are a bright, blinking crimson.

She disappears inside Rusty's Surf Ranch. Who is she meeting? Maybe her best friend; they hang out a lot in the evenings. Either way, Devin will make sure she gets home all right.

He knows Amber loves the Twilight Saga—she has all four books and an Edward Cullen poster in her apartment—and he's pored through the series, learning what she likes and doesn't like. One thing he's learned is that Edward is always, always trying to keep Bella safe, just like Devin tries to protect Amber.

Devin pulls his baseball cap down over his eyes and enters the beach-themed restaurant. "Can I—" a hostess begins, but he brushes her off and heads for the bar.

He sits on a stool with his back to the room and orders a beer from a muscular, white-toothed bartender. He's learned to dread service industry people like this after a lifetime of them soliciting his father with their headshots in restaurants.

Once Devin has his beer, he turns and scans the room for Amber. He keeps his face hidden behind his glass and the visor of his cap. This is out of consideration for Amber's feelings; he's perfectly entitled to be here. The restraining order expired three months ago and they won't renew it unless he threatens Amber's life, which of course he'd never do. Now that there's no restraining order, Devin hopes they can move into the next phase of their relationship.

If this were *Twilight*, they'd be at the part of the book where Edward is keeping an eye on Bella, but Bella can't find out without risking the Cullen family's secret. It's a risk Edward is willing to take. That's how much he loves Bella, and this is how much Devin loves Amber.

There she is, tucked into a booth near the stage where a

singer wails along with her acoustic guitar. Amber sits close to her companion, a handsome, well-dressed Asian man. *Who the fuck is this?*

As Devin watches, she awards the man a sunny, blue-eyed smile, baring snow-white teeth. Her wavy mop of blond hair cascades over her shoulders and around her cleavage.

Hot, angry heat burns through Devin's limbs.

This is too much. He needs to take control, like Edward did in Port Angeles when Bella almost got herself raped by that gang of guys. Yes, that's the part of the story they're in, the part where Edward takes control.

Someone sits at the bar a few stools down from Devin. He glances over and snorts out a laugh. It's the middle-aged woman again. She gives him a shy smile.

He wants to tell her she's wasting her time, that he's already got a girl twenty years younger than her and twenty times hotter, but she takes a flip phone out of her purse, opens it and puts it to her ear. A flip phone? Really? She's poor *and* old. Well, she can dream.

Amber and the asshole finish their dinner and go on the Ferris wheel. They play games in the arcade. They stroll around the wood-planked pier. This piece of shit is barely taller than Amber. Devin himself is six foot one.

Amber and her date take a seat on a bench at the end of the pier near a street musician with an electric guitar and a parrot. Beyond the musician, the dark ocean laps peacefully, and a full moon shines down on the water. She rests her head on her date's shoulder.

Devin can't feel his hands or feet. The jealousy that sweeps through his gut drains blood from every other part of his body.

Eventually they get up and stroll back toward the entrance to the pier. She leans into her date's ear and says something, points to the arcade. The douchebag finds a pole to lean on. Amber turns into the arcade—oh, this is perfect. She's going to the restroom.

Devin hurries past Little Dickwad, fighting the urge to punch him. He trots through the noisy arcade, past teenagers playing foosball and girls in a video game dance-off. The back door releases him into the empty, restless night. A women's restroom sign flashes brightly against the concrete beams and the stacks of empty crates and pallets. He slinks along the side of the building. He waits for voices, the flush of toilets, anything to indicate there are more women in the bathroom with Amber. Nothing.

He tiptoes through the door into the brightly lit, urine-and-bleach-scented ladies' room. A row of four stalls stretches off to the right opposite two dingy sinks. One of the stall doors is shut.

Softly, carefully, he pulls the exterior door closed behind him.

The tinkling of urine hitting toilet water echoes around the concrete room. He hopes she's using a seat protector. He doesn't want to catch any diseases.

The toilet flushes. He tucks himself behind the door of the first stall. She should have a chance to wash her hands.

She opens the stall door and click-clacks toward the sink. He can see her in the mirror; her cheeks are flushed, and a small smile plays on her red lips. She dispenses soap and washes her hands in the sink. When she turns to use the hand dryer, she spots him.

It's on.

Her cheeks go white. She gasps, trips over her feet and starts to fall. He jumps forward, heroic, and grabs her by the throat. She writhes in his grip, which makes her cleavage jiggle appealingly.

"No," she screams. She thrashes, makes an animal sound, frees a hand and scratches at his face. Her eyes are wild, panicked. He ducks from the clawing fingernails. She wrenches herself sideways, topples to her knees. He dives down, scrabbles to catch her wrists, her waist, but she spins away. Her shoes go flying. She launches to her feet and explodes through the exterior door, another scream tearing the moment apart. He jumps up and bursts through the bathroom door a half second behind her.

One of her hands grips the door frame and she takes a hard, graceful leap into the arcade. She pushes through a crowd of boys surrounding a basketball game. Devin follows. Blind fury. Rage. Bella doesn't run from Edward. Bella *loves* Edward.

A foot sticks out and Devin crashes forward, bashing his chin on the linoleum floor. He rolls onto his back, hands clutching his face, bleeding, groaning in pain.

"The fuck you doing?" A group of Latino teenagers towers over him. The one talking wears a bandanna around his shaved head and has a neck full of tattoos that snake up onto his cheeks. The clang and clash of arcade games echoes against a loud background pop song and the smell of popcorn.

"You chasing that white girl?" The boy's eyes are black in the colorful light.

"No," Devin says.

"Looked like you were."

"She's my girlfriend. We got in a fight."

"Uh-huh." The boy glances at the front entrance, where Amber has disappeared out onto the pier.

Devin pulls the neckline of his T-shirt up, presses it to his bleeding chin. "It's fine. Everything's fine."

"Everything is going to be fine when you get your ass up and walk calmly out the back door and let your lady go on with her business." The guy points back the way Devin came, which is bullshit. It's going to be so hard to catch up with Amber if he goes out the back.

He glares up at the guy, assesses the group of friends with face tattoos and says, "Fine. Can I go now?"

"Go on, then."

Devin gets unsteadily to his feet. His chin isn't bleeding that much, but it hurts. It *hurts*. This is Amber's fault. How could she? How *dare* she?

The bandanna guy shoves him away. "Don't be a fucking psycho" are his parting words.

Furious, humiliated, bloody, Devin shoulders his way through the arcade. He turns right out the back door and heads toward the Ferris wheel, which towers overhead, heavy with lights and laughter. Shoulders crowd him on all sides— did he accidentally get in line for this thing? "Excuse me," he growls. He pushes through tourists and teenagers.

"Hey," protests a young woman whose breast he'd accidentally elbowed.

Someone pinches his back, hard. He cries out and claps a hand to it, but it's like someone is stabbing him with a pencil. "What the fuck," he roars, but the world tilts sideways and all the oxygen is sucked from his lungs.

The middle-aged woman from the bar. She's right beside him. She's the one poking him. She gives him a cold, dangerous look, and the sharp thing stabs deeper into his back. He tries to grab at it, but his hand doesn't work. His legs go limp. He grabs someone, clings to a young woman for help. She cries out. He drags her down with him, gasping like a

dying fish. His body is in a vacuum; his lungs are being vac-
uumed out of his chest.

Pain sears his stomach and wraps around him like a snake.
He opens his mouth to scream and vomit explodes from it.
The vomit is frothy, dark with blood. He digs his nails into
the splintered boards beneath him. His hand closes on a small,
waxy paper cardboard rectangle. His eyes blur. Pain sucks his
vision into a tiny pinprick. Voices swirl around him, panic
and fragments of sound.

"He's not—"

"Call 911!"

"I think he's having a heart attack. What do you do for
that? CPR?"

"What's he holding?"

Someone yanks the rectangle from his hand. "It's a playing card."

MONDAY

3

JAZZ

THROUGH A LAYER of beige smoke high up in the atmosphere, the sun filters hot and hazy down onto the asphalt, and the air smells like burning plastic and stale campfire smoke. I almost get trampled by the horde of preteens stampeding out of my old middle school, a Spanish-style monument to the former opulence of East LA. A line of cars inches past, all of them covered in a fine layer of white ash.

The kids don't spare me a glance; I look like many of their parents, tattoos and all. A pair of girls brushes past me so close one of them jostles my shoulder.

"Watch it," I snap. The girl gives me a dirty look.

A stocky man pushes a refrigerated cart through the crowd, beads of sweat rolling down his face. "Paletas!" he calls to the kids. A Popsicle sounds amazing in this nasty heat, but I'd never eat something sweet in front of Joaquin. I always tell him if he can't have it, I won't eat it, either.

Where is this kid? I pull my phone out of my back pocket

to dial Joaquin. It goes straight to voice mail, which is what it's been doing all weekend. At the beep, I say, "Where you at? You better not have lost your phone. I have your insulin and I'm out in front of Hollenbeck."

I shove my sunglasses on, fix my bangs and search the sea of dark-haired heads for Joaquin's. I spot Miguel and Antonio and wave at them. I expect Joaquin's face to materialize between them, but when they approach me, he isn't there.

"Hey, Jazz," Miguel says. I pull him into a hug and rub his shaved head. Grinning, I say, "Damn, you're getting tall. What's your grandma been feeding you?" Antonio gives me a faux punch on the arm, and I kiss him on the cheek. He's a serious soccer player and is small, dark and wiry.

"Where's Keenie?" I ask. It's the name we torture Joaquin with.

"He's absent," says Miguel. "I figured you were here to pick up his homework or something."

"Absent? Why?" I look back and forth between them. They shrug. A vague foreboding takes root in my stomach, and I get my phone out to text him. I ask, "Did you talk to him this weekend?"

Antonio says, "We think your mom took his iPhone. We haven't talked to him since Friday at school."

I look up from the screen. "Wait—really?"

He nods solemnly. It's clear this is a fate hardly worth contemplating.

"She can't do that. I pay for that phone."

They give me sympathetic looks. The injustice is not lost on them.

I heave a frustrated sigh. "She's gone religious again. That's probably why. She took his posters down and stuff."

"Ohhhhh," they groan.

A horn beeps. A man beckons impatiently from a double-parked Ford. Antonio hefts his backpack. "That's my uncle. I got soccer practice."

"You're practicing today? It's not healthy to exercise in this." I gesture to the dirty brown sky.

"Got a game next weekend. Can't take a day off!" He runs to the car and I say goodbye to Miguel. I return to my truck for a sweater to cover my tattoos and button it up as I weave through groups of kids congregated on the sidewalks. I catch a whiff of bad weed as I hurry up the stairs and through a high arched entryway into the administration hallway. A familiar stretch of rust-brown linoleum leads me to a glass-windowed door at the end of the hall. Above the door, a sign reads *Administration*. It's silly, but this office still gives me the heebie-jeebies.

Inside the main office, a grumpy-looking white lady behind the counter regards me over a set of turquoise reading glasses. "May I help you?" She obviously does not relish the prospect.

"May I speak with Mrs. Galleguillos?"

"Mrs. Galleguillos retired. We have a new assistant principal. What is this regarding?"

"My little brother. Joaquin Coleman. I'm supposed to drop his insulin off, but he was absent today, so I thought I could leave it for him in the office to pick up tomorrow. I've done it before with Mrs. Galleguillos."

"And your name?"

"Jasmine Benavides."

"Take a seat." She heaves herself up from the desk, pushes off and limps toward a hallway on the left.

I sink into the proffered plastic chair with my purse on my lap. Inside is the white CVS bag containing Joaquin's prescription, my precious cargo. A teenager occupies the chair next to me, a baby on her lap and a little girl in a stroller sucking on a chili mango lollipop. I flex my fingers, and the blurry skull and crossbones on my ring finger stretches.

A brown-haired woman in black slacks and a crisp white blouse emerges from an office. "Jasmine?" she calls, her eyes searching the waiting room. "Jasmine Benavides?"

I raise my hand hesitantly like a kid in a classroom. "That's me."

"Oh." Her eyes scan me from head to toe as though the sight of me takes her aback. I realize I'm still wearing my giant aviator sunglasses, and I push them up onto my head. She smiles. "Sofia Russo. Come on back."

I follow her through the short hallway to the office I remember from my own days here. A new placard has been stuck to the door that declares her to be *Ms. Russo, Asst. Principal.*

I sit in a wooden chair across from the desk, and she sits in her office chair in front of the computer. "What's your brother's name?"

"Joaquin Coleman."

Ms. Russo clicks a few things with her mouse and types some words in. She leans toward the screen. She's young, around my age or just a bit older, and has pretty Mediterranean features with thick dark brows, high cheekbones, a wide mouth and lots of dark lashes. Her neck and chest are golden-tan against the pristine white of her shirt. She's one of those women with perfect finishes.

"Here he is." She click-clicks. "What grade is he in?"

"Eighth. He's thirteen."

Her eyes light up. "Oh, I know Joaquin. He came in third in the science fair. He's a great student."

"Yeah, he is." A little prideful smile teases at my lips.

Just a couple of months ago, I walked in on Carol reaming

him for mixing household chemicals into a giant dirt volcano in the backyard. "But it really erupts," he was protesting.

Ms. Russo says, "I have you listed as an emergency contact. Jasmine Benavides. Correct?"

"Call me Jazz. Please. I hate Jasmine."

"Okay. Jazz. But I don't have you listed as a guardian. That's...Carol Coleman? Your mother?"

No. Not a mother. I want to scrub that word from her mouth. "That's our foster mom. Joaquin's adoptive mom."

"Do you want to call her? I can't dispense medication without her permission, but we can just conference her in, and then I can—"

"Don't call her." My head feels light. I don't like sitting in this chair of judgment and laying out the details of our fucked-up family for this woman's examination. Old feelings associated with being a foster kid are overwhelming me. Always the charity case, the subject of pitying looks, of disgust when I got lice first, of whispers when my clothes weren't clean, when I got into fights.

"Are you all right?" Her voice is kind and warm, and I hate it.

I pull it together. "I've done this before. Mrs. Galleguillos knew us. Carol isn't good with Joaquin's meds, so we kind of worked around her."

A knock sounds on the door frame. It's the front desk woman. She hands Ms. Russo a few forms. Ms. Russo scans the forms and shoots her a sharp look. "When did these come in?"

"Counseling office just sent them over." She exits unceremoniously. Ms. Russo bites her glossy lip and scowls at the pages in front of her. She flips through them quickly, one-two-three, then looks at the front page again.

"What is it?" I ask.

Her eyes flick down to my collarbone, where my chest piece, a set of wings that stretches from shoulder to shoulder, pokes out of the neckline of my sweater. Hesitantly, she says, "I don't want to upset you. You're clearly very attached to your foster brother, and you've—"

"Just brother," I correct in a sharper voice than intended.

"Oh. I'm sorry. I assumed—"

"Same mother, fifteen years later. What's this?" I gesture toward the papers.

She drums her fingers on her desk. "I'm struggling with the confidentiality protocols."

"Why? What is it?"

"This is disenrollment paperwork."

I'm confused, and I stare at her blankly for a few seconds. "Like, he isn't enrolled here anymore?"

"Correct."

My head spins. "But...why?"

"So he can be homeschooled, or that's what it says here."

"Homeschooled by *Carol*? She's not a teacher. She can't do math to save her life. She didn't even finish high school."

"I don't think that's a requirement to homeschool your children."

I rack my brain, trying to make sense of this information. "But we already have his high school picked out. It's a science and technology charter school. He's so excited." My heart pounds, panicked, furious.

"Do you think he's in any danger? If so, we can call DCFS."

"And say what? That I don't think my ex foster mother is going to keep a close enough eye on my brother's diabetes? That she's not going to homeschool him well enough?"

"Well, sure."

"Are you kidding me? Do you think they're going to—" I'm breathing too fast. Even if DCFS took a call like that seriously, which is laughable, what's the alternative? Sending Joaquin to some foster home where I'd never see him, where he'd have to start over the way I did, where unknown horrors might be visited upon him? It's not like they'll let me have him; it's not like I haven't tried.

I can't be here.

I get up and leave. I pass the secretary, making her jump, and slam through the office door into the hallway, banging it so hard I almost break the glass. I push through a circle of kids milling around a single plate of nachos in the hall, taking the stairs two at a time. "Wait," a voice calls from behind me. I ignore it. A hand grabs my shoulder to stop me. I spin, muscles tense, and yank my arm away hard.

The hand belongs to Ms. Russo. She steps back, the look on her face wary and a little afraid.

The kids watch us with huge eyes. One of the boys claps a hand to his mouth.

I lift my hands in the air. "I'm sorry. Just don't grab me. I'm sorry."

The boy chants, "Fight, fight, fight," loud enough to set the girls into giggling.

Ms. Russo shoots him a stern look that shuts him up instantaneously. To me, she says, "Let's go back inside. I want to help you."

"No. I'm going to Carol's. I'm going to find out what she thinks she's doing."

"All right. I'll contact social services first thing in the morning. We'll get this figured out."

"I'm telling you right now, they're not going to do shit."

"Why don't we take it one step at a time? I'll call them, we'll see what they do, and then we'll figure out what's next?"

She's being nice. She's not mad at me for being angry or for swearing. I feel bad. She's just trying to help. "Okay. Call them. Thank you."

"I have your phone number, correct?" she asks. "On Joaquin's emergency card?"

"Yes. That's my cell."

"I'll let you know how it goes."

The brown, apocalyptic sky feels like an omen. This isn't good. It's not good at all.

I clutch the white CVS bag and tiptoe into the bank of knee-high weeds around the side of Carol's house. Dusk is sinking slowly onto the city, cooling the air before it cools the ground. The thing about smoke in the air is that it makes for a beautiful bloodred sunset. I pause outside the house to watch the ruby turn to purples and grays, and then it's just a dim, starless sky.

I turn toward the backyard and let myself silently in through the waist-high chain-link gate. As I sneak underneath the kitchen window, my phone buzzes in my pocket. I pull it out. Andre.

I swipe right and put it to my ear. "Hey, dude, let me call you back," I whisper.

His voice booms out of the phone. "Where's the pile of cables we set aside? The extra long ones? Matt can't find them."

I turn the volume down. "They're piled up by Dao's pedal board."

"They're not there!"

"Well then, I don't know! I gotta go. I'll see you at the venue." I hang up on him and return the phone to my pocket.

I creep through the tall grass to Joaquin's window. This is how I communicate with Joaquin when Carol's being really unhinged. We cut a flap out of the screen a long time ago. She went through a fasting phase last year and never understood that kids with diabetes can't go without meals, so I sneaked him food through the bars every day. It was funny; she couldn't figure out why he was gaining weight. She thought Jesus was feeding him with the Holy Spirit. Nope, it was Jazz, messenger of God, feeding him In-N-Out.

I lift my hand up to knock on the glass, but I stop. The window looks different. It's a strange shade of dark.

I set the CVS bag down, grip the wrought iron bars and pull myself up to get a closer look. The window looks brown somehow, patchy.

Wait. Is it…is it boarded up?

I jump down, get my phone out of my pocket, turn the flashlight on and shine it up through the bars.

Holy shit. It's boarded up from the inside.

My body snaps into action. I grab the CVS bag, wade back through the dead grass, slam the gate open and charge up to the front door. I press the bell hard, once, twice, three times.

She answers quickly. Maybe she saw me coming. She doesn't open the steel-and-mesh screen but stands behind it, one hand on the doorjamb.

"I need to talk to you," I say.

"What about?" Her thin hair is tied back into a low ponytail, her chest gaunt under a baggy pink T-shirt.

"About Joaquin. What do you think? Why the fuck is his window boarded up? Why does his school say he doesn't go there anymore?"

She sighs, opens the screen and comes out onto the porch with me. She's wearing her usual eighties jeans and dirty white sneakers. She gestures that we should sit on the stoop, and I sink down onto the concrete step beside her.

She looks me in the eyes. Hers are faded gray and lined at the corners. "I know you care about him. No one doubts that. But I am his mother. Not you."

Those words are the hardest pill for me to swallow, and I'll never, ever get used to them, no matter how many years go by.

My voice is rough. "Since you're such a mother, do you want to do the doctor's appointments? Deal with the insurance? Check his dosages? Because you've spent the last ten years pretending his diabetes doesn't exist."

"He hasn't had any symptoms in years, Jasmine."

"Because he's been on meds!"

"You have this need to be involved, to control him. You need to let go. He isn't sick. It's you."

The urge to do violence swells huge inside me, but I have to stay calm. I take a deep breath and force my fists to unclench. "Every holiday, it's this bullshit again. You trying to give him candy he can't eat, trying to prove he's fine. He isn't fine, Carol. He could die. Is that what you want?"

"Doctors can only fix the symptoms. God is the only one who can heal."

"Diabetic ketoacidosis. It takes two days to set in with no insulin and would kill him in a week. Do you think this is a fucking game? Do you not remember what happened?" I'm on my feet now; I can't help it. My heart is being raked from my body, my naked soul slick with fury.

Three years ago, before Joaquin got good at taking care of himself, one horrible Christmas found me kneeling over him in his bed, trying frantically to shake him awake. A urine stain spread out around him on the sheets, and his pulse was thready and irregular. I'd slung him over my shoulder and run out to my truck. That drive to the ER was the longest car ride of my life.

Unwelcome images flash through my mind—Joaquin limp and covered in piss, flopping around under the seat belt while I tried to see the road through tears that fogged my vision almost to obscurity—

"'And the Lord will take away from you all sickness,'" Carol continues. "He needs to grow his faith, and he can't do that while being fed lies at school, lies by you. He needs to be surrounded by the Word."

"Is that what they told you at church? After they collected a tenth of your benefits check? Don't you remember what the doctors told you last time? Or do you think it's God's will that Joaquin should die in a diabetic coma before he can go to high school?"

She stands up and brushes her hands on her jeans. "Romans 1:26."

"Stop."

"'And God gave them over to shameful lusts. Even women exchanged natural sexual relations for unnatural ones.'"

I push that aside to deal with another time. "This is not about me. You can think whatever you want about me, but—"

"I'm exhausted by you, Jasmine." She lets herself back in the house and shuts the door behind her.

I bang my fist on the steel screen. "Do you want him to die? Is that what you want?"

I stumble backward down the steps, pull my keys out of my pocket and grip them so tight they cut into my palm. I'm in my truck without knowing how I got there. I thrust the key into the ignition and crank the manual gearshift into first gear. The truck peels away from the curb too fast. At Cesar Chavez Avenue, I slam the brakes, grip the steering wheel and scream at the top of my lungs.

4

JAZZ

THE CEILING ABOVE the crowd sparkles with strings of golden lights. They twinkle just bright enough to illuminate the faces. I adjust a microscopic issue with my toms and run my fingers through my bangs, straightening them over my eyes. The guys are tuning up, creating a clatter of discordant notes in the monitors. When they're done, they approach my kit for our usual last-minute debate about the set list. Dao humps his bass in his ready-to-play dance, black hair swishing around his shoulders. "Dude, stop," Matt groans and readjusts the cable that connects his Telecaster to his pedal board.

"Your mom loves my dancing," Dao says.

"You dance like Napoleon Dynamite," Matt retorts.

"Your mom dances like Napoleon Dynamite."

Andre raises his hands. "Y'all both dance like Napoleon Dynamite, and so do both your moms, so let's just—"

I wave a stick at them. "Guys. Focus. The sound guy is watching. We're three minutes behind." I have no patience for this shit tonight. This all feels extra and stupid. I should be doing something to help Joaquin. His dwindling supply of insulin sits at the front of my brain like a ticking clock.

The guys get into their spots, the distance between them set by muscle memory. Andre leans forward into the mic and drawls, "Arright DTLA, lez get a little dirty in here." His New Orleans accent trickles off his tongue like honey.

The room inhales, anticipates, a sphere of silence.

"Two three four," I yell. I clack my sticks together and we let loose, four on the floor and loud as hell. I'm hitting hard tonight. It feels great. I need to hit things. My heart beats in tempo. My arms fly through the air, the impact of the drums sharp in my joints, in my muscles, the kick drum a pulse keeping the audience alive. This is what I love about drumming, this forcing of myself into the crowd, making their hearts pound in time to *my* beat.

Dao fucks up the bridge of "Down With Me" and Andre gives him some vicious side-eye. The crowd is pressed tight up against the stage. A pair of hipsters in cowboy hats grabs a corresponding pair of girls and starts dancing with them. I cast Dao an eye-rolling look referring to the cowboy hats and he wiggles his eyebrows at me. I stomp my kick drum harder, pretending it's Carol's face.

The crowd surges back. Arms fly. A guy in the front staggers, falls. A pair of hands grips the stage, and a girl tries to pull herself up onto it.

Matt and Dao stop playing. The music screeches to a halt.

"What's going on?" I yell.

"Something in the pit," Dao calls back.

Andre drops his mic and hops down into the crowd. Dao and Matt cast their instruments aside and close the distance to the edge of the stage. I get up and join them. Together, we look down into the pit.

A clearing has formed around a brown-haired guy lying on the floor. Andre and the bouncer squat by him as he squirms and thrashes, his arms and legs a tangle of movement. Andre's got his phone pressed to his ear and is talking into it urgently. The bouncer is trying to hold the flailing man still, but the man's body is rigid, shuddering out of the bouncer's grip. He flops onto his back, and I get a good look at his face.

Oh, shit, I know this guy. He's a regular at our shows. He whines and pants, muffled words gargling from his throat. Some of the bystanders have their phones out and are recording this. Assholes.

The man shrieks like a bird of prey. The crowd sucks its whispers back into itself, and the air hangs heavy and hushed under the ceiling twinkle lights.

Andre is still talking into his phone. The bouncer lifts helpless hands over the seizing man, obviously not sure what to do.

I should see if Andre wants help. I hop down off the stage and push through the crowd. "Excuse me. Can you let me through? Can you stop recording this and let me through?"

I'm suddenly face-to-face with a man who is trying to get out of the crowd as hard as I'm trying to get into it. His face is red and sweaty, his eyes wild. "Move," he orders me.

Dick. "You fucking move."

"Bitch, *move*." He slams me with his shoulder, knocking me into a pair of girls who cry out in protest. I spin, full of rage, and reverse direction to follow him.

"Hey, fucker," I scream. He casts a glance over his shoulder. "Yeah, you! Get the fuck back here!"

He escalates his mission to get out of the crowd, elbowing people out of his way twice as fast. I'm smaller and faster, and

I slip through the opening he leaves in his wake. Just before he makes it to the side exit, I grab his flannel shirt and give him a hard yank backward. "Get the fuck back here!" I'm loose, all the rage and pain from earlier channeling into my hatred for this entitled, pompous asshole.

I know I should rein it in, but he spins to face me and says, "What is your problem, bitch?" And that's it. I haul back and punch him full in the jaw.

He stumbles, trips over someone's foot and lands on his ass on the cement floor. His phone goes clattering out of his hand, skidding to a stop by someone's foot. "The hell!"

"Oh, shit," cries a nearby guy in a delighted voice.

"Fucking *bitch*," the guy says, and this is the last time he's calling me a bitch. I go down on top of him, a knee in his chest. I swing wild, hit him in the jaw, the forehead, the neck. He throws an elbow; it catches me in the boob and I flop back off him with a grunt of pain. He sits up, a hand on his face, and opens his mouth to say something, but I launch myself off the ground again, half-conscious of a chorus of whoops and howls around us. I throw a solid punch. His nose cracks. Satisfaction. I almost smile. Blood streams down his face.

"That's what you get," I pant. He crab-shuffles back, pushes off the ground and sprints for the exit. I let him go.

My chest is heaving, and I have the guy's blood on my hand, which is already starting to ache and swell. I wipe my knuckles on my jeans.

His phone lights up and starts buzzing on the floor. I pick it up and turn it over in my hand. It's an old flip phone, the kind I haven't seen in years. The bright green display says *Blocked*.

Back in the pit, the man having a seizure shrieks again, and then his screams gurgle to a stop. I put the phone in my pocket and push through the onlookers. I watch as his back convulses like he's going to throw up, and then he goes limp. A thin river of blood snakes out of his open mouth and trails along the cement floor.

The room echoes with silence where the screams had been. A trio of girls stands motionless, eyes huge, hands pressed to mouths.

The flip phone in my pocket buzzes. I pull it out, snap it open and press it to my ear. "Hello?"

A pause.

"Hello?" I repeat.

A click. The line goes dead.

A set of paramedics slams the stage door open, stretcher between them. "Coming through!" They kneel down and start prodding at the man curled up on the concrete. His head flops back. His eyes are stretched wide and unseeing, focused on some point far beyond the twinkling ceiling lights.

Next to him on the concrete lies something... What is it? It's rectangular and has red and—

It's a playing card.

5

RICKY

"HURRY UP," RICKY whispers. Andrew is busy jimmying the locks open.

"Keep a lookout," Andrew murmurs back.

Ricky obeys, eyes flitting left and right along the deserted outdoor hallway. The neighboring apartment building's parking lot flickers under a dying security light, casting the walkway into uneven shadow. The night is bright, all the city light reflected by the smoky sky. It smells like fire, but not in a good way, not like barbecue or a campfire. It smells nasty, like when they burn furniture at the Dockweiler beach pits on the Fourth of July.

A low rumble builds from the east. Both Andrew and Ricky freeze, eyes on the sky. A helicopter swoops over the roof and roars west, a spotlight trained down on the ground below. Far away, sirens echo through the night.

"It's not for us. They're looking for someone," Ricky says.

Andrew returns to his work on the dead bolt. "This lock is a motherfucker. It's reinforced or something."

"Maybe we should just go."

"Don't be a pussy." With a grunt of triumph, Andrew turns the door handle and pushes it inward. The apartment is dark and releases a cloud of hot, stale air into their faces.

Ricky follows Andrew in and they close the door behind them. Andrew's eyes glint in the light filtering in through the cracks in the blinds. He's tall and thin, his head shaved like Ricky's. They look alike—you can tell they're brothers—but Andrew has always been the better-looking one.

Ricky says, "I know they got a TV and computer in the bedroom. I saw through the blinds."

"Let's get to it." Andrew sounds excited.

He follows Andrew through the living room into the bedroom. The apartment looks clean, like no one lives here, which Ricky is pretty sure they don't. He's been living three doors down with his mom for ten years—when you get your Section 8 housing, you stay put—and during the last six months since this new person moved in, he has only seen them one time, when he was coming home from a party at three in the morning. Even then, he only saw a dark shadow hurrying down the stairs.

The bedroom is hotter than the living room. It smells like moldy carpet, which probably hasn't been changed since that old lady died in here a few years ago. It was sad; they found her all starved to death and shit.

The bedroom has a bed, a desk, and that's it. The desk is empty.

"What the fuck?" demands Andrew.

"It was here!"

Andrew yanks the desk drawer handle, but it's locked. He

inserts his pick into the lock, jiggles it, and the drawer comes open with a click. "Oh, shit." Andrew's grin is white in the semidarkness.

"Is it there?"

Andrew pulls a sleek black laptop out of the drawer and sets it on the desk. He reaches in and pulls out another object, a small black box, and frowns at it. "What's this thing?"

"It's some kind of router, or maybe a hot spot?"

"Nice." Andrew sets it aside. "This laptop looks new. That's good!"

Ricky could swear there was a TV in here. He crosses the room to the closet and slides the doors open. The rod is completely empty; no clothes hang inside here at all. He sees the TV up on the top shelf. "I found the TV!"

His eyes focus on something stuck to the back wall of the closet. He gets his phone out of his pocket and hits the flashlight button. It illuminates a web of lines, words and photographs.

He steps forward.

Thirty or forty index cards are pasted to the wall in a six-by-six-foot circle. On each index card are two photographs and some information written next to the pictures. He reads one that says *Norma Peterson. Age 66. Retired Teacher.* Beside her photo is that of an older man. *Christiano Peterson. Age 68. Retired Bus Driver.* The index cards are taped to the wall, and lines are drawn between them with blue painter's tape.

With his finger, Ricky traces the painter's tape that leads from Norma and Christiano's card to another card with a man and a woman on it. This man and woman are younger. From this card runs a strip of painter's tape to another card, this one with two women on it, and from them to a middle-aged man and woman. From one card to another, from one pair of people to another.

His eyes drift down to the floor of the closet, where a cardboard box sits with its flaps open. He turns his phone on the contents. It shines across a collection of identical clear plastic… What are they? He kneels down to get a closer look. They're needles, the kind the doctor uses to give you a shot.

"What are you doing?"

The words make Ricky jump to his feet. He presses a hand to his chest. "Fuck, you scared me."

"Pussy."

"Look. This is some serial killer shit right here."

Andrew leans forward to examine the web of pictures. "Huh. Whatever." He grabs the flat-screen TV off the top shelf.

A click. From the living room.

They stare at each other, breath held.

"Did you close the door behind us?" Andrew whispers.

"I thought so!"

"You're a fuckup. You know that?"

Andrew shoves the TV at Ricky and pulls his gun out of the waistband of his pants. "C'mon, son."

"Wait, man—chill. Maybe it's not even—"

"Shh." Andrew points the gun at the ceiling like *CSI* and tiptoes toward the door. "Grab the laptop," he whispers.

Ricky stacks the laptop on top of the TV and grips them tight to his chest. He can barely see anything, just Andrew's white tank top in the darkened room. They tiptoe past the dark, silent bathroom into the living room.

Light filters in through the blinds, spilling stripes onto the carpet. The room is empty.

Andrew releases a sigh of relief. "All right, maybe I'm the one who needs to chill."

Ricky laughs. "You got spooked!"

Andrew heads back toward the bedroom. "Imma grab that router thing."

Ricky shifts the TV and laptop in his arms. He feels proud. Maybe now Andrew will stop—

The bathroom door creaks.

Something cold and wet covers his nose and mouth.

He lets go of the TV and laptop. They crash down onto his foot. Pain flashes hot and bright in his toe, and he sucks in a breath. A cold chemical fog rushes into his lungs. His head spins, and he crumples to the floor.

Andrew is running. Andrew's right above him. "Ricky? What're you—"

Something white snakes around Andrew's face, covers his mouth. Andrew's gun flashes, but a hand whips out and knocks it to the ground. Andrew squirms, thrashes, crumples down on top of Ricky.

A pinch in Ricky's neck. A bee sting.

A hand—a body, crouched above. Something shiny and slender touches Andrew's neck.

And then the burning, shimmering pain.

TUESDAY

6
JAZZ

THE LAWYER'S GLASSES are dirty like the Plexiglas covering his beat-up desk, but behind them, his brown eyes are kind. "Can you prove she's not giving him his insulin?"

I sit forward, elbows on knees. "It's kind of hard to prove something is going to happen in the future. Which is what brings me to you."

"Say she doesn't give him his insulin and he does get sick. Can't you just call in DCFS then?"

I say, "Juvenile diabetes isn't like type two diabetes. With type two, you can live with it untreated for years, and you can go without your insulin for a while if you watch your diet. Joaquin has type one, and his is especially unstable. If he goes a few days untested, untreated, he could die fast. There isn't time to wait for him to get sick. He already almost died once, and DCFS didn't do shit to Carol, just told her to be more careful."

"All right. Give me a moment to review." He bends his

head forward to examine my paperwork, and the strands of hair he'd combed across his bald spot tumble forward in front of his glasses. He pushes the hair back into place. Embarrassed for him, I let my eyes drift around the office, from the seedy vinyl client chairs to the crooked bookshelves to the vintage phone on his desk. I drum my fingers on my knees, catch myself and fold my arms across my chest. Outside the window, faint sirens wail a plaintive song. Their volume squeals to a crescendo as they pass us, and then it fades into the distance as they continue west.

He turns a page. "So you have a criminal record."

I feel my hands tighten around my biceps. "Yes."

"Lots of fighting." He points to something in the paperwork. "Jesus, girl. How many bar fights have you gotten into?"

Shame and pride vie for my attention. "Some."

He shakes his head and flips the page. "You need to go to anger management."

"I've been."

"Maybe you should go into boxing or something, try to channel that energy toward—"

"I've done all that. I used to teach jujitsu. Now I play the drums. I'm all chilled out now." Kind of. Sort of.

He returns to the paperwork, reads through a page and snorts. "You kidnapped your brother. That's great."

I'm not going to punch my lawyer. That would be bad. "There were extenuating circumstances."

"The judge didn't see it that way."

"The judge was an asshole."

He looks up. "You want to run the clock out acting like a teenager, or you want to tell me what happened so I can help you?"

He's right. I am acting like a teenager in the principal's office. I look down at the tattoos peeking out of the wrists of my Trader Joe's sweatshirt. I wish I could scrub them off. I wish I could scrub every word off those papers in front of him.

"Tell me why you kidnapped your brother," he says, gently this time.

I pull the folder toward me and shuffle papers until I find a faded manila envelope. I pull a single piece of paper out of it and slide it across the desk toward him.

He reads it and his eyes go wide. "Oh."

"Yeah." I rub my mouth with a hand to hide the expression on my face.

"I'm sorry." His voice is soft and compassionate. "Tell me what happened."

I have to blink hard to keep my eyes dry. "Carol beat my ass. It was a really bad one. I freaked out. I grabbed Joaquin and ran. I thought I could keep him away from her. Keep him…" Tears threaten to consume me. "Keep him safe from her." I clear my throat. "But anyway, I was nineteen, and I already had some shit on my record, so, yeah. Five years' probation."

"Did they charge Carol with assault?"

"Carol?"

"If she assaulted you, I assume they charged her."

"No. She was the victim. I was the one who took—" I can't say the words *her kid*. I won't. Instead, I say, "She denied it. She said I had gotten into a fight, that I was drunk, and that I just, you know, snapped. They believed her." I search for a joke, anything to get the pitying look off his face. "I mean, I didn't exactly inspire their confidence. You should've seen me at nineteen. I was like the Tasmanian devil."

He doesn't smile. I don't blame him; it was a weak joke. He says, "Carol is his adoptive mother, correct? Not foster?"

"Yeah."

"In that case, she does have the right to homeschool him. There's not much you can do about that." He closes the folder and consults the notes he's been taking in a yellow legal pad. "At this point, I think the only thing you can do is work with DCFS directly about the diabetes. If they'll create documentation, that will help your case later if Joaquin does get sick."

"You're telling me to call DCFS."

He holds his hands up in a helpless gesture.

I stand up and start gathering the paperwork. It's worn and tattered from all the handling. How many lawyers have I had look at this? They all tell me the same thing.

The policewoman holds a hand up. "Ma'am. I have already told you. This is not *Minority Report*. I can't take action on a crime you think is going to be committed in the future. You understand?"

"Fuck!" I pound the counter with my fists. I back up, almost tripping over a woman in line behind me. She has a black eye and two toddler boys asleep in a double stroller.

I find myself on the top of the steps. I'm breathing too fast, sucking in the stale, trapped-fire air that tastes as bad as it smells. I have to get an Uber home, but is going home accepting defeat? Is there something else I can do? Across the street, tents have been set up against a chain-link construction fence. A man emerges from a tattered blue one and starts rifling through a collection of plastic bags he has hanging from a loaded shopping cart.

My purse buzzes and my heart leaps. Joaquin. I dig around inside it and pull my iPhone out, but the screen is dark. My purse keeps buzzing, and then I remember the flip phone I accidentally stole from that asshole last night. I find it in the deepest pocket and pull it out. I flip it open and press it to my ear. "Hello?"

A soft voice half whispers, "Are you alone?"

"Excuse me?"

"Are you alone?" the voice repeats, like a goth phone sex operator.

"Am I alone? No, I'm not alone. I'm standing here in front of the fucking police station. Are you that asshole who called me a bitch, like, five times? Did you learn your lesson?"

The line goes dead.

I snap the phone shut. "What a piece of shit," I mutter. I shove it back into my purse just as my iPhone starts buzzing. Again I hope for Joaquin, but it's a 310 number I don't recognize. I swipe the answer button. "Hello?"

"Jasmine? Jazz?"

"Why? Who's this?"

"This is Sofia Russo from Hollenbeck Middle School. I'm just now driving home, so I thought I'd call you on the road. Do you have a moment?"

"Yeah, I'm just leaving the downtown police station. What happened with DCFS?"

"I filed a report, and they'll make sure someone checks in on Joaquin soon. I just spoke with them a couple hours ago."

"What's 'soon'?" I ask bitterly. "Two weeks? A month?"

"They wouldn't specify, but I made it clear we'd follow up tomorrow and we expected to see some progress. I gave them your phone number so they could check in with you as well."

They won't call me. They'll do a home visit or they'll do nothing. I wonder if Joaquin will tell them anything. Probably not; he doesn't want to end up in some random foster home any more than I want him to.

"Jazz? Did I lose you?"

"I'm here." My voice is small. I feel small.

"Do you need help? Is there something else I can do?"

"I'm fine. I need to go. I Ubered over here. I have to order one to get home. I'll talk to you soon."

"You said you were at the Central Police Station?"

"Yeah. Why?"

"I'm on the 5 near downtown. You want to get a beer? I can give you a lift home after."

I pull the phone away from my ear, stare at it and then return it to my ear. "Are you allowed to do that?"

"What do you mean, allowed?"

"You're a principal. I don't know!"

She laughs. "I'm not a nun. Do you want a drink or not?"

A pair of police cars jolts out of the parking garage. Their lights turn on and their sirens whoop to life. They screech out of the driveway and down the street, swerving around cars, heading west.

"Jazz?" Her voice is tiny in comparison to the sirens.

"Hang on!" I wait for the cops to make it down the street, and then I say, "Sorry. What were you saying?"

"I was saying, if you don't want a drink, that's fine—"

"Oh, I want a drink."

"I'll pick you up. I'm, like, five minutes away."

We hang up and I return my phone to my purse. I guess I'm giving up for tonight.

I can all but see Joaquin's vial of insulin. I imagine it's almost empty.

I push the image aside. What else can I do right now? Tomorrow I can call DCFS. I can go to their offices.

There has to be more. There *has* to be.

I start down the steps and almost collide with a woman rushing up. "Sorry," we chorus.

"It's all right," she says in a British accent. She turns to continue up, and a gun and badge peek out of her open blazer.

7

PATEL

DETECTIVE PATEL ALMOST knocks the young woman over in her hurry to get up the steps. "Sorry," they say in unison.

"It's all right," Patel replies. She jogs up the steps to the Central Police Station and through a side hallway. Nielsen, her partner, catches up with her outside the conference room they've taken over with their investigation. His cheeks are pink, corn-silk blond hair tousled.

"You got my text?" he asks.

"Yes. We got another one?"

"Santa Monica jurisdiction. They just called it in. It happened Saturday. You should have an email."

"Saturday? What took them so long?" She pushes through the conference room door and flicks the light on. They've made a mess in here with files and photos and laptops. "And where's Gonzalez?"

"She's on her way over to Santa Monica. I was just downstairs talking to Forensics. These crimes scenes are a fucking nightmare. More DNA than a public bathroom."

"I don't think that's an accident." She sits in front of her laptop and flips it open. Nielsen comes to stand over her shoulder and watches as she opens her email. The victim is Devin James, age twenty-six, killed at the Santa Monica Pier at nine twenty Saturday. Poison. They're waiting on lab work to confirm.

"You talked to the boss?" Patel asks.

"He's gonna do a press conference. Too many calls coming in. Press is going nuts. You seen Twitter?"

"You know I don't look at that shite."

He shows her Twitter on his phone. "It's trending. #LAMurders, #JusticeforDevin. I guess Devin James was the son of a director and he has an actor friend who's making a stink. This is blowing up huge."

She snorts. People are ridiculous.

"What?" Nielsen asks.

"Justice for bloody Devin? Really?" She gestures to the screen in front of her. "Do you see his record? The man had three sexual assault allegations and an expired restraining order."

"The charges were dropped. Innocent until proven guilty."

Thank you for mansplaining the presumption of innocence to me, twat. Nielsen collapses into the chair next to her, and they read the rest of the report together.

"Look at this." Nielsen points to the bottom corner of the screen. "I was wrong. Former conviction of stalking. I guess he is guilty." He gives Patel a meaningful look. "Is this a pattern?"

"I don't know, but I'm already completely knackered." They've been working this case for forty-eight straight hours.

Nielsen opens his mouth to say something, but a young man in uniform explodes into the room. Eyes wide, a grin of pure glee stretched across his face, he says, "Got another one. Number six! Someone poisoned in the Burbank Walmart."

Number six.

"Goddamn," Nielsen murmurs. "This is going to be huge. I can feel it."

8

JAZZ

TRUE TO HER word, Ms. Russo pulls up in a beige Toyota five minutes later. She rolls the passenger window down and waves at me. I let myself in. The car is spotlessly clean except for the fine layer of ash on the hood. "Hi," I say. I try to get my face to give her a smile, but I only get halfway there. I twist to get the seat belt and spot a car seat in the back. "You have a baby, Ms. Russo?"

"Yes. She's almost two." She pulls away from the curb. "And for the love of God, call me Sofia."

That feels weird, but fine. Sofia. "You don't have to get home to your daughter? It's getting late."

"She's with her father." The words draw her mouth into a pinch.

I study her profile, then guess, "Your ex?"

She nods. "We're just... We're still figuring out the custody situation."

I lean my head back against the headrest, filled with gratitude at the solace and shelter of the car. We drive down the one-way streets in tired silence.

She points out the window at a corner pub. "Been there before?"

"I don't think so, but it looks good to me."

She finds a parking spot a couple of blocks down, in front of a gated-up newspaper stand. Self-conscious next to her polished work outfit, I shrug out of my baggy sweatshirt and leave it on the front seat. That leaves me in a black tank top and jeans, but it's better than a Hawaiian-print hoodie with *Trader Joe's* across the back.

I watch her with curiosity as she jaywalks across the street in front of me. So does a guy who's walking down the sidewalk in the opposite direction. He actually does a double take and rubbernecks to get a better view of her ass. I can't blame him, but he could be a little more subtle about it. She's taller than me by a couple of inches, more with the heels, and has maybe ten or fifteen pounds on me, all in the right places. I can't imagine having a teacher or principal like her; they were always old ladies, or at least old to my young eyes. Sometimes you'd have a dude, usually a perv with a mustache.

The tiny bar is just hipster enough to have rustic wood walls but not hipster enough to use mason jars instead of glasses. We settle ourselves at the bar under a small TV tuned to the local news and order drinks from a young bartender with a bow tie, suspenders and a belt, which seems excessive. His eyes flit back and forth between us, bright with interest like he thinks we're on a date. Embarrassed, I scoot farther away from her and try to make it clear with my body language that I am not hitting on her.

He slides a wooden menu toward us. I have many choices

of artisanal beer, and I pick a lager at random. She orders a glass of red wine, which seems to suit her.

When the drinks come, we clink glasses. We drink, eyes on the TV, which is playing a news story about a gas station robbery by USC, and then she rubs her forehead with her fingertips like she has a headache. Her hair looks a little tangled and her makeup is worn off, cracking the perfect veneer.

I wonder what Joaquin is doing right now. The image of him in his room, no Miley Cyrus poster, no phone, no music, no friends, no school tomorrow, brings up a wave of sadness, and I ball my hands into fists on the bar. I hate feeling so helpless. I want to *do* something.

Sofia pushes my pint glass toward me. "Less thinking. More drinking."

I sip my beer. It does help. She finishes her wine and raises an elegant hand to the bartender, signaling for another round. A diamond ring on her middle finger glints in the low bar light. It's not a wedding ring, not on the middle finger. I wonder how much it cost—thousands, probably—and who bought it for her.

She watches me above the rim of her glass. "What are you thinking about?"

"Joaquin." I force my eyes back onto the TV. An anchorwoman is standing in front of the Santa Monica Pier. The banner beneath her reads *Death Count Across LA County Grows*. The bartender crosses to the TV, grabs a remote and turns on the volume.

"...right here at the Santa Monica Pier," the anchorwoman says. Her face is drawn into an expression of deep concern. "The victim was the son of Austin James, director of the Oscar-nominated film *Taking Over*. The victim's family asks that anyone with information reach out to LAPD or Santa Monica PD."

"Did you hear about this?" Sofia points to the TV with her bling hand.

I shake my head.

The reporter says, "...the Burbank Walmart, the Santa Monica Pier, a club downtown called Villains, the Koreatown Metro station...these killings have one thing in common—they're happening in crowded places."

"Wait—did she say Villains?" I ask.

"I think so. Why?"

"I was there. A guy died, but he wasn't murdered. He had a seizure or something."

"You saw it?"

"I was right there! I play the drums and I was playing that show. I saw the whole thing."

"Oh, wow. What was it like?" she asks in a hushed voice.

"It was fucked up. I'm telling you, there was..." I remember his screaming, the blood leaking from his mouth. "He was, like, squirming around. Thrashing. I can't imagine someone could have stabbed him or something. It wasn't like that."

She pulls her phone out and Googles it. I lean in, and we read a *HuffPost* article together. She points to the screen. "It was murder, Jazz. Poison."

"Poison? Damn. I didn't think poison would be like that."

"Did you actually see him die?" she whispers.

I nod.

"Was it scary?"

I search myself for any emotion. At last, I say, "It was sad, but it was sad because of how small it was. It didn't feel like this huge thing. No Hollywood music, no giant revelation about how short life is. Just this...just these empty eyes." Without my consent, my brain constructs an image of Joaquin, lifeless like the man at Villains. I try to push it away, but it's burned into the backs of my eyes—a premonition? No. No, no, no.

I jiggle the dead bolts and open the front door for her. "The bathroom's through there." I point across the living room unnecessarily. It's not like she's going to get lost; there isn't even a hallway, just a living room separated from the little bedroom alcove by a waist-high wall.

Her eyes travel around the space. "This is really cute. Did you paint it yourself?"

"Yeah. It was this awful Pepto-Bismol pink when I moved in." I lock the dead bolts out of habit even though she's leaving again in two minutes.

"I love your hardwoods. These are original, right?" She continues into the bathroom and calls out, "Oh my God, I love the vintage tile!" before shutting the door.

Vintage. That's funny. I wonder if she'd think my rusty shower knob is vintage. Or my clunky Darth Vader window A/C unit.

Speaking of which, I flick the unit on. It delivers its signature "chunk-chunk-hummm" that signals the arctic cooling of the area immediately around the window. I pull the fan over in front of the window unit and turn it on rotate, which delivers feeble wisps of cool air into various parts of the living room.

I toss my purse on the little Ikea dining table, plug in the Christmas lights that string across the ceiling and fill the electric kettle. I'm choosing from my collection of Trader Joe's tea when she returns, heels clacking across the "vintage" hardwoods. "You want tea?" I ask.

"Sure." She sinks into one of the small dining chairs and sets her purse down. "Do you like living here?"

I cast her a sarcastic look. "It's a fucking palace."

"I just mean you're a young woman living alone. Do you feel safe? You're so close to downtown, and it's not a security building."

"What's someone gonna do, grab a blowtorch and melt the bars off my window?"

"No," she protests. "I don't know. Living alone makes me nervous."

I fold my arms across my chest and lean on the counter next to the kettle, which is making rustling sounds. "You're not wrong about the neighborhood. It's a little shady. But it's cheap, which lets me set money aside for Joaquin to go to college."

She stares at me like I've grown another head. "You're saving up for Joaquin's college education?"

"Yeah. He's a good student. He has real potential. I don't want him to worry about anything except studying." I look down at the rose that wraps around my left wrist and trace the thorns with my fingertip. Will he still go to college? If Carol homeschools him, probably not. If she keeps him out of school, he'll be full of rage and rebellion when he turns eighteen. Who knows what he'll get into?

Fourteen thousand, three hundred and fifty-two dollars. That's how much I've saved over the last five years since Carol kicked me out. I've saved it at the expense of everything—travel, a newer car, better clothes, a nicer apartment. Five years I've been picturing the pride I'll feel writing those tuition checks, finally making up to Joaquin for all the mistakes I made, mistakes layered on top of each other until they all blend together into a careless, reckless, thoughtless life.

"What's wrong? Are you okay?" Sofia asks.

I try to find a joke, can't. I clear my throat. "Joaquin. Carol.

The whole homeschool thing. I'm just fucking helpless." She looks stricken by my words. I say, "Hey, I don't mean to be a downer. I appreciate you inviting me out tonight. It was nice of you. And thank you for calling DCFS and everything."

"You don't have to thank me for making a phone call. That's my job."

"It's more than most people would do. I just…" I shake my head. I can't get the words out.

"You just what?"

"I miss him," I manage. I press a hand to my mouth and pull as hard as I can on the sorrow that's going to run me off the road.

She takes a deep, shaky breath, and then she brings her hands up to her face. She crumples forward, and for a moment I'm so shocked, I almost don't register that she's crying, a faint, contained gasping like she's choking on the sobs to keep them in. Her caramel-brown hair spills onto her tanned arms.

My own sadness forgotten, I move forward and drop to my knees in front of her. My hands hover awkwardly in the air and then land softly on her knees in my most no-homo way. "Hey, hey. What's wrong? Is it my shitty apartment?" I'm trying to be funny the way I always try to be funny for Joaquin. "It's really not that bad. I mean, there's the cockfighting, and sometimes I have to wrestle wild pit bulls on my way down to my car, but other than that."

Her shoulders shake in a different way—she's laughing and crying at the same time. She sits up and wipes at her mascara, which turns her fingertips black. "Oh my God," she groans. "I'm so embarrassed. Can we forget this happened?" She wipes her fingertips on her black slacks and blots her eyes with the heels of her hands.

"It's fine. It's been years since I made a girl cry. I thought I had lost my touch."

She takes a shaky breath. "I lied earlier. In the car. About my daughter. I'm not in the middle of a custody battle with my ex."

"Oh." I'm not completely sure how to respond.

"The battle's over. I lost." She presses her open palms to her eye sockets, hard enough that I think she might be hurting herself.

I gently pull at her hands. "Hey. Careful. Tell me what you mean."

"He's a lawyer, and he knew the judge, and there was a bunch of bullshit…and he won. So she's with him now. I have supervised visitation every other week for an afternoon. Of my daughter. My *daughter.*"

"Fuck. Sofia." I don't know what to say. I feel so bad for her.

"I don't know why I'm telling you this. What is wrong with me?"

"I think you're just upset about not seeing your daughter. It's only natural."

She twists her fingers together. "I guess I thought you'd understand. Because of Joaquin."

"I understand better than you realize."

She cocks her head, looks me in the eyes. Her nose is a little red, her eye makeup smeared. "You're really nice."

I search around for a joke, a way to deflect the compliment, but I come up empty.

She stands. "Now that I've finished humiliating myself, I think I'm going to go. Thanks for keeping me company." She grabs her purse, and I gather my keys off the table.

I walk her down the block to her Toyota in silence. The air is crisp around the edges, like it wants to be cool, but the fire is forcing warmth into it. Sofia looks too polished for this neighborhood, and I feel embarrassed by the apartment buildings' dilapidated facades and the shopping carts tipped over in the median strip.

At the door of her car, she asks, "Want to hang out again sometime? I promise to be in better spirits."

I'm surprised, but I shrug. "Sure."

She gives me a quick straight-girl hug. "Good luck with Joaquin. I'll let you know if I get any news from DCFS."

I watch her taillights glow red and disappear around the corner. I stand there for a long moment, looking at the darkness left in their wake. The air smells like smoke. The fire is still burning. Somewhere far away, sirens echo through the night.

I wish Sofia would come back. I wish anyone would come. I feel left behind.

Sofia's grief of separation is a heavy weight she handed me, and now I'm standing here holding it only to realize it's identical to the weight I already had.

I can't lose Joaquin. He's my only family, the one thing tethering me to this earth.

A homeless man from the tent city on the next block hurries past. He looks busy, like he's on a mission. He passes me fast, but then he turns around and yells, "No!" like I asked him a question.

I turn and walk back toward my apartment, my feet leaden inside my boots.

Back inside, I head for the bathroom and wash my face. From the living area, a faint buzzing filters over the sound of running water. I turn the water off. The buzzing stops, then starts up again. I check my back pocket. My iPhone is there, but it's silent and dark.

I remember the flip phone from Villains. I hurry for the

kitchen and pull it out of my purse. It buzzes in my hand, and its little screen glows bright. *Blocked*, it reads.

I snap it open. "Hello?"

"Jasmine?" a voice replies, warm and low.

I hesitate. How would anyone calling this number know my name?

"Jasmine?" the voice repeats.

"Why? Who's this?"

"Jasmine, I represent an organization to which you have been referred." The voice is neither female nor male but somewhere in-between, and I realize its owner is using a voice disguiser, the kind you hear on crime shows. The voice resumes. "You've been referred in response to the situation with your... mother? Your foster mother?"

"Are you from DCFS?"

"Not exactly. Are you alone? Are you at home?"

"Why do you keep asking me that?"

"We deal with sensitive, personal matters. It's important that we have privacy to discuss this."

I pull the phone away from my ear and examine it, like this will help me understand what the fuck is happening. I return it to my ear and say, "This is creepy. You have two minutes to explain what you're talking about or I hang up."

"I know, and I promise to explain everything in just a moment. Please, don't hang up."

I surprise myself by saying, "All right."

"Thank you. Before we can continue, I'll make you aware, in case you are not already, that recording a call without all parties' consent is a felony under California Penal Code Section 632, and I want to further state that I do not grant permission to record any part of this, or any subsequent conversations. Any recordings of conversations will not be admissible in court. Do you understand?"

"I guess. Why—"

"Let me explain. Now, Jasmine, I understand Joaquin's in quite a bit of danger with his adoptive mother, Carol, and you're in a bind trying to get him some help. Does that sound right so far?"

"So you are with DCFS."

"We are an underground network of helpers. We have access to all kinds of information. But we aren't part of any government institution." I'm silent, trying to process this, when the voice says, "We were quite worried when you got ahold of this phone, but when we looked into you a bit more, we realized you might be a great candidate to join our organization."

"Dude, I don't know who you are, but you need to tell me what the fuck you're talking about."

"This is just a first conversation, and you may feel uncomfortable. That's fine. We've all been in your position, Jazz. I myself more than anyone know how you're feeling."

"How I'm feeling?" I repeat.

"You've reached a breaking point, haven't you? And through no fault of your own. We offer people in your situation a permanent solution."

"What kind of permanent solution?"

"We can offer you a solution to your problems with Carol that would leave you free to live out the rest of your life with Joaquin as you see fit. A life without Carol."

"Without Carol? What do you mean, like, Carol…dead?"

"I think that's enough for now. Why don't you think about it? I'll call you tomorrow. It's very important you don't share any of this conversation with anyone."

"Okay," I hear myself say.

"Good night, Jazz. It was nice to meet you."

The phone goes silent.

"What the fuck?" I whisper.

9
JAZZ

WEIRD PHONE CALLS or no, Joaquin needs his insulin, so here I go.

It's the middle of the night and the street is quiet. Sepia-tone streetlight casts geometric projections of palm fronds onto the asphalt. I grab the backpack from the front seat, get out of the truck and press the door shut until it latches with a low click. I ease open the tailgate and slide out the extendable ladder. I shoulder the ladder and leave the tailgate open to save the noise of closing it.

I make my way around the house until I'm facing the back porch and, above it, the attic intake vent. I telescope out the ladder and lean it carefully against the house.

When I'm up the ladder and level with the vent, I pull a screwdriver out of my pocket and get to work on the screws that anchor the vent to the frame. The moon is my coconspirator, shining enough light on my project that I don't need a flashlight. I'm closer to the palm trees up here, and I can hear the rustle of their fronds as they toss around in a high, cool breeze.

The moon. The breeze.

There's no smoke. Either the fire has gone out or the wind has changed.

Encouraged, I have the vent off in two minutes. I peer into the attic. It's dark and smells musty. I've been up here before. We had a mouse problem when I was younger, and it was my job to set traps and collect the tiny corpses.

The opening is small, and it's an awkward angle. I can't go in leg first; it's not big enough for me to then get my other leg around. I guess it's going to have to be face-first.

Joaquin, you're lucky I love you. I set the backpack inside. I grip the rough wood frame and pull myself in.

It's pitch-black in here, and the air is close and hot. I pull a flashlight out of my backpack, flick it on and shine it around.

Ew. Gross. Piles of rodent droppings and crumbled insulation litter the rough wood floor. The attic beams show through the disintegrating insulation. I wait for giant rats to scamper out and attack me. Nothing moves.

I slip my arms through the backpack straps. I can walk if I hunch over, but I'm right on top of Carol's bedroom, so I crawl through the rat shit and insulation on my hands and knees. I remember reading something on the internet about how, back in the day, torturers used to trap a rat in a bowl on people's stomachs so the rat would burrow into their guts to try to escape. The thought is not helpful.

When I finally make it to the crawl-space door, I force myself to hold still and listen. If I'd woken Carol up, she'd be opening doors, looking for her baseball bat, calling out to Joaquin across the house. All I hear is muffled silence so deep it makes my ears ring.

Alrighty then.

I get to my feet, brush off my hands and grip the pull tie on the crawl-space door.

I pull the door up and set it aside. There is no attached collapsible ladder like some attics have. I've always just used a kitchen chair to get up here. I grip the frame and lower myself in a slow reverse pull-up until my feet dangle a couple of feet off the carpet. I take a deep breath and release my grip. I drop to the ground and let myself crumple down flat with a muffled clump, like a bag of oranges falling out of the groceries.

With my face pressed into the old carpet, memories invade my brain through my nose. Lying on the carpet watching TV—Joaquin as a baby puking on this carpet and Carol yelling at me for not catching the spit-up—push-ups in my room at night—rolling around, tickling Joaquin while he shrieked with joy—Carol, standing over me, my body on fire with pain—

I push myself up to standing and brush my hands off on the butt of my jeans. I tiptoe across the dark hall to Joaquin's bedroom door. I push through it silently. With the window boarded up, this room is as dark as a cave. Bitch. How dare she kennel him up like this?

I close the door behind me and feel my way to his bed. I trip over the nightstand and knock something off with a clatter. Blankets rustle nearby. "Joaquin?" I whisper.

"Jazz?"

I shed my backpack and rush toward the sound. I trip on his metal bed frame and collapse right on top of him. "Ow," he protests quietly.

"Sorry." I feel my way to his face in the darkness, run my fingers through his hair. I fold him into a tight hug, and my heart smolders with love so deep it hurts.

"You're squashing me," he mutters.

"Move over." He scoots aside and I snuggle up next to him. "So you're still alive," I whisper.

"How'd you get in?"

"I climbed in through the attic like Jack fucking Bauer, that's how."

He snorts. "It's not like you broke into the Pentagon."

"Shut up. I'm here to deliver your insulin. I'm your damn delivery girl."

"Seriously?"

My eyes are adjusting, and I can see the glimmer of his eyes on the pillow beside me. I turn to face him. "Why are you surprised?"

There's a pause, and when he answers, his voice sounds young. "I just thought maybe you gave up or something."

I want to cry. I want to hit things. I want to bust into Carol's room and beat her fucking face in. Instead, I grip Joaquin's chin. "I'm obsessed with you. Okay? I would never give up. I'm like the worst stalker girlfriend."

He hisses a little laugh.

"You know that, right? I'll bulldoze a hole in this wall before I'll let anything happen to you."

He's quiet, and then he whispers, "I don't want the insulin, though."

I sit up. *"What?"*

He sits up, too. "If I get sick, they'll take me out of here. They'll let me come live with you. You're my only family."

"Joaquin, no, they won't. Believe me, they won't."

"A social worker came here," he says, his voice rising a little. "Shh."

He drops his voice back down. "She said they don't send you to a foster home if you have family who can take you."

Fuck that social worker. "No, honey, they will. You have to trust me on this."

"Why? Don't you want me?"

My heart is going to break. "Of course I want you. I even have our bunk beds picked out."

"Nerd."

I consider my words carefully. "You know I have a record. I'm not the kind of person they give kids to."

In the darkness, I can sense him lifting his chin stubbornly. "The social worker *said*. Why would she lie?"

"Because she wants you to talk to her!" I take a breath. "I'll figure out a way to help with Carol. For now, I just need you to take care of yourself."

"No. Let her get me sick. Then they'll finally find out what she's like."

I'm frantic to make him understand. "No, dude. I know Carol's awful, but you don't understand what some foster homes are like. And you're a teenage boy from East LA. They're not sending you to the nice ones. They'll send you to one of the homes you don't want to go to, believe me. Please. You don't know how bad it can be."

"No."

I'm stunned. "Joaquin. You could enter a diabetic coma. It's not a gradual thing. Remember last time? You could *die*."

"I don't care." His voice cracks. "I'm locked in this room like a prisoner. I have nothing to do. No books. No TV. No friends, no music, no—" He's crying, I can hear it, and I reach out for him, but he pushes me away. "Don't! You did this, too. You know she's like this, and you left me here. How could you leave me here?"

I stare at his silhouette helplessly. My throat is tight with tears. "I'm sorry," I whisper.

He takes a few breaths. "No. I'm sorry. That was messed up. How could I expect you to stay with the way she treated you? I'm such a dick."

I grab his hand. "No. NO. I would have stayed, even with all that. I don't care. I'm tough. I can take it. She wouldn't *let* me stay. She kicked me out. She said she'd file a restraining order if I didn't go, and then I'd never be able to see you."

We've been through this, a hundred times. We're making the best of a shitty situation. We always have.

"Take the insulin. Please," I murmur.

"Not until I get out of here."

A light flashes. The door swings open, crashes into the wall. Carol's silhouette is black against the blinding hall light behind her.

"I knew it," she shouts, and her voice is full crazy.

"Whoa," I say. "Just be calm."

She's got her bat. I hop off the bed, draw her away from Joaquin.

"You come into my house," she snarls. She runs at me, bat raised, swings it, connects with my legs. I go down hard onto the carpet.

Joaquin cries out.

"Stay there," I yell. "Carol, stop."

"You come into MY HOUSE." She swings again. I roll. The bat hits the carpet with a thunk. I try to push myself up but she swings again and connects with my stomach. I fall back, the wind knocked out of me.

"Stop!" Joaquin screams.

I grip my stomach, try to separate myself from the pain. Pain is just a sensation. I can rise above it. "I'm sorry," I manage to tell her. "I came to see Joaquin. I missed him."

"You don't get to miss him," she screeches. Gone is the pale, dishwater-bland woman. In her place is a wild-eyed beast of rage, white nightgown fluffy around her. She swings again, catches me on the shoulder, knocking me forward. My temple hits the corner of the bed frame.

Blackness. Pain. Memories of the carpet—

—Crying into the carpet when she pulled Joaquin from my arms, my tears and drool wetting the dirty wool beneath me—Bleeding into the carpet, my busted nose on fire, pain pounding from my broken wrist—

I roll onto my back. I hear myself groaning. The bat thumps into the carpet next to my head.

Joaquin leaps out of bed and onto Carol, and he's her same size now. "Stop it!" he shouts. He's wrestling for the bat, and he's almost winning.

I try to push myself to my feet. My head swims. My cheek is warm and wet.

"Joaquin, leave it," I say. "Go into the living room."

"NO!" He wrenches the bat from Carol in an impressive display of testosterone. He heaves it aside, knocks all the shit off his nightstand. "You're a crazy fucking bitch!" he screams in her face. "I hope you die and go to hell!"

I stumble to my feet, almost passing out from the wave of pain from my forehead. I press my hand to my head and blood slides warm and wet across my palm. Carol turns to me, and we look at each other in the yellow hallway light.

"Get out of my house," she commands.

Joaquin says, "Go ahead, Jazz. Go get your head looked at. I'm fine."

I leave the backpack. I hope Joaquin will take the insulin. I'll go to Carol's church and pray to her twisted-ass God if that will get him to take it.

As I limp past Carol, I stop to look at her. She's small, and old looking, and she's taken everything from me.

If I could shoot her in the face right now and never get caught, I would. Without hesitation.

WEDNESDAY

10
GREG

I CAN DO THIS, Greg thinks, but he isn't altogether sure he can. His whole body quakes, shivers racking his arms. The syringe clutched by his side trembles against his leg. He checks his watch. 7:12 a.m. *Any minute now.*

The underground 7th and Metro station downtown is hot with the scents of cologne, weed and body odor. Commuters push past Greg as they rush to the escalators, shoulders bumping as they push past each other to get their connections to the yellow line.

Greg's heart pounds maniacally: thump-thump-thump-thump. He checks his watch. Seven fourteen.

He pulls the visor of his baseball cap down over his eyes. The brown spray they'd given him to conceal his shock of bright red hair rubs off on everything, and the inside of his cap is already sticky with it. It's funny. Where he grew up, in Chicago, his red hair was unremarkable, but here in LA, red hair is so unusual and recognizable, they had him disguise it.

They also gave him a temporary sleeve of tattoos, a hideous collection of brightly colored dragons. The idea is that, if people describe him, they'll focus on the dragon tattoos and pay less attention to facial features.

A thought slides into his head, bringing with it a new wave of panic: when this is over, he will have become a whole different person. Never again will he be someone who hasn't killed someone. From here on out, for the rest of his life, he'll be a murderer.

Doesn't matter. He'll be free from Catelyn. No more plates thrown at his head. No more mocking, no more threats. No more waking up with her on top of him, eyes wild, hips thrusting. He'll be a free man, and he'll take the burden of conscience over the chortling of policemen any day as he files report after report that all go uninvestigated. After all these years of feeling like half a man, he's going to take control.

A little voice tells him, *"You can't do it. You're weak."*

He checks his watch. Seven eighteen.

Where *is* this guy? He should have been on that last train, the red line from NoHo.

Greg searches the crowd for gray hair. Has anyone else had a hard time finding their quarry in these crowds? Of all the things he's worried about, it never occurred to him that he wouldn't be able to find the guy in the first place.

And there he is.

Relief washes through him. He's in business.

The man walks by Greg, eyes on the escalator, forehead drawn into a frown. Gray hair, gray suit, briefcase clutched under his left arm. Greg has stared at the photo of this man so much over the last twenty-four hours, he would recognize him anywhere. It's time. Now. *Go.*

He pushes himself off the wall, joining the flow of traffic

just a few people behind the man. He bumps into a crowd of teenagers and mutters, "Sorry." His heart knocks against his ribs.

He follows the gray-haired man through the crowd and gets on the escalator ten steps behind him. The man hurries off the escalator across the platform headed for the 7th Street station exit. Greg picks up his pace. He can't let him get past the next escalator, where the crowds thin out and then it's the open street.

The man's legs are long, and he has a head start. Greg jogs after him. He gets on the escalator right behind the man. This is his chance.

He bends down like he's tying his shoe, pulls the little plastic stopper off the syringe and stabs it into the man's calf, depressing the plunger.

The man kicks, knocking the syringe out of Greg's hand. It clatters into a crack in the escalator. The man spins, looking for the source of the pinch. Greg dives back down the way he's come, pushing past people going the correct way up the escalator. Shouts ring out around him as he pushes a group of women out of his way. He's in a blind panic, has no idea which way he's going, slams into a Metro cop. "Sorry," he gasps and dives into the open door of a gold line train just as it closes.

He presses his back to the door. His chest heaves. He's sweating. His whole body shakes. The train lurches and picks up speed.

He locks eyes with an old lady in a handicapped seat. Her eyes widen and she drops her gaze. He must look crazed. Everyone conspicuously ignores him, studying their phones and the toes of their shoes. Only a young man with tattoos on his shaved head looks straight at him, one corner of his mouth pinched into a smirk.

Greg shoves his hands in his pockets, afraid someone will notice the latex gloves.

How much poison does it take to kill someone? He barely got any into the man, not even a fourth of the syringe.

"Oh my God," he gasps as a horrible truth collapses down upon him. He forgot the playing card. It's still in the Ziploc baggie in his back pocket.

With unsteady hands, he pulls out the flip phone and dials the 800 number. He keys in his six-digit code and snaps it shut.

The train shudders, slowing. "Chinatown station," the speakers tell the passengers. The train jostles to a stop. When the doors whoosh open, Greg jumps out into a clean, clear morning. The San Bernardino fire has been put out, and the sun shines bright in a cloudless blue sky.

He hurries down the stairs of the two-story train station decorated like a pagoda. The phone buzzes. He flips it open. "Hello?"

"Hello, Greg?"

His voice trembles and cracks. "I fucked up. Okay? I'm sorry. I fucked up."

A pregnant pause, and then the voice says, "Calm down and tell me what happened."

He lowers his voice to a whisper. "I tried to inject him in the leg but he kicked it away. And I forgot the card. I'm not sure I got enough poison in him."

"We told you very specifically to inject into the trunk of the body. Were you unable to do so?"

"I forgot!" Greg cries, only now remembering this part of their instructions. If Catelyn were here, she'd have so much fun mocking him about it. He can hear her laughter, feel it in his bones. "I don't know if I can do this. Maybe I just don't have it in me. Why do I fuck everything up?"

"You need to calm down, Greg." The command comes through hard and dry.

Greg takes deep breaths. He feels like he's hyperventilating.

The voice goes on. "You understand, this is a complex organizational system. If one single person fails to complete their assignment, the rest of the chain falls apart."

"I'm so sorry," Greg moans. "I don't know if I can do this."

A metallic sigh hisses through the voice disguiser. "Go ahead home. I need to regroup. Do you have any plans for the rest of the day? Tomorrow?"

"I told my neighbor I'd take her to Costco tomorrow so she could use my membership card. But I can cancel."

"No. Go ahead. It's important not to draw any attention to yourself by making changes to your schedule. We'll check in with you tomorrow. And, Greg?"

"Yeah?"

"Keep the temporary tattoos for now."

"Okay." This is good. This means they're going to give him another chance.

The voice says, "I want you to think about all the people who now have to wait for justice because of you. Because you didn't follow through today, women and children will go to sleep tonight—and tomorrow night and the next night—separated from each other, victimized, tormented. This is what you've stolen from them, Greg—freedom."

11

JAZZ

I WAKE TO a dull buzzing. Through the darkness, pain in my head flashes sharp and bright.

I pull my face up. It's been squashed against the rough fabric of my couch. My body feels stiff and sore. I touch the bandage on my forehead, remember with a flash the clinic, the nurses, the stitches. Only four. Not bad.

The buzzing resumes. It registers that the sound is coming from my purse on the kitchen counter. The bright light shining through the curtains and bars on the windows tells me it's late morning.

I drag myself off the couch. The room buckles around me and my head goes fuzzy. I grip the couch arm and wait for my vision to clear.

Panic flares—did I forget to call in to work? A blank space where memory should be. And then it comes back. Right. Yes. I texted Carlos from the waiting room last night. Relief.

I look down at myself. My tank top is crusted with dried

blood, and my skin and jeans are filthy from the trek through the attic. I strip out of my clothes and replace them with a pair of boxers and a T-shirt.

I catch a glimpse of myself in the mirror that hangs on the bathroom door and straighten up to get a better look. My eyeliner is smeared, casting my eyes into shadow under my shaggy bangs. I hate the way I look in mirrors. I feel bigger from the inside, tougher, stronger. Sometimes I'm caught by my own reflection and shamed by my own smallness, by how vulnerable and female I must look to the world around me.

My head throbs. I press a hand to the stitches. I never let them prescribe me opiates out of fear of being like my drug addict biological mother, but I got a bottle of ibuprofen 800s at the clinic and I need one of those bad boys stat. I find my purse on the kitchen counter and pull the prescription bottle out of it. I take one of the pills with water from the sink. I gulp down the entire glass of chlorine-scented tap water gratefully. I fill the glass up again and chug it. Blood loss always makes me thirsty.

My purse starts buzzing again. I search through it, cursing my need to have seventeen lip balms, and finally come up with the flip phone. I stare at it in blank surprise, and then I remember yesterday's phone conversation and open it. "Hello?"

"Jasmine," the warm, genderless voice purrs. "Are you alone?"

"Yeah."

"You're in your home or car, somewhere you can't be overheard?"

"I'm in my apartment."

The voice says, "Are you all right? You don't sound well."

"I'm fine."

"Have you had a chance to think about our offer?"

I gather my thoughts. "So you give people a permanent solution to their problems with people like Carol."

"That's right."

"You know how shady this sounds. You call me on this weird burner phone I found the night some dude was murdered, using a voice disguiser, and you want me to believe you're just a nice and helpful organization who wants to help me, like, murder my foster mother?"

"You're right about us wanting to help you. We really do."

I should know better than anybody—there are no easy solutions. No one wants to help you, not for free. Everything comes at a price, and I don't even want to know what this person has in mind.

"Jasmine?"

"You know what? I think I'm good. Thanks but no thanks." I snap the phone shut and set it aside. I feel a twinge of regret, which is stupid.

I get out my French press, scoop Trader Joe's coffee into it and pick at my nails while water boils in the electric kettle. I'm a little angry with Joaquin for not wanting to take his insulin, but I also remember being his age. I was thirteen when they placed me with Carol. Jesus, Joaquin's two years younger than I was when he was born. I can't believe how young I was. I felt like I was so mature and world-weary, but I was just a kid.

The kettle clicks off, and I fill the French press with boiling water. When the coffee is ready, I pour some into my mug and sip it. It tastes like heaven.

The flip phone starts buzzing again. I drink my coffee and watch it, contemplating the green light glowing from the little rectangular screen in which shines the word *Blocked*.

I pick up the phone, open it and snap it shut.

The phone buzzes again. I gulp my coffee, flip open the phone and snap it shut.

A pause. Buzzing. I snap it open. Shut.

Pause. Buzzing. Open. Shut.

After the tenth time, I fumble the phone open before it starts buzzing and try to find the power button. I'm pressing things at random when the phone buzzes again, and I accidentally answer it. A tinny, faraway voice emits from the speaker.

"Don't hang up, Jazz, or your son will die."

The phone is a venomous snake in my hand. I bring it slowly to my ear. "What did you say?"

"We've done our research, Jasmine. We know he's your son."

I set my mug down with a clunk. "How?"

"I saw the paperwork. It looks like you gave him up without a fight."

"Fuck you!" I cry. "What the fuck do you know?"

"I know a lot, Jazz. I know your biggest fear is to be like your biological mother, and yet here you are, not living with Joaquin, not taking care of him, his life at the mercy of DCFS. How are you so different from her after all? How is his life any better than your own?"

The words slice and burn their way through me. I feel the phone drop from my hand. I press my face into my palms, dry sobs choked behind my teeth. How do they know all this? Who are they? I'm so scared, my chest gritty like my heart has been ground up into pieces.

I wish I had been smarter, stronger for Joaquin. When he was born, I was only fifteen. DCFS said it would be best if they placed him in foster care with Carol so we could stay together, so I signed the paper. But then Carol said she'd kick me out if I didn't let her adopt him—she'd always dreamed of having a baby of her own. I would have done anything to stay in the same house with Joaquin, sign any paper, and without even realizing it, I signed my life away.

I pull myself together. I have to think straight. I pick the phone up. "Are you still there?"

"Still here." The voice is patient and warm. "I'm so sorry to say those things, Jazz, but sometimes we have to be cruel to be kind. I can't watch another child die at the hands of someone like Carol. She won't do a day in prison. You know that, don't you? Not a single day. After he's dead, she'll say she followed the advice of her church, and the law protects parents whose children die this way."

I press my hand to my mouth so I won't cry out loud.

"So are you ready? Shall we get to work?" they ask gently.

I remember what they called it: a permanent solution. Are they some sort of hit-man service? They find out all this personal information about you and then blackmail you into doing something illegal? What's next—will they record me agreeing to hire them and then I'll go to jail for the rest of my life? Fat lot of good I'm going to do Joaquin behind bars.

I snap the phone shut.

It stays silent for a minute, and then it starts buzzing again.

I grab my keys off the table. I take the phone outside and, barefoot, walk it down the street to the storm gutter. I crouch down and throw it between the grates into the cavern where the raccoons and rats live, down into the sludge where no one can reach it. I hear it plop into the muck, and for a moment I want to get it back, but I can't. It's gone.

12
SOFIA

SOFIA OPENS HER mouth to interrupt Anahit's quiet reading of the documents, and then she restrains herself; she must be calm and collected. She must be taken seriously. She brushes a speck of lint off the knee of her slacks and straightens the seam of her shirtsleeve.

At last, Anahit pushes the stack of paperwork aside and folds her hands on the glossy mahogany desk. Sofia meets the brown eyes and wonders how old this woman is. Forty-five, perhaps, but the Botox makes guessing harder. Through the window behind Anahit, the hills of Encino glow orange in the late afternoon light. The sky is clear, the smoky haze swept away like it never existed.

Anahit retrieves a heavy-looking gold pen and pulls a legal pad toward her. "I see you attempted to get restraining orders a number of times. Were you ever successful?" Her voice is lightly accented, the syllables soft and round.

Sofia shakes her head. "They said he needed to explicitly threaten me."

"And he didn't?"

"He was always hurting me. I thought that was enough." Sofia's voice is bitter.

"When you say 'hurting,' what do you mean?"

It's shameful and painful to say the things out loud. "He'd grab me. Push me. Slap me."

"Were you ever hospitalized?"

"No."

Anahit makes a note on her legal pad. "When you were married, did you report the abuse?"

"No." Sofia forces herself to maintain eye contact. Her body is vibrating with shame.

"Why not?" Anahit's eyes feel judgmental, and Sofia has to look away, out the window at the view of the hills.

"I was embarrassed and afraid," she says at last.

Anahit flips through the papers again. "Help me understand what I'm seeing here. *Are* you an alcoholic?"

Sofia grips the carved wood arms of the chair she occupies. "I'm not. That was something Charles invented for court."

Scribbling. Face averted. "But he had witnesses corroborate that you had a habit of drinking when your daughter was with you. Is that not what happened?"

"No, it isn't. I never have more than a glass of wine when I have Olive. Those witnesses were his buddies. They just said what he told them to say." She prays the truth shines clear in her voice, silently begs Anahit to intuit the authenticity of her words.

Anahit frowns. "You didn't bring witnesses of your own to testify on your behalf? Couldn't you have asked your own friends to rebut his claims?"

This hurts, a spike through her stomach. "No," Sofia says. "He sent all our friends those photos. Said they happened while we were married, that I was cheating on him. All our friends…they were really all his friends. I wasn't allowed to make friends he didn't approve. The ones I had before we got married were a 'bad influence.'" She does air quotes. "I haven't spoken to any of my college friends since Charles and I started dating."

When Anahit gets to the envelope with the photographs, Sofia holds out a hand. "Please don't look at those. There's no need."

Anahit sits back. "So let me make sure I understand. You fired your lawyer because of the outcome of this case." She gestures to the stacks of paperwork on her desk.

"Yes."

"Your ex-husband, Charles, is a family law attorney? In Los Angeles?"

"His office is in Woodland Hills, yes."

"And he hired a private investigator to follow you to prove you weren't properly caring for your daughter. The PI provided photographic evidence of, um…" She clears her throat. "Sexual activity, and evidence that you were living…"

"A wild, promiscuous lifestyle," Sofia finishes. "It was crap. None of those photos were taken when I had Olive. They were all taken on Charles's weekends."

"And there was evidence of chronic alcoholism, and prescription drug abuse."

Sofia's heart pumps harder. "I've never even heard of those drugs he mentioned in court."

"So the judge said, what? You should test yourself with the Breathalyzer every day, get drug tested weekly? Take parenting classes? And then you can get some visitation back after six months or so? That seems reasonable. Perhaps we can discuss a visitation schedule you'd be happy with."

Anger cracks like a whip. "I hold two master's degrees, one in early childhood education and one in educational administration. I am a good mother. I don't need parenting classes. I was never promiscuous. I slept with three people while I was separated, over a period of six months. Does that sound promiscuous to you?" Anahit drops her eyes to her own wedding ring and doesn't answer. Sofia contemplates the averted face. "Let me ask you a question, Anahit. How many partners would be appropriate for a woman in my situation? Since three is obviously too many." Underneath the forced calm, her voice is tight.

"I don't believe that's for me to say."

"Just say what you think. How many? Two? One?"

Anahit sighs heavily. "Well, if you're in the middle of a contentious divorce with an ex-husband who has the resources to create problems—"

"How many?"

"If you were my client then, I'd have advised you to abstain from dating until after the divorce was finalized. Until after we were done in court."

"So zero. I should have slept with zero people."

Anahit shrugs.

"Do you think Charles's lawyer would tell him the same thing? That he should go a year or two without sex so it doesn't make him look slutty in court?"

"I'm not able to speak to that."

Fury and rage sweep through Sofia's intestines, hot enough to burn her alive. She wants to scream like an animal, throw all these papers in Anahit's face, trash this office, beat Anahit into a bloody pulp. She wants to torch it all, burn this building to the fucking ground.

And then she realizes.

This is a farce. She's been fooling herself.

She's wasted enough time and money on Charles. She doesn't want to expend another minute on this rigged game.

Maybe that's why she came here. She needed to know she was finished before she does something she can't take back. She doesn't just want justice.

She wants revenge.

13
JAZZ

I GET UP and approach the DCFS reception counter. My butt is sore from the plastic chair I've been in for the last two hours. I fix my bangs, straightening them so they cover the Band-Aid that hides my stitches. I wait behind a girl with a baby on her hip, and finally the woman at the counter beckons me forward.

"I've been waiting for two hours," I tell the receptionist, a middle-aged lady with gray roots.

"Name?"

"Jasmine Benavides."

She types it into her computer. "There are three people ahead of you. Is there anything else I can help you with?" This means I need to sit down and shut up.

I hesitate; I don't want to piss her off. "I'm sorry. I know you're busy. But my brother needs someone to go check on him. He's not getting his insulin. It's—"

She holds a hand up. "Ma'am. I am not a social worker.

You do not need to give me this information. When you get called, you can tell the social worker all of this." She looks behind me at the line. "Next, please."

I return to my seat. It's like the DMV in here, but everyone looks nervous and alone, especially the women surrounded by children.

The last time I was here, I came in with a black eye and my arm in a cast to beg them to give me my parental rights back. I got a big fat no on that one. I should have reported Carol much earlier, when the ink wasn't so dry on all the paperwork. By the time I was nineteen, I had a string of offenses on my record starting in middle school. Carol was a nice, sweet, unassuming foster mom. Looking at the two of us, I don't know if I'd have believed me, either.

Before Joaquin came along, it was always slaps in the face and evenings in my room without dinner, which was nothing compared to the shit I saw in other foster homes. But when Joaquin came and Carol claimed him as hers, having me around seemed to drive her into rages of increasing intensity. It infuriated her to see me with Joaquin, to see the bond we shared, the similarities between us. She hated to let me hold him, to let me feed him. One night when I was sixteen, she caught me curled up next to him in his crib, sleeping with his little body nestled against mine, and that was the first time she lost it and I ended up with a broken collarbone. She said if I reported her, she'd send me to a different foster home and I'd lose Joaquin forever.

Now I think she was bluffing. I should have told DCFS everything. I should have begged on the street, sold my body, anything to get enough money for a lawyer. I might have still had a chance back then.

But then the first time turned into the third time, which

turned into the fifth time, and then I was throwing Joaquin in my car and crossing state lines, and any chances I ever had to get him back from her were gone.

My iPhone buzzes, and I pull it out. It's Andre, wanting to know if I'm coming to rehearsal.

I reply, Probably not, but I will if I can. Working on some family stuff.

We have a show coming up, don't forget, he says, and I scowl at the screen.

"Jasmine Benavides?" a voice calls. I snap my head up. A grandmotherly woman is scanning the crowded room.

I stand, nervous, and raise a hand.

An hour later finds me slamming out of the glass door onto the sidewalk. My chest heaves unevenly. I think I'm having a panic attack. I have to get away from this looming tower of oppression. I turn my feet toward the street and walk so fast I'm almost running.

I fumble my keys out of my purse and shove one of them into the door of my truck, and then I hop in. I pull the door shut behind me, and I'm safe in a hot little cocoon that smells like cherry air freshener and old leather seats. I turn on the engine, crank the A/C, and sit staring out the window at the packed sidewalks and colorful restaurants of Koreatown. I feel like people can see me in here. I don't like it.

I lie down sideways on the bench seat and pull my knees up to my nose. I wrap my arms around my legs and lace my fingers together, which always makes me feel calm, like an orphaned baby elephant holding on to its own tail.

In the darkness against my knees, I breathe.

The grandmotherly social worker had taken my report and then closed the folder. She said they already sent a social worker to see Joaquin, and he was perfectly healthy. His doctor confirmed his prescription had been picked up, and he isn't due for a checkup for four more months, so everything is in order. She doesn't have an army of social workers to do daily checks on kids when everything looks fine.

"*I* picked the prescription up," I cried, pounding a fist to my own chest. "I did. She won't give it to him."

"Where is the medication now?"

"At Carol's house. But—"

"That's good, then! So he has his insulin, and I'll keep my eyes on this. We'll let you know if we need anything else from you."

Why am I surprised? Why had I thought it would be any different this time?

Eventually I sit up. I feel dirty with emotion. I slap myself in the face, hard. My cheek bristles.

Better. Again, with the other hand this time. It stings, but now I'm back in the present.

Cheeks burning, I turn the car on. Fine, then. If DCFS won't check on Joaquin, I'll do it. I'll go there every goddamn day.

Carol's house is dark. Even though it's dusk and the palm trees are fading into black silhouettes against the purple sky, the windows show not a hint of light. In the median strip in front of her house, a pair of abandoned shopping carts lean into each other like drunk girls leaving a club.

I frown at the house for a moment, and then I cross the street, march right up to the metal front screen door and bang on it. I pound and pound with my fist, but nothing happens except the neighbors' dogs start barking.

My eyes land on the rusty mailbox, which is attached crook-

edly to the porch railing. It's overflowing with mail and cat-
alogs.

That's weird. Carol is super paranoid about identity thieves—
why, I don't know; she has a net worth of, like, four dollars—
and she collects the mail the moment it arrives, which is always
around ten o'clock in the morning.

Hmm.

If it were Sunday, I'd say they could be at church, but her
church is too small to have midweek services; it's a one-room
schoolhouse type of place. I know she's not going to a new
church because Joaquin specifically told me "she's back at that
snake charmer church," the little church in the row of warehouses near his old elementary school.

I step off the porch and make my way around the house.
The ladder is still here, leaning against the back wall. I bang
on the back door. Nothing.

I push the ladder back up to the vent, which is still open and
probably will be forever until I close it. I climb up and topple into the attic, coating my clothes in dusty rat shit. I don't
even try to be quiet. I tromp straight to the trapdoor, release
it and jump down to the hallway with a crash. The house is
dark, silent and stale.

"Hello?" I yell.

Nothing.

My heart stutters as I imagine dead bodies and cults and
murder-suicides and victims of poisoning. I cross the hall and
push through the door into Joaquin's room.

At first glance, it looks normal. Messy. I switch on the
overhead light. My black backpack is still crumpled into a
pile on the floor. I squat down and open it. The white CVS
bag is gone.

That's good, right? That means he took the insulin with him wherever he went.

The dresser drawers are partway open. I pull one open all the way, and then my chest freezes.

It's almost empty.

I pull open drawer after drawer. Underwear, almost all gone but for a few old pairs. Socks, only a handful of mismatched, holey black ones left at the bottom. All his favorite T-shirts are gone, leaving only the ones he hates—the school T-shirts they make them wear for spirit day, the dorky polo shirt Carol bought him for church.

I leave his room and hurry down the hallway toward Carol's room. I flick the light on.

The drawers are like Joaquin's: ajar and pretty much empty, her favorite shirts gone, most of the underwear and jeans cleaned out.

I check the tiny en suite bathroom that adjoins Carol's room. I open the medicine cabinet. The toothbrush is gone.

A white bag is crumpled on the floor by the toilet. I kneel down and pick it up. It's the CVS bag, Joaquin's prescription label stapled onto the side. On the floor are little piles of shattered glass—the insulin bottles, violently crushed, their silver caps bent and scattered. My eyes travel to a pair of Carol's ancient sneakers that lie nearby. I pick one up. Glass shards are embedded in the thinning rubber sole. I flip the shoe over and see blood inside. She cut her foot. That's how hard she stomped on the insulin vials.

I storm from room to room. Hall bathroom—Joaquin's toothbrush is gone. In the kitchen, I pull the fridge open. It's empty. Not a single item remains.

I press my hands to my mouth.

Carol has no family. They're all dead. She's from Tennessee. She doesn't really have friends. I guess she could have met someone at church?

I take a deep, shaky breath.

Alone in this silent house, the epicenter of the worst things that have ever happened to me, I feel more helpless than I have ever felt in my life.

14
JAZZ

I'M IN KNOTS when I get home. I take my clothes off, yank on leggings and a tank top, and pull on my Nikes and gloves. I lock the door on my way out. I need to move; I need to run. I need to sweat and burn off fear. I need to think, and I can't think while I sit still.

I live on the second floor, and at the end of the exterior walkway, at the top of the stairwell that leads down to the front, is a rusty service door. I'm the only one except the landlord with a key to it. The hallway leads to a dirty, dark stairwell. I jog up the thirteen stairs. Crisp evening air prickles my cheeks as I emerge onto the flat, tar-papered roof.

Tucked behind the stairwell just above my apartment is my punching bag. I pay my landlord an extra fifty bucks a month to keep it up here, and it's worth it to be able to work out alone overlooking the hills of Echo Park and the outskirts of downtown.

The skyscrapers in the distance glitter against the clear night sky. I usually love to look at them, but tonight I don't care about the city sparkling like Christmas. I care about hitting the punching bag as hard as I can. I want to hit it so hard it hurts *me*.

I strap my gloves on with my teeth and start with some combos. As my breath comes faster and my muscles start to burn along with the stitches in my temple, I think about Joaquin. I let the pain have me, let it get its teeth deep inside me. Cross, cross, jab, jab, roundhouse. Jab, cross, uppercut.

A roar builds from the east. I think it's an earthquake, but then a helicopter shoots by, wind from its blades blowing my bangs into my eyes. I watch it pass, always sort of fascinated by them. I wipe my bangs off my face and get back to working out.

I can't believe Carol took Joaquin. Where could she have gone? I could call DCFS, but I'd have to confess to breaking and entering, and besides, she hasn't committed a crime. It's not illegal for a mom to take her kid somewhere. For all DCFS cares, she could go back to Tennessee. She could go to fucking Mexico if she wants.

I hit the bag hard enough to feel it in my shoulder joints. My head throbs. I don't give a fuck. Let it throb. Let the stitches bleed.

Eventually I wear myself out, and I catch my breath. I drop my keys off at my apartment, taking my main house key off the ring and tucking it into my sneaker, and run down the stairs. The walkway lets me out onto Lucas Avenue, which I follow around a wide curve, past a high school, a pawnshop, a Laundromat, a liquor store, and a row of tents and shopping carts. I turn left at 4th Street and jog down to weave my way through the skyscrapers.

By the time I make it back up the hill and to my apartment, I'm gasping, drenched in sweat, all my pain siphoned into muscles and tendons and bone.

I stop to glare at a beat-up couch someone has put on my front lawn. How do any of the people on my street even have couches inside their apartments at this point?

My quads shudder as I climb the steps, and I don't notice the cardboard box on my doorstep until I squat down to dig my key out of my shoe.

I flip the box over. It has an Amazon label and is addressed to me. I must have ordered something and forgotten.

Inside, I toss the box on the kitchen table, lock the dead bolts and turn on the lights. I fill up a glass of water and drain it in one gulp. I'm just kicking off my Nikes when the box starts buzzing.

The hell?

I slip my Trader Joe's box cutter out of my purse and cut through the Amazon tape. I open the cardboard flaps and peer inside.

Nestled in a little bed of cardboard is a flip phone just like the one I got rid of. The green light from the little caller ID window lights up the box. *BLOCKED.*

"Oh, shit," I whisper.

I back away until I hit the couch, and I plop down onto it. The springs squeak in protest.

The package was on my doorstep. They know where I live.

Of course they know where I live! They know everything about me! The court documents where I'd signed over my parental rights were supposed to be sealed; I was a minor. If they know that, they can find my damn address.

Did they actually order this from Amazon, or do they have some fake Amazon packaging materials?

Who is *they*?

The box starts buzzing again.

I get up. I cross the room, grab the phone out of the box and snap it open. "Hello?"

"We know where they are," the voice says.

I can't speak for a full five seconds, and then I gather myself together and say, "Excuse me?"

"We know where Joaquin and Carol are."

It takes me a moment to sort through my thoughts, but then I say, "Where are they, then?"

"That's not how this works. We deal in permanent solutions. Do you want a permanent solution or not?"

"Fuck." I press my face into my hand, clutch at my sweaty bangs. At last, I say, "So, what, you're like a hit man? You want a bunch of money from me?"

"We are a support service. We are not hit men. We help people help themselves. Imagine if a complete stranger took care of Carol for you. No money would ever have to change hands if you simply returned the favor for someone in the same situation."

"How do I trust you? How do I know anything you say is real? I don't know you!"

A pause. "What time is it? Is it eight o'clock yet?"

The question feels like a complete non sequitur, but I look up at the wall clock. "It's, like, three minutes till eight. Why?"

"Good! See? This is meant to be. The timing is perfect. Turn on Channel 11. This will help you understand."

"You want me to watch TV?"

"Do it now or it'll be too late."

I don't know why I obey, but I turn on my old-ass TV with the remote that only sometimes works. It sparks to life, and I abuse the channel button until it changes to eleven. I pick up the phone again. "Fine. There. I'm on Channel 11. It's a beer commercial. Are you suggesting I need a beer? Because you aren't wrong."

As I say that, the commercial ends, and the camera zooms out to show a handful of people in suits and police uniforms. The banner below them reads *LAPD Deputy Chief Antonio Vela, Chief of Detectives, Live in Front of LAPD Headquarters.*

A middle-aged man in a suit steps forward to address a roomful of reporters. He says, "I'm here with my colleagues, Detectives Patel and Nielsen, and Lieutenants Nguyen and Washington." He gestures to the line of people behind him. "We're going to walk through the basics of this case with you and answer all the questions we can. First, I want to go ahead and disclose that it seems we have a serial murderer selecting victims at random in public places. So far we have six victims across the LA Metro area."

A flurry of activity from the audience. He continues. "We can't release many of the details. But this is a public safety concern, and we want to be as transparent as possible without hindering our investigation." He flips through a handful of note cards, and I realize he is nervous. His voice shakes a little, and the way he handles the cards is clumsy. "This is an opportunistic killer. We think he selects his victims by location. We're working with the FBI's profiling team, and they believe we're looking for a mass shooter type, someone who wants to make his mark, most likely a white male aged twenty-four to forty." He looks up from his cards and addresses the camera. "People need to be careful. We've confirmed murders in two Metro stations, the Universal CityWalk, the Burbank Walmart, the Santa Monica Pier and a nightclub downtown. People should be aware of the behavior of those around them when they are in crowded places. Do not take drinks offered to you by strangers. Be on the lookout for people holding strange objects, objects you wouldn't expect to see people carrying around. Be aware of your surroundings. Call any suspicious behavior in to the number on your screen." An 800 number for LAPD replaces the biographical information in the banner.

The reporters erupt with questions. Vela points to someone off camera.

"Are all the victims men so far?" the reporter asks.

He leans toward the microphone. "So far, all victims have been men, but that doesn't mean the killer's intent is to stick with men only. Women should be on the lookout as well." He points to someone else.

"What is the murder weapon?"

"Poison."

"Given in food? Or are we talking about an agent dispersed into the air?"

Vela covers the microphone and looks at the row of people behind him. A woman in a black suit comes forward to whisper something in his ear. He returns to the microphone and says, "The poison was administered as an injection. But the same poison could be administered orally, so people should be conscious of what they eat and drink. These are crimes of opportunity, and we expect this killer to improvise if need be."

The reporters turn the room into chaos. He holds his hands up and raises his voice. "I can't answer any other questions about the murder weapon. Let's move on."

Another reporter says, "Three of these victims had police records. One was accused of spousal abuse, one of sexual assault and one of stalking. Are you sure these are random killings, or is this a pattern?"

Vela's sharp brown eyes jump back toward the line of people behind him. "We are very sure there is no connection between any of these victims, and we're treating them as random killings at this time. However, if anyone has information, they should call the hotline and we'll take every tip seriously. Now, that's all we have for you tonight, but we'll be keeping the public updated as the investigation progresses."

Vela makes a final hand-raised gesture and backs away from the mic. The reporters are respectful; they stop asking questions as soon as he gives the cue, except for one, who raises her voice above the bustle.

"Can you tell us about the playing cards?"

Vela freezes, turns, glares into the audience. He leans down into the mic and says, "No."

I'd almost forgotten about the phone, frozen in my hand. From it, the warped voice says, "Jasmine? Turn off the TV, please."

I reach for the remote and punch the power button. The picture sucks itself into a tiny rectangle in the center of the screen and disappears into the dark.

From the phone, the voice says, "I understand you have reservations. You're right to be worried about working with an anonymous person such as myself. But you need to understand what you're passing up. You have a chance to be part of a movement. Do you think you're the only person lawyers won't help? The only person police turn away? We're fed up, and we're taking back control. We want to help you get your life back so you can be a proper mother to your son. Isn't that what you want?"

I swallow against a dry lump that stops up my throat.

"It costs you nothing. You help someone and then someone helps you. It's quick. It's easy. Anyone can do it. And you'll never be a suspect in the assignment you commit because you're a complete stranger to everyone involved. And when it's Carol's turn, you can arrange to have an alibi, so you'll never be a suspect in that death, either. It's rock solid. *This* is how justice gets served, Jasmine."

I have a friend at work, an ex-gangster from El Salvador whose sister was raped on a first date. The guy who raped her disappeared shortly thereafter. No one asked what happened to him. No one ever needed to. This is that same kind of justice, the kind that finds you, the kind that hunts you down.

At last, I say, "You really know where Joaquin and Carol are?"

"We really do."

"How does it work? What do I do? I trade murders with someone else? Do I meet them?"

"No. It's more of a relay system. I assign you to someone, and then I assign someone to you, but you never know who you're helping, and the person who's helping you never knows who you are. It's completely anonymous."

"Except *you* know who I am," I point out.

"You'll have to trust me."

"Right. Great. Awesome. I have to trust the creepy voice disguiser serial killer phone stalker. Perfect." I'm losing it. I'm totally and completely losing it.

"There's a package for you on the roof by your punching bag. Go get it. I'll wait until you return."

I snap my face toward the door. "By my punching bag? I was just up there—there was no package."

"There wasn't, but there is now. Go ahead and grab it. I'll wait."

This is so creepy, my skin actually crawls. They were here, just a little while ago. They could be nearby, sitting in a car or an apartment building.

"Jasmine? Can you go get the box, please?"

I hear myself say, "I'll be right back." I set the phone aside. I get my keys, let myself out and lock the dead bolts behind me. I head down the exterior walkway. The rough, peeling paint floor is cold on my sock feet as I run up the dark steps, half expecting someone to jump out at me like in a horror movie.

I check around behind the maze of half walls and piles of tar paper. No one's up here; nothing looks different, except that on the ground next to my punching bag sits a cardboard box.

A faint wail. Sirens. A few blocks away.

I freeze. Was it a trap? Are the cops about to show up?

The sirens swell and fade, and then they're gone.

I retrieve the box and run downstairs like someone's chasing me. Inside my apartment, I set the box down on the table and twist the dead bolts into place. The phone waits faceup on the table, and I pick it up. "I have the package," I say, and suddenly I want to laugh at the ridiculousness of me, grocery store employee, saying these words into a burner phone like the world's worst knockoff James Bond.

The voice says, "What you have there is a kit containing everything you need in order to take care of your target. We'll send you information on the target later, but for now, it's important for you to practice."

Like the one the phone came in, the box has the paper Amazon tape, but this time there's no shipping label.

"Practice?" I repeat.

"You'll see. Now go ahead and open it."

I cut the tape with my box cutter and pull apart the cardboard flaps. "I see a few oranges? Are you serious?"

"You'll need those. You can pull them out and set them aside."

They're squishy and overripe. I set them down on the table. "This is like a fucked-up Blue Apron."

The voice dissolves into chuckles. "Oh, Jasmine. That's quite funny."

I return to the box. "I see…a Ziploc bag with…" I pull it out. "A playing card inside?"

"Do not open that yet. It's very important to leave it in the bag. You'll open that with gloves on at the scene."

"The four of spades. Okay, then. Suuuuper creepy." I set it aside. "A Ziploc bag full of latex gloves." I pull it out of the box. "What's next? A mask made out of human skin?"

"Set the gloves aside as well. Don't open them inside your apartment and get any forensic evidence from your apartment on them. Otherwise, you might transfer something from your apartment onto the playing card later. What else?"

"I see a… I don't know how to describe it. A plastic box. No, like, kind of an EpiPen case?"

"There should be two of those. Those are called sharps containers and are used to store syringes. One of them should be blue and one should be yellow with black markings on it. Why don't you pull them out, but do *not* open them."

I lift the first one out. It's clear with a blue plastic cap, and inside rests a large empty syringe. The second one, which has a yellow cap, is emblazoned with a black-and-white poison symbol, a skull and crossbones like the one tattooed on my ring finger. *Biohazard*, the sticker reads.

"What—the—fuck," I breathe.

"The blue container is your tester. That's your practice needle. You'll be practicing on the oranges. The yellow one is what you'll be using to take care of your target, and that one is quite lethal, so you'll need to be very careful. Do not open it until you are at the scene and wearing gloves. And for God's sake, don't poke yourself with it."

I sit in one of the kitchen chairs. This feels surreal, and I

THE KILL CLUB | 113

suddenly want the whole thing to go away. I ask, "What's to stop me from chickening out and bringing all this shit to the police? I can't believe you trust me enough to just send me a needle full of poison. And how do I even know it's real poison? What if you're setting me up somehow and I get to wherever you send me and the poison doesn't work?"

They don't miss a beat. "Jazz, if you take those things to the police, you'll immediately be implicated in the deaths that have already happened. Like it or not, it's already too late for you to back out. Unless you think the police will take you at your word that you just happened to innocently get your hands on the exact same poison used to kill six different people, including one right in front of you at Villains."

I whisper, "Fuck."

"But don't worry. You're going to do great. I want you to practice tonight. Let the orange roll around and inject it with water from the blue syringe over and over until you feel confident. I assume you know how to get water into a syringe?"

"I'm good with needles." My heart is pounding. I'm freaking out a little. What have I gotten myself into?

"I'll give you the rest of the information tomorrow when I give you your assignment," the voice says. "Please don't start Googling anything related to this. We'll give you all the info you need. And the most important thing is, you can't talk about this with anyone. Not a friend, not a colleague, not a lawyer, nobody."

"First rule of murder club. Don't talk about murder club. Got it."

A pause, and I think I hear them trying not to laugh. "Now, I need to know your schedule for the next week so I can plan your assignment. Can we go through that now?"

I give them my work schedule, my rehearsal schedule. They

want to know if I have any dates lined up, any "social engagements," as they put it. They want to know if I have doctor's appointments; a significant other; plans to go to the grocery store. To that, I say, "Why would I go to a grocery store? I literally work at a grocery store," and the voice says that must be nice, and the total insanity of this comes crashing down on me again. "Hey," I say. I try to find the right words for this. "Joaquin—he doesn't have a lot of time. If he stops taking his insulin now, he might only have a week before keto-acidosis kicks in."

"I fully understand. I'm hoping to send you on your assignment tomorrow or the day after, which means Carol would be taken care of within a few days of that. We're looking at a full resolution within the week."

I don't know if I feel afraid or relieved. The skull and crossbones on the yellow sharps container stares me down. "How bad is that poison? What does it feel like to die that way?"

"It's similar to the lethal injection that is used by correctional facilities. It immediately incapacitates, and the target passes on within a few minutes. It's very humane."

I open and close my mouth, choosing from a thousand questions, and eventually say, "You said you know where Joaquin is. Is he in LA?"

"Yes, they're local enough for us to make a move very quickly when it's time."

"I bet they're staying with some people she met at that church."

"Possibly," the voice says, and I feel like I've hit the nail on the head.

"Okay," I say, and in that one word is contained an ocean of acceptance. This is where I am. This is what I'm doing.

I've already made my decision, and now all that's left is to walk it out.

When we get off the phone, I sit with the sharps container in my hand. It's quiet in here.

Where will Carol be when they kill her? Church? The grocery store?

I think about what the reporter said, that the people who have been killed have had records of stalking, domestic violence. It actually sounds like the voice on the phone is who they say they are.

They invented a serial killer. The police are searching LA for a murderer that doesn't exist.

I don't know how I feel about this, morally. Is it bad to kill someone like Carol? Does she deserve the death sentence? Do I have any feelings about her being dead?

I pick up the yellow container and peer through the clear plastic at the syringe. The liquid inside is a bright, sickening yellow, and the outside of the syringe is stamped with another skull and crossbones. The plunger is bright yellow, too; everything about it is designed to look dangerous.

Down on the table, the four of spades sits inside its Ziploc bag. I flip it over. The back is decorated with tiny antique-looking blackbirds nestled in flowering vines and a maze of paisleys.

I realize they never answered my question about what it feels like. I remember the guy I saw die at Villains. I heard him scream. It's definitely not painless.

But then I remember Carol with her baseball bat crunching through my bones like glass, and I think, *Good.*

THURSDAY

15
SOFIA

HERE IN THE bathroom stall, Sofia wills herself into calm. The wig clings to her head like an itchy vise, trying to distract her, but she has years of experience maintaining a state of calm in the middle of a hurricane of distractions. She taught middle school English for five years.

She closes her eyes.

She summons an image of Charles from Olive's baby days. He'd come home from work late, still on the phone. Olive crawled up to him and tried to pull herself to a standing position on his leg. He looked for the source of the interruption and kicked Olive off his leg, then took his phone to the patio. Olive lay there on her back, eyes wide and stricken. Sofia threw the lettuce she was washing aside and scooped Olive into her arms. Their hearts beat together, and Olive cried quietly into Sofia's neck. "There, baby girl," Sofia crooned. "You're so good. You're so pretty." And then, "I'm going to get us out of here, okay, sweetie? Mama's going to find us a way out."

Sofia opens her eyes. She is the mother bear, the terrifying maternal beast. Today, she is not the victim. Today, she is the thing to be feared.

She pulls a mirror out of her fanny pack and checks her disguise. It consists of big ugly glasses, a gray-haired wig underneath a pink sun visor to hide her face from surveillance cameras, and a false stomach under a velour jogging suit. She looks like a retired PE teacher.

In the spirit of the character she's playing, Sofia has a bundle of canvas tote bags. She loops the handles over her shoulder and conceals the syringe in her hand behind them.

It's time. He should be here soon. She lets herself out of the bathroom.

She's instantly engulfed in the chaos of Costco. Children in carts crying; a woman on a motor scooter; a couple lugging a giant color television. Sofia makes her way through the crowded aisles to the front of the store, where she pretends to study a display of cereal and keeps an eye on the front door.

Her target walks in ten minutes later. She recognizes him right away from the photos she was sent this morning. He's six feet tall, with a messy head of bright red hair and a hideous collage of brightly colored dragon tattoos all down his left arm. His companion is an older woman, perhaps an aunt or family friend given the age difference. As Sofia watches, the woman leads him past the dry goods aisle straight for the deli and meat section at the back of the store.

Sofia doesn't want to be seen on camera following or watching them, so she goes the opposite way, looping slowly around an aisle full of wineglasses, toasters and space heaters before coming to the deli aisle from the opposite side. She weaves between families and old people, passes a couple arguing about shrimp, and spots her target and the woman in deep conversation over a case full of smoked salmon. Sofia edges nearer. She casts a furtive glance around. No one is looking at her. She reaches into her fanny pack, withdraws the playing card from its little Ziploc baggie and walks it over to the salami case. She pretends to search for the perfect salami and drops the card down the side onto the floor. Nobody notices. She moves toward her target.

The man is in line for a sample. His red hair is clearly visible above the other heads around him. Sofia joins the crowd. Someone jostles her from behind, pushing her forward. Her target is just ahead of her in line. This is her chance.

Her heart is pounding, a wild staccato rhythm.

She flicks the rubber tip off the syringe with a latex-gloved thumb. The needle is naked now, dangerous.

She pretends to stumble into him, getting as close as she can. Quick and calm, she stabs him in the waist and depresses the plunger.

He cries out, but nobody notices. She withdraws the syringe as he spins to search for the source of the pain. She looks straight ahead and drops the syringe into the bag on her shoulder. He cries out again and grabs his back like he's been stung by a bee.

"This is ridiculous," Sofia hisses in her best angry grandma voice, and she turns and pushes her way out of line. She moves toward the front exit. She's passing the clothing and candy when she hears shouts from the other side of the store. The kids working the doors are unimpressed; they glance lazily over their shoulders and then resume checking receipts. Sofia slips past the lines of shopping carts and out into the parking lot. She doesn't want to hear the screams. She can't let herself think about that part of it.

The evening sky is a deep, rich indigo. A quick, cool breeze dances forward and whips the bangs of the wig around her face.

I did it!

She picks up her pace, crosses the lot toward the side street she'd parked on. She inhales the ocean-scented air. The houses on this street are quaint and well kept, their midcentury facades newly painted, low-water gardens planted in the front yards. An airplane roars faintly overhead, released into the atmosphere by the nearby LAX.

It's a beautiful evening. It's a great moment to be alive.

Charles will be dead within a week.

Already, she's mentally rearranging her apartment to make a spot for a toddler bed, organizing closet space, planning a new day care closer to work. She imagines Olive at the dinner table with her, Olive on hikes in Griffith Park, Olive at the beach and the movies and snuggling in front of cartoons on Saturday mornings.

I did it!

Twin tears course down her cheeks, and a sob escapes Sofia's throat. It's been a long, hard road, and it's finally almost over.

16
JAZZ

LEAVING LOS ANGELES feels like a balloon deflating in my chest. As the snarl of the city unfolds into the wide-stretched streets of Orange County, I roll down a window to combat the car sickness generated by two hours on the 5 surrounded by 18-wheelers.

The directions have me get off the freeway in Fullerton, which is a city in north Orange County I've seen on maps but never visited. It turns out to be a bubble of idyllic suburbia, and I pass at least five frozen yogurt shops on my way through the winding streets lined with eucalyptus trees instead of the palm trees I'm used to.

Why would they send me here? They said they were glad to have me because my assignment was impossible for most of their members to do, but now I can't help but wonder what they were thinking. They didn't give me a disguise or anything.

I have to use paper directions I'd scrawled on a napkin; I

can't use Google Maps and have this trip on my Google history, and anyway, my iPhone is powered off lest it ping a nearby cell tower.

I turn off a six-lane boulevard onto a smaller street lined with warehouses, an animal shelter, a liquor store and at last a dive bar. I think I've found the rough side of Fullerton, if that is even possible. I bump into a cracked asphalt parking lot lit red by a neon sign declaring the dive bar to be the Last Stop Roadhouse. Strains of "Hotel California" drift into my truck like a toxic gas. I turn the engine off.

I sit here in my safe, cozy truck, eyes on the crooked neon sign, hands clamped on the steering wheel.

I don't know if I can do this.

I wonder if the other people feel this way, the others who have done these murders. At work today, I read an article that said the killings are up to eight. That's eight people who have been successful. If they can do it, I can do it. Tomorrow, there will be a ninth murder on the news, and then Carol will die and that will make ten, and then more murders will happen, and mine will be lost in the jumble. With Carol dead, I'll be Joaquin's next of kin. He'll be mine, like he always should have been.

I'll need to find a bigger apartment.

I laugh, a brief, choked sound. It feels so real when I think about it like that, and suddenly I'm full of confidence. How many times have I given Joaquin injections while he squirmed and thrashed? I'm sure the other eight people didn't have this much experience with needles.

I dig the flip phone out of my purse along with my little piece of paper. I type in the 800 number, wait for the beep and then press the six-digit code I was given, which they say identifies me. It's kind of like a pager, I guess. I try to remember the last time I paged anyone.

The flip phone rings a minute later, and I open it. "Hello?"

"Hello, Jasmine," the voice greets me. "Where are you?"

"In Fullerton at this roadhouse place." I survey the bank of motorcycles parked in front of the entrance. "This is a biker bar, I assume."

"Yes, it is."

"I was wondering why you were sending me, of all people, to Fullerton. This makes more sense."

A chuckle. "All right. Well. It's time to give you information on your target. I've sent you a photograph. Please confirm when you've received it."

The phone buzzes at my ear. I open the picture message, which comes through old-school on SMS. It's a worn-out white lady in her fifties or sixties. She has a dirty blond mullet and reminds me of Carol a little bit. "She looks like a tweaker," I say.

"Good guess! She actually deals methamphetamines out of this bar. She's quite the mastermind and has proven a very difficult target to catch. She stays away from crowds except for this bar, which she frequents nightly."

I take another look at the photo. The woman's eyes are cold and hard. This might be a mug shot, actually.

The voice says, "We're so glad we found you. We've struggled to find someone who could infiltrate a venue like this without sticking out like a sore thumb."

"I mean…thanks? I guess?"

"I suppose that didn't sound very complimentary. Sorry about that. Now, can you verify that you have what you need?"

I check my purse. There's the yellow syringe in its plastic container alongside the baggie containing the skin-toned latex gloves. Another little baggie contains the blackbird playing card, the four of spades. "I have everything," I confirm.

"And you know what to do with the card, when to put the gloves on, how to handle the syringe? Do you have any questions?"

I run through all the things I was told to do, which is hard with my heart pounding its way outside of my chest. "I remember everything. To be honest, I'm just nervous as fuck."

"That's very normal."

"Have you ever had anyone panic at the last minute? Like, chicken out?"

"Everyone feels nervous, but if you hold fast to your motivation, you'll find you're stronger than you know. Plus, we've made it very, very easy."

I try to quiet the pounding of my heart. "Okay," I say.

"Jasmine, have you ever heard the song 'Blackbird' by The Beatles?"

"Of course."

"Do you remember the lyrics?"

"Yeah, I guess so."

"I'm sure you've wondered why we do what we do. You can imagine that this organization doesn't run itself. It's expensive, and it requires a significant investment of time on my part."

"Well, yeah, I guess it must."

"I do this because I want to help people take power back. I want you to be that blackbird singing in the dead of night. I want to empower you to take your broken wings and learn to fly. That's why I do this. To give you what no one could give me when I was in your position."

It's so cheesy; it makes me cringe and squirm. I want to make a joke. But the voice is so earnest, so solemn and warped.

"Now, let's talk logistics," the voice says, businesslike again.

"I'd like you to go inside without your items to make sure the doormen won't be searching your purse and to make sure she's here tonight. She travels with an entourage. Getting to her will be no easy task. It may be a matter of ambushing her in the bathroom."

"Got it." I pull my wallet out of my purse and stash the purse under the seat.

"Why don't you call to check in after you've done a little reconnaissance? When you come back to your truck for your purse. Good luck!"

"Thanks." I close the phone and put it in my pocket. I flip the sun visor down and look at myself in the mirror. I straighten my bangs so they hide my Band-Aid.

I let myself out of the truck. The roadhouse is long and low, like a warehouse-sized mobile home. A group of men in black leather jackets and vests stands around a bank of motorcycles, and I feel their eyes on me as I walk past them to the entrance. I show my ID to a giant bouncer with a long, scraggly beard, and he nods me through the door.

"Caught in a Dream" by Alice Cooper blasts from the ceiling speakers. It's packed full and even more biker on the inside than the outside. It has a familiar stale-beer, old-carpet smell that reminds me of pool halls and pubs. The women wear low-necked tank tops and Levi's; the men wear leather jackets. Some of them have patches sewn onto their jackets that tell me they're more than hobby riders. The room is centered around two pool tables with a bar along the longer wall. No bar stools are open, so I tack myself onto a corner and wave my hand to get the bartender's attention.

She's in her forties and has seen better days. Her hair is teased into a style similar to that of the target in the photo, and when she smiles a silver canine twinkles blue in the black light. I order a Budweiser and sip it while I let my eyes wander around the room. I wonder how I'll be able to find this lady in here.

I take my beer with me to search the pool table areas. Women scatter themselves around like decorations; she could be among them. They laugh and chat while their biker boyfriends get way too serious with the cues. I make accidental eye contact with one of the dudes who's shooting, a bearded Hispanic man with long, stringy hair and a black leather jacket. Immediately, a heavyset woman in her forties detaches herself from her group and approaches me. "The fuck you looking at? What're you tryna stare at my man for?"

I keep my voice neutral. "I'm just looking for my boyfriend. I'm not trying to look at your man."

"Well, you ain't gonna find your man here, bitch, so move on."

I walk away, resisting the urge to make a smart-ass comment. Why women get so possessive over these tired-ass gangsters will be forever beyond me.

I follow a hallway that I assume leads to the restrooms, and I discover a whole outdoor patio. People surround a row of firepits like moths, their faces glowing orange with reflected firelight. I let my eyes travel from one firepit to the next, and then I see her.

She's in a place of honor, surrounded by bikers in leather jackets and vests. She converses intensely with a man at her side. Like she senses my gaze, her eyes dart to mine and I'm pinned by a glittering, dangerous stare.

I let my eyes roam, as though I haven't noticed her attention. I make my way to a nearby firepit, smile at the women surrounding it and make a comment about wishing I'd brought a jacket.

The voice on the phone was right. This is not going to be easy.

I return to the hallway to scope out the ladies' room. It has two stalls and a single, dingy sink.

She has to go to the bathroom sometime, and if not the bathroom, the bar. I should find a place at one of the firepits, watch her, and follow her wherever she goes. I can get her in the crowded bar area, or I can get her in here.

Fine. That's my plan. Time to get my purse from my truck. I'm ready to get this over with.

I straighten my ponytail and square my shoulders. I nod to myself in the mirror. My ponytail bounces peppily, like a cheerleader. I should never nod like that again.

I leave the bathroom and pass through the main room on my way out. I'm by the pool tables when I accidentally make eye contact with the bearded man again. This time he gives me a grin and a wink. I shake it off, making a point of ignoring the wink in case his psycho old lady is looking.

At the bar, I get waylaid by yet another bearded man, this time a six-foot-five mountain of a guy with a blond Gandalf beard that ripples over his belly.

"What's up," he yells at me over the music.

I try to step around him. He sidesteps, blocking my way to the door.

"What do you want?" I ask.

"I like your ink! Did that hurt?" He points at my chest piece with a fat, dirty index finger that someone needs to snap right off his hand.

Instead of being the one to do the snapping, I force a smile onto my face. "You bet it did."

"I got one, too." He stretches the neck of his T-shirt down to reveal a giant Old English tattoo across the white, hairless skin of his chest. It's clumsy but has enough black ink in it to make me wince. He sees this and grins. "Fuck yeah that hurts, amiright? Lemme buy you a drink. Why haven't I ever seen you here before, li'l mama?"

I take a deep breath for patience and say, "I'm on my way to meet my boyfriend, actually. Sorry!"

He groans and clutches at his chest like I've wounded him, and finally he lets me move around him toward the door. I hurry past the bouncer and out into the cool night air. The guys near the rows of motorcycles are still there, smoking cigarettes. When they see me, their eyes widen.

I dig around in my pockets for my keys. The biker guys have gone silent. I look up, my senses tripped by a premonition of danger. Their eyes flit back and forth between me and the far corner of the building.

I follow their gaze. A line of women walks toward me. In front marches the woman who'd stepped up to me at the pool table. She looks pissed.

"Shit," I say.

One of the bikers laughs. "Shit's right."

"What did I fucking *tell* you?" the woman hollers. She closes the distance between us.

I open my mouth to protest, and she pops me in the jaw with a punch that tosses me back onto my butt on the asphalt. She squats down to speak close to my face. "Did I not give you a warning?" Her voice is raspy with decades of smoking. "Did you not just look at my man *again*? Are you fucking stupid?"

"Honestly, it was an accident. I was—"

"Looking for your boyfriend? You got no man here. I don't know who you tryin' to find, but you need to learn your place, girl." Her fist draws back and hits me square in the cheek. My head smacks asphalt. Lights erupt behind my eyes. She hits me again, in the forehead, in the stomach, and then she stands up and kicks me. I hide my face in my forearms, curl up and deflect blows. Pain explodes in my head, my gut.

I can't argue or fight; they'll murder me. I know gangsters. And what am I going to say, anyway? "I'm gay—I don't want your man"? To a bunch of bikers? I'd rather get my ass kicked by these bitches than raped by this group of onlooking men.

A hard blow lands on my neck and unconsciousness sucks me down. I fight it, grip my hair, protect my face.

The woman kneels down next to me and says, "That was your last warning, bitch. It'll be a lot worse next time." She's out of shape, panting with exertion. I wish it was just me and her.

I feel them walk away. I'm left in front of the motorcycles, curled around my pain, holding it in my hands like a gemstone. When the throbbing in my gut recedes enough to inhale, I touch my face with my fingertips. It's always my first worry; I have nightmares that Carol catches me in the face with her baseball bat and I'm disfigured for life. A lump is rising on the back of my head. My stitches must have been ripped out; warm blood trickles into my eyes, and my neck aches from the blow they'd landed in the side of it. I press my palms to the asphalt and push myself up. Blood drips from my nose. It trickles thin and salty down the back of my throat.

Darkness approaches and recedes. Close at hand, a dude says, "Bitch fights, man."

"I know," a voice replies. "Nasty."

I get to my feet, hunched over, gut aching. I fumble the keys out of my pocket and unlock my truck. I pull the door open and haul my body up into the cab. I slam the door shut behind me. I turn the key in the ignition. I'm getting blood on the seats. I pinch the bridge of my nose with my left hand and, with my right, I crank the truck into first gear and bump my way out of the parking lot. I drive around the corner, down the street, and pull around the back of one of the warehouses.

I pull the flip phone out of my pocket. My fingers slip and miss as I dial the numbers. A faint beep, and I press the code I've memorized by now. I snap the phone shut and rest my pounding head on the seat. I stretch the neckline of my shirt up to my nose and use it to wipe some of the blood off my face.

The phone buzzes. I flip it open. "I'm sorry," I say, voice muffled through the shirt. "It got fucked up."

The voice says, "What happened?"

"I just got my ass beat by some biker bitches."

"Where are you?"

"I'm around the corner from the bar. I just need to rest for a minute before I can drive. I think I actually have some ibuprofen in here," I realize aloud. I pull my purse open, feel around in the side pocket, and sure enough, there's the bottle of ibuprofen 800s I got at the clinic. My hands tremble as I press open the childproof cap. I shake a pill out and swallow it dry.

"What happened?" the voice asks. "Did you get caught in the act?"

"No, nothing like that. Some bitch thought I was looking at her man. Old-ass dude. He wishes." I groan, press a hand to my head. "I gotta get this stitched up again."

"Are you injured?"

"Nothing's broken. It's just bruises. And these stitches came out, but those were from Carol." My nose seems to have stopped bleeding.

"You didn't call anyone for help, did you? You can't let anyone know you're down there."

"No, I didn't call anyone for help. What do you think I am?"

"You said you needed to get stitches? We should make a

plan for what you'll tell the ER. Can you make it back up to LA? We can't have you on record at an ER down in Orange County."

"Chill. It's fine. I'll drive myself up to the clinic I always go to. I pay cash—there's no drama."

"Oh." The voice is surprised.

A long, pregnant pause, and then I say, "What do we do next?"

A sigh, which sounds mechanical through the disguiser. "We don't normally give second chances. We expect our participants to take their responsibility seriously."

"I do take it seriously. I got literally attacked. I was on my way to do exactly what you—"

"Listen," the voice commands. "Do not interrupt me while I am talking."

"I'm sorry." *Sorry* isn't even a big enough word for the sadness I feel at this failure.

"As I was saying, we do not usually give second chances. But this time and this time only, I will reassign you. You clearly weren't at fault, and this was a difficult target. I knew it would be a challenge."

"I tried," I say quietly.

"I know." The voice is softer. "Go to your clinic. Get stitched up. I will make the arrangements necessary, and I'll contact you soon. But, Jasmine?"

"Yeah?"

"There are no third chances. Do you understand?"

A chill sweeps through me. "Yes."

"Good."

"I'll do better next time. You don't have to worry."

"I know you will." The line clicks, and the call ends.

17

JAZZ

SCRUBBED CLEAN AND bandaged, I say goodbye to the nurses at the twenty-four-hour urgent care. There's something wonderful about nurses. My whole life, they've been the ones to stitch me back up. Doctors can kiss my ass; they have the attitudes and the lectures, but nurses are always just…there for you.

"No more boxing," orders the main nurse, Sue. She's in her seventies and has fun pink streaks in her gray hair.

"Sure thing, Sue," I say cheerfully, and she rolls her eyes. She's known me for a long time.

The sliding doors let me out onto Vermont. I'm parked just a block away, which is a miracle for this part of town. Headlights whiz by as cars fly over the speed limit, exhilarated to drive without traffic. A homeless man with a shopping cart shuffles by. An upright, proud-looking Chihuahua is perched on his shoulder. The man doesn't have any shoes on. There's something sweet and sad about his bare feet.

My purse buzzes. It's the flip phone. I snap it open. "Hello?"

"I hear street noise. Are you alone?"

"Gimme a sec." I get into the truck and shut the door. "Okay. Go ahead."

"What did you tell the doctor?"

"Oh, this urgent care thinks I still do boxing and jujitsu, so they're used to me coming in with all sorts of injuries. It's fine."

"I'm glad it was you and not someone else. I'm not sure I'd trust anyone else to handle this so well."

I feel warm all over. They aren't mad at me. "Thanks."

"So let's talk about your assignment. I'd be more comfortable giving you a few days to recuperate, but I'm sure you're worried about Joaquin. Do you think you can handle being reassigned in the next day or two? We have a few potential alternates."

"Yes. Reassign me. Nothing's really wrong with me, just bruises and a few stitches."

"Excellent. We'll be in touch tomorrow. Do you have rehearsal? Would evening be all right?"

"No rehearsal tomorrow. I get off work at four."

"Perfect."

We hang up. I turn on my iPhone. As it powers up, I wipe half-heartedly at the dried blood smeared on my seats. It should come off with Windex. I don't think anything sticks to fake leather.

The little apple icon pops up followed by a text notification. It's from Sofia, at eight thirty.

Do you want to keep me company? It's wine o'clock. :-D

A drink actually sounds fantastic, but it's ten thirty; that might be too late. I reply, Sorry, I— I stop, consider. I fell while loading up my drums and had to get a few stitches. I'm down to get a drink if you're still around.

Three little dots appear, and then Oh no! I'm so sorry! Are you okay?

I'm totally fine. Not a big deal.

Well, come get me, then.

It only takes me fifteen minutes to get to Studio City; the 101 is clear, and she lives right off the Laurel Canyon exit. It's probably best not to arrive covered in dried blood, so I dig around in my truck for the bag that contains some spare clothes, which I keep on hand so I don't have to go out after work in my Trader Joe's uniform. I trade the blood-soaked white tank top for a clean black one. My windows aren't really tinted, but I'm too worn down to care if anyone sees my black bralette. It's not like I have any boobs to hide anyway.

Sofia lives in one of those modern buildings that takes up a whole block. It has a security entrance, and I look her name up in an electronic directory. I press the numbers on the little pad and she answers, "Hello?"

"It's Jazz," I say into the speaker.

"Come on up. Take your first left and the elevator is on the right."

Her directions take me past a ritzy pool area and into an elevator alcove where two teenage girls giggle incessantly over something on one of their phones. Sofia's apartment is down a carpeted hallway that smells like air freshener. I'm fascinated by the way people decorate their front doors in nice buildings. They put inspirational signs, even little entry tables, in the hallway. In my building, that shit would be stolen the second you closed the door behind you.

I knock on apartment 215, and a shadow passes by the peep-hole. A chain disengages and the door swings open. She looks relaxed; she is barefoot and wears a simple black dress. Her hair swings free and wavy down her back.

"Show me the stitches" are the first words out of her mouth.

This makes me smile. I lift my bangs to display the bandage. "Is that my ticket inside? Showing you my injuries?"

"Yes. Now you may enter." She beckons me in. I follow her down a little hall to the kitchen, which is all granite countertops and stainless steel appliances. The black dress she has on is made of clingy T-shirt material, and I get an A for effort as I try not to look at her ass. I set my purse down on the counter.

She hands me one of two glasses of red wine. "Cheers. To getting stitches where your bangs will cover them."

I clink my glass against hers and sip. I always forget how rich and thick red wine is, like blood. For some reason it makes me think about Joaquin, somewhere out there. Is he safe? I pray to a God I don't know if I believe in that Carol takes pity on him, that she keeps him alive.

Sofia reaches out with a bare foot and nudges my calf through my jeans. "Jazz? Hello, fun? We're having fun. We're not worrying about things."

I force a smile onto my face. "You're right. Sorry."

"Yeah. You should be." She's happy and sparkly, a completely different Sofia from the one I saw the other night. I'm going to need a lot more alcohol if I'm going to avoid bumming her out completely.

I try to rally. "I mean, we have red wine in fancy glasses and a completely sterile, silent house. It's basically a music video."

"My house is not sterile! It's…" She looks around at the kitchen, which is so clean and free of clutter, it looks like we are the first people to ever set foot in it.

"Fucking party time with the principal. Everyone be real quiet and swirl your wine." I make a show of inhaling the wine fumes.

"I am an *assistant* principal. It is totally different."

"Right, I forgot. Assistant is way cooler."

"*Way* cooler."

I smile into my wineglass. I feel a little better. "Thanks for inviting me out. Seriously. I needed the company. Even if you make me write standards, it will be better than sitting alone in my apartment worrying about Joaquin."

"Good! Same here. Actually, no. You know what? Today has been a good day. In a weird way. I think."

"I can tell. Do you want to talk about it?"

"Nope." She takes another drink of her wine. "I just want to enjoy not feeling horrible for the first time in ages."

"All right, well, should we go hit up a bar? You know the area. What's around here?"

"There's a wine bar down the street."

The long day, hours of traffic, and physical exertion overwhelm me suddenly. I set my glass aside. "If I drink too much wine, I'm going to fall asleep. It'll have to be cocktails. Where do women like you hang out, anyway, besides wine bars? Like if you want an actual drink?"

"Women like me? What does that mean? Principals?"

I grin. "Studio City women. Yoga women."

"*Yoga* women?" She laughs. "Screw you, Echo Park. You don't know my life."

I fold my arms across my chest. "I want you to look me in the eyes right now and tell me you do not do yoga."

She looks down at her tanned feet, which are meticulously pedicured. "Yeah, fine, I do yoga."

I cackle. "Ha! I knew it. You're one of the yoga women

who come through my line and ask me why we're out of kale chips."

"Why *are* you guys always out of kale chips, anyway? Just order more. I don't understand." She pulls a drawer open and sets the corkscrew carefully inside.

"Women who have matching utensils!" I yank open the drawer, revealing a neatly organized row of black-and-red KitchenAid utensils in size order from biggest to smallest. "Oh my God. Sofia. This is pathological. It's worse than I thought. You need help."

"Shut up!" She grabs a spatula and threatens to hit me with it.

I dodge. "Wait—I have to see. I have to know the extent of your psychosis." I pull open a deeper drawer and reveal a matched set of Tupperware containers with coordinated lids separated from the tubs by a custom drawer divider. "Oh my God! You're a fucking serial killer!"

Sofia giggles helplessly. She fans at her eye makeup. "Why are you so mean? I didn't make fun of your hipster apartment!"

"All right, all right, I'm sorry. I'll stop. Let's get going. Find us a bar and I'll call us an Uber."

"There's an English pub up Ventura Boulevard. I think they have a full bar."

"Perfect. Fair warning, I'm not sure I can keep up with your good mood. Are you really not going to tell me what happened today?"

She fidgets with her diamond ring. "I can't tell you, but I feel less... I don't know. Less powerless somehow. Like I'm in control of my own life again after a long time." She pushes off the counter. I think she's heading to the hall to get her shoes on, but she steps toward me. She puts a hand on my arm. "I feel like me again. Does that make sense?"

No. Not at all. Why do women communicate like this? Just say what you fucking mean.

She trails her hand down my arm. I watch the path her fingertips trace, past the pirate ship and onto the skull and crossbones. Her touch burns like dry ice, leaving a trail of goose bumps in her fingers' wake. "What—" I begin.

She leans forward and kisses my cheek. Her face is silky smooth, and I'm intensely aware of the curves of her body. "Sofia, what—"

She kisses my lips, softly. Her hair tumbles down over my shoulder and envelops me in the fresh scent of conditioner.

Fuuuuck. I grip her upper arms and pull back to make eye contact. "Are you drunk? Were you drinking before I got here?"

"Of course not." A frown darkens her face. "Why would you ask that? What about me makes people think I'm this— this alcoholic?"

"No no no. It's not— I'm just— I'm trying to make sure— I'm trying to understand." *I'm trying to understand why you would want me*, I finish in my head. I feel naked, soaked through with hope that she'll touch me again.

She sighs, a soft sad sound like she can read my mind, and she brushes her lips against mine. Hers are full, soft, and I feel mine move slowly against them. Her fingers sneak up under my shirt, across my bare stomach and up my sides. It tickles, and I hiss a little breath, which makes her smile. She kisses me harder, her tongue velvety smooth. Her breasts press against me, warm, soft. I run a hand up the back of her hair and grip the roots. Her breath catches and I feel a snap of satisfaction. Our kissing deepens, quickens.

I spin her around and press her back against the fridge. My hand runs up her skirt, traces the curve of her hip. She messes with my ponytail and the rubber band goes flying. My hair spills loose around my shoulders. She tugs at the hem of my shirt. I lift my arms obediently and she pulls it off me, tosses it aside. She makes a little sighing noise, runs her hands across my chest and kisses me again. I wedge my thigh between her legs and push forward, grip her hips and bring her toward me, kiss her slower. Her leg wraps around my hip. I let my hands get up under her skirt onto her ass and pull her tight up against me. I get a little moan out of that one, which sets my chest on fire.

A sound comes from the hallway. Is someone knocking? It's more of a rustling… Did Sofia lock it?

"What's wrong?" Sofia asks. She pulls my face back to hers, kisses me again.

"Did you hear that?" I release her ass, which is an actual sacrifice, and cross the kitchen to the hall to peer out the peephole. I see the top of a head, like someone's crouched in front of the door.

The hell? I yank the door open.

A man is stooped forward, a handful of flyers in one hand, a roll of tape in the other. He's in the middle of taping one of the flyers to the door. He's in his late thirties, a slim, soft sandy-haired man with a corporate haircut and jeans that look awkward with his leather shoes.

"What are you doing?" I demand.

Sofia presses past me and looks down at the man. "Oh—my—God. You're pathetic," she says in a tone I can imagine terrifying any number of eighth graders. "Where's Olive? Did you make the nanny stay late so you could come here? Pathetic."

"Is this your ex?" I ask Sofia.

"Do you know?" he asks me, a little grin on his thin lips.

He stands up. He's a head taller than me. His voice is a low baritone.

"Know what?"

"She's a whore." He points at Sofia. "Has she told you? Do you know?" His eyes are wild. Under the polo shirt, his breath comes fast and furious. He shuffles through the flyers in his hands, showing them to me one at a time. "This is her. See? Here." He points to the woman. She's straddling a man, and I realize the photo is of Sofia, taken by someone peeking in through the space left open at the edge of the closed blinds. The photo shocks me, all of Sofia's bare skin and breasts and hair pixelated in this cheesy grayscale flyer. "See?" He points again, flips through photos. He says, "See? Here's her with— See?" Now he shows me a photo of Sofia with a woman, their bodies a tangle of breasts and hair on the same bed as the photo with the man. It must be her own bedroom.

I turn to Sofia, who looks grim. "What's going on? Why does he have these? You want me to call the cops?"

Charles pages through the flyers, obsessive, frantic. "You like this one?" He shoves it into my face, rubs the paper across my cheek.

I smack it away. "You're gonna want to back the fuck off, Abercrombie."

"Charles, look," Sofia begins in a hostage negotiation tone.

"Shut—*up*." He backhands her across the cheek with a sharp crack. She stumbles back into the wall.

My vision goes white. I kick his feet out from under him and shove him hard. He hits the ground shoulder-first with a grunt. I drop onto him with a knee in his kidney and grab his right arm, pull it up behind him. He lets out a yelp of pain.

"Jazz, stop," Sofia cries, scrambling up from the floor.

"Call the cops. I got dipshit covered." He thrashes, tries to buck me off. I don't have weight advantage, so I lie on top of him and crook my elbow around his throat in a rear naked choke. "I will put you to fucking sleep," I tell him. His body writhes and struggles against me. I grip my left bicep with my right hand and tighten my hold on his neck. His chin is hot and scratchy on my forearm. He stops squirming and starts to go limp.

"Jazz, stop!" Sofia yanks at my shoulders, tries to get me off him.

"What is wrong with you? I'm fine. Call the fucking cops!"

"Let him *go*," she begs.

"Why?"

"Jazz!"

I release my hold and push up off him. He gasps for breath and gets his arms underneath him. He shakes his head like a wet dog and gets unsteadily to his feet. I'm ready for him to come at me swinging, but instead he turns on Sofia. "Mistake," he snarls, and then he turns and strides down the hallway.

"What the fuck?" I breathe.

"It's fine," Sofia says, to me or to herself, I can't tell.

"It's not fine. Is he stalking you? *Photographing* you? We have to call the cops. They won't believe you if you don't call them right away." I step forward, try to touch her face where he hit her.

She backs away. Her eyes are fixed on the images taped to the door. "You need to leave." She starts pulling the pictures down savagely, her fingernails tearing at the paper.

I try to put my hands on her waist. "Hey. Come on. What—"

"Just go!" She pushes me off.

The rejection hurts so much worse than it would if she had

actually hit me the way Charles had hit her. That would be a relief, the pain that only lasts a minute. That's the kind of pain I can handle.

FRIDAY

18

JAZZ

CARLOS SEES I'M in a mood and kindly schedules the last three hours of my shift in the dairy case. I pull my fleece jacket and gloves out of my locker in the back room and let myself into the walk-in fridge. I focus on hefting plastic crates full of milk and juice, checking expiration dates and pulling soon-to-expire cartons off the shelves. My breath comes in foggy puffs and my muscles ache and then burn, but I lift the cases higher, harder. There's something comforting about this work, about the expenditure of energy and strength, the pure exertion with no thought except organization. I don't want to think about Sofia. I don't want to remember her cold, hard tone telling me to leave. I don't want to think about Joaquin, or Carol.

It's not until Kevin lets himself in an hour later that I drag myself out of my reverie. He's a beautiful light-skinned black man twenty years older than me with a soft, scary voice and shocking clear blue eyes.

"Cool if I smoke in here?" Kevin asks, ever the gentleman.

I gesture to the corner underneath the whirring vent fan. "Go ahead."

He starts to roll a cigarette using his pouch of tobacco. He sprinkles white powder into it from a tiny plastic bag and lights up. He blows the smoke up into the fan while I use my box cutter to open a case of vanilla yogurt. He takes a few hits and offers it to me. "You want?"

"I'm good, but thanks."

"You heard about the serial killer?"

It knocks me off my groove, and I drop a carton of milk to the floor. As I retrieve it, I say, "Of course. Who hasn't?"

"Some crazy shit."

"Crazy," I agree. I pull my gloves off so I can get the small containers of yogurt out of the case. He blows meditative smoke rings up into the fan.

One of the glass doors opens, and a woman calls inside, "Do you have fat-free half-and-half?"

I call out, "Yes, ma'am. It's to your left on the second shelf."

"Can someone please just help me?"

"One sec." I pull a carton of the precious fat-free half-and-half off the second shelf. I walk through the storeroom, through the swinging back-room doors, and out onto the sales floor. I find her huffily checking her Apple watch. She's a middle-aged woman with a side-swept blond bob everyone calls the "I'd like to speak to the manager" haircut. I hand her the half-and-half. "Here ya go."

"You should put it on display so people don't have to ask for it." She places the carton in her packed cart, which she's parked right in the middle of the aisle.

Another woman just like her tries to get her cart past and can't. She says, "Excuse me. You're blocking the aisle."

"Excuse *me*. I'm in the middle of a conversation."

"Excuse *me*, but others need to get by you."

I press my lips together, my first smile of the day fighting to escape.

The original woman succumbs to the pressure of twenty watching sets of eyes; it's rush hour and the store is shoulder-to-shoulder packed. From the front, a flurry of bells rings over and over again. Carryout, return, price check. No wonder Kevin's hiding.

I retreat to my cold cave of milk and eggs. "I just saw two moms throw down over a carton of half-and-half," I tell Kevin. My pocket buzzes. It's not my iPhone; it's the flip phone in my left pocket.

Kevin watches me get it out, stubbing his cigarette out on his shoe. "Fucking 2005 or what?"

"Yeah, 2005, when you started getting your senior discount," I retort, and he laughs on his way out.

I flip the phone open. "Hello?"

The voice says, "Jazz, are you alone?"

"I'm in the dairy case at work. No one can hear me, but it's not exactly private."

"What time do you get off?"

"Four."

"Can you page us in the car before you go home?" The tone is different than usual, not quite as calm.

"Sure. Everything all right? I thought you were going to call me tonight?"

"We've gotten your reassignment, but we need to move quickly. If I understand your schedule correctly, you're free tonight, correct?"

"Yeah, that's right."

"We've given you some additional items for tonight's assignment. You'll find a box up by your punching bag when you get home."

When I hang up, I get my iPhone out and stare at it for the twentieth time today. No messages from Sofia. No missed calls.

I hesitate, and then I open up text messages and compose one to her.

I'm really sorry about last night.

I hit Send.

I remember Sofia begging me to get off Charles. I hadn't listened. I'd just plowed forward like I always do, stubborn and stupid and thoughtless. Look at me. I'm a mess, covered in tattoos, never been to college, a crew member at Trader Joe's, with a shitty apartment and an even shittier truck. It's no wonder someone like Sofia doesn't want me. What was I thinking? Did I really think I could date her? Am I going to pick her up for dinner in my fucking gardener's truck? It was a hookup for her. That's it.

Three little dots appear by her name. I hold my breath.

The three dots vanish, but no words appear. I wait. The screen goes dark. I poke at it. Nothing.

I throw my phone across the cooler. It clatters down between the boxes. I press my forehead into my hands and take a breath. It's okay. I've been rejected before, and I'm sure I'll be rejected again. It doesn't have to hurt this much. I would do anything, give anything, to keep it from hurting this much.

I feel ridiculous and conspicuous as I walk through the underground parking garage looking for space thirty-two in a flowered muumuu, socks, sandals, a gray wig and a fanny pack—the additional "items" they mentioned earlier. This apartment building reminds me of Sofia's. No. Stop. I'm not thinking about Sofia right now. One thing at a time.

The yellow syringe of death is tucked into my fanny pack along with the playing card and flip phone. On my way over here, I stopped at a gas station in Hollywood, where I put on a pair of latex gloves and rubbed the playing card on every surface, even the inside of the urinal, to get as many strangers' DNA on it as possible, since I'm doing this murder in a relatively clean place. I thought this was a smart idea. Go, shady murder club.

I find the parking space and tuck myself behind a nearby pillar. I pull the flip phone out of my fanny pack. I page the 800 number, enter my six-digit code and wait.

The phone buzzes. I answer it by saying, "Do you make everyone dress up like old people, or are you trying to humiliate me in particular?"

The voice chuckles. "The only person who will see you will be dead in minutes. I'm more concerned with your exit strategy than your appearance. Tell me about your plans to get out of there when you're done."

"There's a gate to the pedestrian walkway about...like..." I measure the distance with my eyes. "It's five parking spaces away from me. Fifty feet or so."

"Does it seem safe?"

I survey the parking structure. The fluorescent lights illuminate the tinted windows of the expensive cars. "I mean, worst case, someone sees me walk out afterward, right? I'm in disguise and I don't know anyone around here anyway."

"That's what we think, too. And, Jasmine..."

"Yes?"

"We need you to make this work. This is a dangerous man. Be careful. We're counting on you."

"He's a bad one?"

"Very. Remember, as soon as you complete your assignment, Carol will be added into the queue. You're almost there. You're so close."

"Okay. Good. This is good."

"Are you ready?"

I take a breath. "Totally. I'm ready."

I get off the phone, tuck it back into the fanny pack and pull a pair of latex gloves over my hands. I get the syringe out of its plastic container and squat with my back to the pillar and my thumb on the depressor. The needle is a bright silver snake, slender and silken in the gray-blue light.

Headlights flash. My heart skips beats. They flicker along the wall in front of me and fade as the car turns a corner.

Not him.

Silence. Dank concrete air.

I pull the playing card out of its baggie. Should I drop it now? Or should I wait until after I inject him?

After, I decide. I slip it back into its plastic bag.

Headlights, brighter than before. My heart palpitates again. This time, the lights slow as they approach, casting shadows onto the wall, and the car turns toward me. I could reach out and touch the passenger's side door as it slides into space thirty-two. It's a silver Lexus, brand-new with dealer plates.

I'm frozen. I don't think I can do it.

A voice from my past trickles into my thoughts, a girl I dated a few years ago. She was watching me work out on the roof with a cigarette between her red lips. "What are you freaking training for?" She laughed, making fun of the intensity with which I attacked the punching bag.

I just said, "Life." I didn't know it, but I was training for this. This moment.

I grip the syringe in my right hand. Thumb on the depressor.

Maybe this is what my life has been leading up to. Maybe all this shit I've been through has been preparation for this ultimate act of sacrifice and protection, for me to be able to do for Joaquin what most other mothers could never do for their children. The thought makes me swell up with pride.

The Lexus's driver's door opens. A tall silhouette makes shadows against the overhead lights.

I creep around the front of the car, duck down and hide in front of the bumper. His back is to me. He pulls a bag out of the back seat, drapes it over his shoulder, turns to close the driver's side door, and the light catches his face.

It's Charles. It's fucking Charles. Sofia's ex.

Oh no.

Why am I being sent after Sofia's ex? Who wants him dead? *Who the hell do you think?* I scream at myself inside my head.

For a second, I'm excited. I *want* to kill him. I remember the slap of his hand hitting Sofia's cheek. I remember the pictures.

But no. Wait. I'm supposed to kill a stranger. I'll be a suspect if I kill Charles. I'll get caught.

He turns and walks toward the elevator. Where my heart used to be, an empty hole filled with panic and fear carves itself into my chest.

What do I do? *What do I do?*

Do I call and ask them for guidance? I don't have time. He's at the elevators now. I need to make a decision.

The syringe is shaking in my latex-gloved hand. I'm gripping it too tight. A tiny pearl of liquid beads at the razor-sharp tip of the needle and drips onto the concrete floor.

I can't be caught sitting in his parking space with a syringe full of poison, for fuck's sake. I maneuver the trembling syringe back into its plastic container and zip it into the fanny pack. Across the garage, the elevator dings. I peek around the side of the car, don't see anyone and head for the exit, keeping low in front of the cars. I let myself out into the grassy walkway that winds between neatly-groomed flower beds toward the street. I pick up my pace. I try to keep myself from running.

I get into my truck. I fumble the flip phone out of the fanny pack and dial the 800 number. It takes all my concentration to keep my hands steady enough to punch in the six digits, and then I wait.

A man jogs past my window. I jump. He doesn't even see me; he's just a normal suburban jogger, and he crosses the street to run up the hill.

The phone buzzes. I flip it open. "Hello?" My voice is shaking.

"Jasmine? Are you all right?"

"I know this guy. Charles. I know him. Should I still do it? No, right? I *know* him." My breathing is fast and tight.

"Let's calm down. Why don't you start from the beginning. How do you know this target?"

I take a deep breath. The wig is itchy, and I brush its bangs off my forehead. "I know his ex-wife. I was just at her house last night. He came by and we had a fight. Like, my DNA might even still be on him."

"You were at his ex-wife's house last night?" the voice demands, and the tone is full of controlled anger. "I thought you were at urgent care last night, Jazz."

"After that. After I talked to you. She called me. She asked if I wanted a drink. I mean, I'm allowed to, like, live and do normal things, right?"

Another pause. "How do you know the ex-wife?"

"We met at Joaquin's school. She works there. We've hung out a couple times."

"Hung out? As friends? Or romantically?"

"I don't know! We kissed. I haven't bought the fucking ring yet."

"Jazz. I asked you specifically if you had a significant other. Do you remember that?"

"I didn't. I don't," I protest. "We hooked up one time and this douchebag Charles showed up at her place, posting naked pictures of Sofia on her door, so I knocked him down and Sofia made me let him go and—" I stop. I take a breath.

The line is quiet.

"Hello?" I say. "Are you there?"

"So you've met Charles in person. You've touched him?"

"Yeah. I mean, I pushed him down and I was choking him out and I was going to hold him there while Sofia called 911, but she told me to let him go. Oh my God, this is why she didn't want to call the cops. Wait—did she do her murder yesterday? Is that why Charles is up today?" I remember Sofia saying she felt empowered for the first time, that yesterday was a good day in a strange way. Holy shit. She killed someone yesterday. Oh my God. The image of buttoned-up Sofia committing acts of murderous vengeance is so weirdly hot, I almost can't stand it.

The voice on the phone is gravelly. "We have two problems here. First. The fact that you have a personal connection to another member of our organization violates our first rule of anonymity. You should have disclosed your connection to Sofia right away."

"How was I supposed to know—"

"Second." The voice is loud and angry. I shut my mouth. "Twice now you have failed to complete the assignment given to you. Twice. There is a string of people relying on you. And now, twice, you've let those people down. Lives are at stake, Jasmine. You are not the only one in a desperate situation. Do you think other people's children, other people's lives, are less important than your own?"

"No, of course not!"

There is a prolonged silence that almost makes me think they hung up, and then, "I need a little time to put together a plan for reassignment. What is your work schedule tomorrow?"

Hope flares inside me. They're going to give me another chance. "I work till four again."

"Can I call you after work? Will you be alone at five o'clock?"

"I'll make sure I am. I'm so sorry. I promise I didn't—"

"It's fine. I understand," the voice says, softer now. "I'm sorry I got so angry. This is a high-pressure situation for all involved. These things are going to come up. In the meantime, please do not give Sofia any indication that you're a part of this organization. Can you do that? Or have you already told her?"

"No, not at all! I had no idea she was in it. First rule of murder club, right?"

"You're sure you didn't drop any hint of your involvement? Did she see the flip phone?"

"No. Not at all. I promise."

"Okay. That's good. Hang tight, Jasmine, and we'll speak tomorrow."

The phone goes quiet. I'm left with my eyes fixed on the little green window. The green light illuminates the tattoo that trails down my left middle finger: *Fool me.*

Once, the other finger reads.

SATURDAY

19

JAZZ

THE TRADER JOE'S customer parking lot is empty—we don't open until nine—but the employee side lot is full, and the delivery truck is parked alongside the back gate. As I pull in, Carlos spots my truck and lets go of the pallet jack to wave at me. It escapes from him, and he has to run to catch it before it crashes into the ramp.

I park behind Phillip's ancient Nissan and drain the last of my 7-Eleven coffee. It's acidic in my empty stomach. I haven't eaten and barely slept. My apartment felt empty and hostile, and I didn't even want to look at the bedroom nook where yesterday I was fantasizing about putting in a bunk bed for Joaquin and me to share. I'm so worried about him, out there in the city somewhere, I don't feel like I can bear another minute of this horrible not knowing. And yet the minutes keep ticking by.

I grab my purse and get out into the cold, gray morning. I shove my arms into my work hoodie and walk past the delivery truck. In the cluttered receiving dock, Carlos and Phillip are unloading a pallet of boxes. Carlos is built like a bully pit, broad and heavy with meaty hands, the back of his shaved head creased with horizontal wrinkles. He tosses a case of beans to little Phillip, who catches it with a grunt and blunders back a step.

Carlos spots me. "Jazzy J! You're not in till eight."

"I couldn't sleep. Need help with the load?"

"Hell yeah, go clock in. Phillip, go help Henry with chips. Jazz'll take over for your weak ass."

Phillip looks happy about this. I clock in in the pit, where a few full-timers are clustered around the computer. The sales floor is bustling with crew members breaking down pallets and stocking shelves. The music is turned all the way up to KIIS FM's morning show. "Despacito" comes on and the team of women stocking produce shrieks in delight. An answering *"Ciaoooo"* from the dudes in frozen echoes over the music, and I actually smile a little.

I make it to the yard just in time to catch a case of salad dressing hurled at me by Carlos. "Asshole," I say, which makes him whoop with delight and launch another box at me, harder this time.

We get into a rhythm. Throw, catch, stack. Throw, catch, stack, in time to the pop music that blares out from the open warehouse doors. The gray fog lifts and the sky lightens. The heaviness of the boxes is satisfying, the burn in my biceps a distraction from the ache in my chest.

It's Saturday, so we're crazy busy from the minute we open the front doors. On my lunch, I don't feel like sitting in the break room, trying to make conversation with everybody, so I eat a burrito in my truck and restock the cold produce cases, which look like Black Friday at Walmart even though we just stocked them an hour ago. I grab a flatbed of lettuce boxes from the walk-in fridge and start facing the ravaged kale section. These people and their kale, man. I just don't get it.

The din around me—overhead speakers playing sixties music, customers arguing with each other, babies crying—forms a shell for me to hide in, and I'm left with thoughts about Joaquin. I check the flip phone for the hundredth time today. I have it in my pocket; I'm afraid to miss a call, but all it tells me is that it's 1:12 p.m.

A guy with dreadlocks, baggy reggae pants and reflective glasses drifts by me, peering at my chest like he wants to read my name tag. I'm wearing the one Carlos made me, which says *Jazzy J*. "Do you need help finding something?" I ask him.

He shakes his head and walks away. I return to my kale.

My worries about Joaquin hit me hard right now, maybe because I'm anxious about the call later, maybe because I'm worried about Sofia or because I didn't sleep. For whatever reason, it's overwhelming, the sadness and rage, and I feel like I'm going to cry. I squeeze the kale, which pops one of the bags open and sends little shards of greens everywhere. I scramble to pick them up, bumping into a woman in yoga clothes that remind me of Sofia.

If Joaquin and Carol are still in LA like the murder club told me, I bet they plan on going to church tomorrow. Carol never misses church. I wonder if I could go check on him, sneak in, stand in the back. Maybe I could even pull him aside and give him his insulin, sneak it into his pocket. I could pull a murder club and just inject his ass when he's not looking.

The reggae guy appears at my left elbow. I'm about to ask him what he wants when a woman taps me on the arm. "Are you out of organic basil?" she asks.

I scan the produce island. All I see is regular, pesticide-infested basil. "I'm not sure. Let me check the back for you," I tell her.

I squeeze through the customers and carts. I have to wait in a crowd near the coffee grinder to get to the warehouse doors, and I'm about to start throwing elbows when I feel a nudge at my back. Someone's getting too close. I try to step away, but a cart blocks me on either side. I look over my shoulder resentfully, sick of customers who refuse to respect people's personal space—

The reggae guy is right behind me. He has a yellow syringe. He lunges at me and tries to poke me with it.

I try to jump back but am blocked by customers. He pushes forward. The needle pokes my stomach, sharp through my shirt.

I thrash away from it, grab the sides of two carts, heave myself up and kick him in the stomach. He flails back into the woman behind him and crashes down on top of her. His syringe goes flying under a produce island. I launch forward swinging and get him in the temple. He catapults sideways onto the floor, scrambles up and bumps into a produce island. It catches his dreads and pulls them off; it's a wig. He has receding brown hair. I clamber over the fallen cart as he pushes up off the floor and leaps away toward the front of the store.

I'm right behind him, vaulting a shopping cart. It crashes to the ground. People cry out. He runs, slips, grabs a shelf and takes a corner wild. I catch his shirt, pull him back, drop a kick to his leg. His face is wild, terrified. He leaps up, sprints out the front door. I make it onto the sidewalk as he takes a hard right and disappears around the corner.

"Motherfucker," I whisper.

My whole body is shaking. I feel like I'm coming apart.

They put a hit on me. They assigned me to be murdered.

20
JAZZ

I REST MY head in my arms on the rickety table. The interrogation room—or interview room, as the cop called it to make me feel better about being in here—is cold. The air conditioner ruffles my arm hair, pimpling my skin with goose bumps. I wonder if this is an interrogation technique, some criminal psychology thing where they make suspects confess by freezing them out. I fold my arms over the baggy scrubs they gave me when they took my clothes.

Should I tell the cops about the murder club? I haven't committed a crime. I have the flip phone in my purse and the murder kit at home in my closet. I could hand it over to the cops and come clean about the whole thing.

But then what? I'm pretty sure Sofia killed someone. She'd end up in jail. And what's to say the police would believe me? It's more likely they'd blame me for the other murders, the ones I don't know anything about.

Could they blame me? I'm sure I have alibis for some of those deaths. That would be enough to convince them I wasn't involved.

It hits me. The murder at Villains. I was there that night. I could totally be blamed for that one.

I'm fucked. I can't tell the cops.

The door opens and a woman in a gray suit steps through it. "Jasmine?"

"Yeah."

"I'm sorry to keep you waiting. I'm Detective Patel. Just give me a moment to catch up while we wait for my partner." Her English accent is soft around the edges like she's been here awhile. She sits across from me and sets a folder and a notebook on the table in front of her. She flips through the file folder, frowning as she reads through page after page of text. She has thick black hair pinned in a high bun and is maybe in her early forties. She looks familiar.

"Hey, I know you," I say as it dawns on me. "I saw you on TV. You were at that press conference." I stop, remembering that I was on the phone with the murder club when she was giving the press conference. Well, she can't know that.

She smiles. "My mum always told me I'd end up famous if I moved to Los Angeles. I'm not sure a press conference about a serial killer was quite what she had in mind, but she takes what she can get." She looks at the file folder. "And you're Jasmine. Nice to meet you." She reaches a hand across the table, and I shake it.

A man enters, pulling the door shut behind him. He's tall and blond with pink cheeks and high cheekbones, maybe Swedish or Norwegian. He says, "I'm Detective Nielsen." He takes the seat next to Patel. He holds himself very straight and stiff. I'd bet he served in the military before becoming a cop.

"Nielsen is my partner," Patel explains. "He's the junior

officer. He mainly makes coffee, but today we're busy, so we thought we'd let him do some real work."

"Pssht." He shakes his head, but I can tell he likes the joke.

She winks at me, flips through her folder and says, "I know you gave a statement to the officer on the scene, but I'd like you to go through it once more for us." She points to a blinking green light and a little screen embedded in the wall above her head. "You'll be recorded, but you'll see me taking notes on points of interest."

I frown suspiciously at the blinking light. "Do I need a lawyer or something?"

"You're a witness, not a suspect, so, no, you don't."

Right. Yes. I totally trust this scenario. This is fine.

Nielsen says, "We want to ask you about this incident at Trader Joe's first, but then we want to ask you about the show you played at Villains. Did you realize the Villains death was connected to the Blackbird Killings?"

"Not at the time. I thought the guy was having a seizure," I say truthfully.

He nods. "You're the first person that we know of who's been at the scene of two of these attacks, and you're the second survivor. We're looking for patterns in the Blackbird Killer's behavior, and we're looking for connections between crime scenes. So let's start with Trader Joe's. Run us through what happened."

My heart is beating hard and feels unnaturally high up in my chest. "Well, I was at work like usual. Stocking the cold produce case. The lettuce."

Nielsen cuts in. "Do you remember what kind of lettuce you were stocking?"

"What *kind* of lettuce?"

"Yes, Jasmine, what kind of lettuce," he says in a tone that makes me want to smack him.

"It was kale. Organic. Trader Joe's brand. Triple washed."

Patel makes an impatient gesture. "Go on."

"Anyway, this white guy with dreads was kind of hanging around close to me, which I didn't think much of at the time because the store was packed. I asked him if he needed help and he said no, and I went back to facing the lettuce. Excuse me. Facing the *kale*."

"Facing?" Nielsen repeats. "What does that mean?"

Jesus. "Pulling the old ones forward and putting the new ones behind. Do you want me to get you a job application?"

Patel snorts a laugh. She covers her mouth with her hand and keeps her eyes on her notebook. Nielsen cocks his head at me, a smile playing around his lips. "I think I'm good for now. Ask me again if we don't solve the Blackbird case."

"Like they'd hire you," Patel says. "How long was he hovering around near you, Jasmine?"

"A few minutes at most."

"And then what happened?"

"Some lady wanted organic basil, so I walked toward the back room, but the dreadlocks guy was there with this yellow syringe. I couldn't run away, so I kind of kicked it out of his hand and it fell, and he ran, and I, like, followed him to try to get him to stop, but he escaped."

Nielsen says, "You didn't just follow him. You attacked him. Other witnesses said you assaulted him."

I look back and forth between them. "Am I in trouble for that? I just punched him. He was trying to poke me with a fucking syringe. I saw the news. I heard the warnings." Mentally, I pat myself on the back. So far, so good.

They seem to accept this. Patel scribbles in her notebook.

On the chair beside me, my purse starts buzzing.

Oh, shit.

Nielsen says, "You can check your phone. I'm sure people are worried about you."

I try to keep my hands from shaking as I search for my phone in my purse. The familiar green light against the black lining tells me it's the flip phone vibrating.

My brain races. I'm terrified the cops can see panic on my face.

Without removing the phone from my purse, I open the phone and snap it shut.

"You don't need to get that?" Patel asks.

"It's no one important."

Nielsen peers at me with his faded denim eyes. "Going back to the attack, so you tried to catch him, but he got away. What happened next?"

"He took off down Third Street, heading west, and I went back inside and we called the cops. Did you guys find the syringe? I think it fell under a produce island."

"Yes, we got it," Patel says. "You got lucky. We have ten confirmed murders by this killer, and as I said, only two survivors including yourself."

"Who's the other survivor?" I wonder if the murder club is mad at the person who let someone survive.

"The other surviving victim was attacked at the Seventh and Metro station downtown. Do you know anything about that?"

"No," I say honestly. "I've only been hearing on the news about people who have died, not about any survivors."

"Well, he's been the only one. Until now."

"I guess I am lucky."

"You're also lucky there were so many witnesses to the

Trader Joe's attack. Without so much witness corroboration, you could have been sitting in that chair as a suspect, not a witness." His eyes are piercing, penetrating, and I get chills at the words. I feel like he's watching me for a reaction, like this was a test and I'm not sure if I passed.

Patel asks, "Have you ever seen this man before he attacked you?"

I lift my hands, helpless. "We're one of the busiest Trader Joe's in LA. A thousand middle-aged white guys come in every day."

Patel pulls a photograph out of her folder and slides it across the table to me. It's a picture of the back of a playing card. It's just like the one in my murder kit, vintage-looking with little blackbirds peeking out of a tangle of vines and flowers. The edges are yellowed and worn.

Nielsen asks, "Have you seen anything like this? At work, at home, anywhere? Maybe that night at Villains?"

I shake my head, willing my face to stay blank. It's better to say as little as possible. "I don't think so."

Patel asks, "Are you sure? This is very important. We've found these at the scene of every murder in this series."

I rack my brain, searching through those minutes with the kale. I think I would have noticed one of these cards if it had been lying on the floor or something, but I had been pretty deep in my own thoughts. At last, I say, "I didn't see a card. But I could have missed it in the crowd."

Nielsen watches me for a second. I don't know what he's thinking, but I feel x-rayed by his too-light blue eyes. To Patel, he says, "Anything else?"

She closes her notebook. "I think that's all I need for now. Jasmine, we'll be in touch."

Something occurs to me. "Do you think you can help me

with something? I tried to get one of your front desk cops to help me with my ex-foster mother. She's not giving my brother his insulin for his diabetes. That's a crime, right? Can't she go to jail for that?"

She spreads her hands. "Honestly, I'm homicide. I don't work with family services. Have you contacted DCFS? They're really the ones to ask about this."

I slump back in my chair. Why did I even bother? Despair and impotent rage fill me up so strong, I almost can't feel my extremities.

Nielsen says to Patel, "Will you go ask someone to grab Gonzalez? I want to touch base with her before I leave."

She meets his eyes, they have a silent conversation, and then she gets up from the table and leaves. When the door swings shut behind her, Nielsen presses a button on the wall. The green light goes off. *He turned off the recording? Why?*

He comes around to my side of the table and sits next to me. "You have a record. So you must not like the police much."

I fold my arms around my waist and grip my upper arms hard. *Please don't come any closer.*

"Would you say that's true?" he asks, his voice low. "You're not a huge fan of police, right?"

I open my mouth and make myself say, "Police are the good guys. I have no problem with police." My voice sounds far away from me, like it's coming from the walls.

"What I'm saying is, you're in a different seat now. You're not in trouble. We're worried about you. If you know anything about these murders, you should tell us. We only want to protect you."

Is the door locked? Am I locked in? If it's unlocked and he comes at me, I can make a run for it. But I'm in scrubs. They'll think I'm a criminal; they'll tackle me in the lobby. Then I'll get in trouble for running, and he'll be hot with rage. He'll bring me back to a room like this and it will be twice as bad.

"Jasmine? Is there anything else you want to tell me? Anything at all? I promise I can help you. Even if there's one little thing, something you think is no big deal, or maybe something you're afraid will make you look bad, you can tell me. I'll make sure you're safe."

"I don't have anything else to tell you."

I feel his stare gouging a hole in the side of my head. *Don't come closer, don't come closer, don't come closer.*

He gets up. My chest expands. I haven't been breathing right. He says, "I'm going to give you my card, and Patel's. Please call us if you think of anything. Are you going home tonight? Do you need a lift?"

"No, I'm good. I can Uber back to my truck. I'm going to try to stay at a friend's house."

My eyes are on his hand, which is on the doorknob. *Open it. Open it. Open it.*

He turns the handle and opens the door, and I grab my purse and get the fuck out of there. As I clear the room and make it into the hallway, my purse starts buzzing again.

21

NIELSEN

NIELSEN PRESSES THE up button impatiently. He's lost in thought. He's thinking about three people.

The first person on his mind is Jasmine Benavides, grown-up foster kid from East LA, and the only person to be connected to two different Blackbird crime scenes.

He doesn't believe in coincidences. Maybe she saw something at Villains, something she doesn't know is important. Maybe Blackbird *needed* to get rid of her.

The attack on Jasmine seemed sloppy, though, like Blackbird had expected her to be an easy kill. But that can't be. Look at that girl. How could Blackbird be so amateurish? Unless the Trader Joe's attack was faked and she killed the victim at Villains. But, if that was the case, why draw attention to herself? She wasn't a suspect. She wasn't even interviewed. There's no motive. It's a circular puzzle, each question bringing up a handful of other questions.

The second person Nielsen is thinking about is Greg Mc-

Cadden, Greg with the red hair and the full sleeve of temporary tattoos who was killed at Costco. There is something very strange about that sleeve of temporary tattoos...

The third person on his mind is the reason he's here at the USC Medical Center: gray-haired Keith Manzano, midlevel management at a real-estate brokerage downtown, victim of attempted murder at the 7th and Metro station.

Gonzalez appears at his side. "You didn't wait for me!" She's out of breath from rushing here across the parking lot.

"You knew where you were going—why did I need to wait?" He knows he's mean to her, but he can't help it; there's just something about her that bugs him. She can't be under forty; the way she bleaches her hair and hairsprays her bangs makes him think of the pathetic older women he's seen trying to lure younger men home in bars.

Gonzalez looks up at Nielsen and smiles. "Two survivors. This is good, right?"

"How so?"

"It could mean he's getting overconfident. He tried to inject Manzano in the leg? And then of course Manzano kicked the syringe away. It seems..."

"Sloppy," Nielsen finishes.

And it does. The two survivors are alive because of mistakes, mistakes of...well... If not for the other ten spotless murders, he'd call these mistakes of inexperience. How can a killer be so cunning one moment and so clumsy the next? Does he have split personalities or something?

A Filipino family approaches, flowers and balloons in hand, to wait for the elevator. They cast him nervous looks.

The elevator dings and the doors slide open. Nielsen holds them open and waves Gonzalez inside. The gesture pulls his suit jacket open to reveal his gun and badge, and the elderly woman carrying a teddy bear gives him a fearful, wide-eyed look as she hurries into the elevator.

The family presses the button for the third floor, and Gonzalez presses number six. The family rides in stifled silence. He can almost feel their relief when they get off on the third floor, leaving him behind.

Gonzalez watches them go, an unreadable expression on her face. It's the NICU floor, and he wonders if she's thinking about her own dead child, the one that got her six months of leave. She's only just come back, and her performance has been mediocre at best. He feels a twinge of guilt. She's been through a lot. He should cut her more slack.

In a forced-soft voice, he asks, "You sent the swabs off Jasmine Benavides to the lab?"

"You know it. She gave me an earful about taking her Doc Martens, but I thought we should take any chance at getting Blackbird's DNA we can get. She's a fighter, hey? He bit off more than he could chew with that one! He'll pick someone easier next time."

"He's killed grown men. There's more to this failure than bad judgment."

She's quiet, chastised.

He says, "We're going to catch this fucker through DNA. Watch."

"We have too much," she protests. "Each crime scene has thousands of profiles."

"Eventually two will match, and then we'll have him."

The elevator dings. He leads the way out, and Gonzalez says, "Good luck taking that to the DA. All you'll prove is that one person was in the same two places."

Nielsen wants to yell at her, but there's no denying the truth in her words. He knows he needs a lot more than DNA, but it's not on Gonzalez to point that out to him. She's lucky to be invited along.

The sixth-floor nurse station is chaos. Women in scrubs swarm the computers, exchanging shorthand arguments about room numbers and patient charts. He and Gonzalez show them their badges. "What's up? Why the commotion?" he asks.

A woman his mom's age snaps him a stern look. "We'll be with you in a moment, Detective." To a young nurse, she says, "Try checking six-fourteen. Then six-twelve." The nurse rushes off.

"Hey," Nielsen says. He snaps his fingers in the older woman's face. "What's going on?"

She glares at him. Her eyelids sag like a basset hound's. "Someone mixed up the patient charts and we're tracking them down."

"That's weird. Do you have new staff?"

"No. It looks like a prank, and I'll figure out who's responsible."

Nielsen digests the gnawing feeling in his stomach. "Where's Keith Manzano? Six-ten?"

"Yes."

"My officer's on duty?"

"Yes!" She throws the word at him and trots off down the hallway with two women at her side.

He leads the way toward the room he'd visited this morning. A pair of nurses hurries out of room six-fourteen, clipboards in hand. One of them says to the other, "These charts are out of order, too. They're all mixed up, and they're from, like, four different people."

"She's gonna freak out," the other girl says. They push past Nielsen and hurry down the hallway toward the nurses' station.

Nielsen stops to consider this.

Four charts mixed together? Pages out of order?

He picks up his pace. As his left foot hovers over a square of yellow linoleum, a rough, desperate scream echoes and bounces around the hallway.

He freezes. His foot lands on the yellow tile. Gonzalez's hand drifts to her gun.

Another scream, a shrill shriek of lingering, agonizing pain. Shouts from the nurses' station.

He throws his feet forward. Gonzalez runs behind him.

Another scream gurgles into silence. He follows the echoes. They lead him to a door.

Six-ten.

He bursts in. Two nurses are right behind him. They shove him out of the way.

The figure on the bed, the gray-haired man in a hospital gown, is twisted into the fetal position, his mouth stretched into a grimace of pure pain. A trickle of blood from his mouth is smeared onto the pillow and around his cheek like face paint. The uniformed officer and nurses shout at each other—"He just started screaming!"

"Help him lie still!"

"Is this—"

Nielsen pulls the officer toward him by the sleeve. Officer Johnson's eyes are stretched wide with fear so that the whites are visible all around the brown irises. "Did anyone come in here?" Nielsen asks.

The officer shakes his head. "No. I mean, nurses, doctors, but no one else."

The nurses.

Nielsen whips around and looks out into the hallway. A pair of women pushes a crash cart toward him, and he and Gonzalez step out of the way to allow it to pass. Another cluster of people rushes from one end of the hallway to the other.

To Johnson, Nielsen says, "Tell me if any of them gave him an injection."

"No! None of them."

"Did any of them come near him?"

The officer says, "Someone came in to check his IV, but they never touched him."

Gonzalez asks, "When did they check the IV?"

Johnson's hands fly up. "Five, ten minutes ago? Right when they started panicking because they had the charts wrong."

Gonzalez says, "It's in the IV!"

Nielsen leaps back into the room. To the nurses manning the crash cart, he yells, "It's poison in the IV! Disconnect it!" Frantic hands grab at the needle in Manzano's hand. His eyes stare unblinking at the ceiling now, his face slack. A trickle of blood sluices languidly down the white plane of cheek.

Gonzalez turns and runs down the hallway to the nurses' station. She yells, "Lock the floor down! Call security. Full lockdown!"

Frantic grabbing of phones, yelling into them, alarms resounding, doors slamming. Gonzalez's voice becomes one in a tangle of female voices yelling.

Five or ten minutes is plenty of time to get away.

He leans against the wall. People rush by him, doctors now alongside the nurses, stethoscopes bumping chests.

So much for two survivors. Make that one.

22
JAZZ

KEVIN LIVES OFF Adams and La Brea in a suburban pocket south of Mid-Wilshire. He obviously can't afford this place with his Trader Joe's paycheck; I think his dad owns it. A lot of the houses here are bungalows with bars on the windows, like Carol's, but they look cleaner, more lovingly maintained, than the houses in her neighborhood. None of the driveways have old cars rusting in them; no ruins of play structures rot on any of these fresh green lawns.

Kevin's house lights are blazing. The curtains shine bright and cheerful through the bars on the windows, and the quiet street is jammed with cars. It's Saturday night; of course Kevin's house is lit.

I check outside the windows of my truck to look for anyone who might be following me. I'm so paranoid right now. I took the most circuitous route here, zigzagging through side streets and making at least ten U-turns. I don't think the cops would be tailing me, but I don't know that for sure, and I don't know if the murder club might have someone watching me. I have to assume they plan to send someone else to finish the job, although it does seem more likely that they'll simply get me at Trader Joe's again, since they like crowds.

They don't only do things in crowds, I remind myself. They'd sent me to Charles's parking garage. So I need to keep my eyes open.

My iPhone buzzes in my purse. It's funny; now I can tell the difference between the two phones' vibrations.

I hustle to get the phone out. I hope it's Sofia, but then I also worry—what will I say to her?

It's a 213 number I don't recognize. I check the clock. It's not going to be DCFS, not at 9:00 p.m. I silence the phone. A small part of my brain worries it's Joaquin, but a larger part worries it's the police. I don't have it in me to answer any more questions, and I think it's smart to stay away from them as much as I can without seeming guilty. I watch the phone until the voice mail lights up, and then I press the button to make it play.

"Jasmine, this is Detective Gonzalez from the Los Angeles Police Department," a chirpy female voice says. "If you could call us back at your earliest convenience, that would be great." She recites a phone number.

Knew it. I think I'll pretend I didn't get that voice mail yet. If asked, I'll just say I was already inside the house and didn't hear my phone ring.

I pull the flip phone out. It's silent, but it's not disconnected. No calls have come through since the police station.

A part of me wants to page the murder club, to see if they'll call me back—but no. What good would that do?

I hunt around in the cab of my truck for my bag of extra clothes and heave a frustrated sigh when I find it. All I have left is a set of workout clothes. That's what I get for not doing laundry.

I can't believe the cops took my Docs. Now I have to buy new ones and break them in from scratch. Assholes.

The thought makes me mad at myself. What a stupid thing to worry about right now.

I slip out of the prison scrubs and pull leggings on over my underwear. I yank on a tank top and shove my feet into my old hiking Nikes. I fix my bangs in the mirror, let my hair out of its ponytail and grab my purse.

The air outside is cool, and I fold my arms across my chest. I don't want my nipples poking out through my thin bralette and tank top when I walk into the den of dudes. I ring the doorbell. As I wait, I cast suspicious looks around the street, half expecting someone with a syringe to pop out of the bushes.

The door opens and a pair of guys poke their heads out like Tweedledee and Tweedledum. "What's up," one of them drawls, eyes raking down my body.

"Is Kevin here?"

"Somewhere," the one on the left says. Their eyes are bloodshot, their voices fuzzy.

I push past them into the living room. It's a regular-sized house with two bedrooms and a bathroom squeezed into about eight hundred square feet. In the living room, a group of people younger than me dances to some old-school R & B. More are gathered in the kitchen—Sofia would call this kitchen "vintage," I think—which is where Kevin leans against the counter, the king in his court, a Corona in hand. A handful of people I don't recognize is chilling around him, close-packed in the tight space.

All eyes turn on me as I step inside. "Hey, old man," I say to Kevin.

"Jazzy J! What are you doing here, girl?"

I approach him for a hug. His powder-blue eyes are bloodshot, his mouth loose in a half smile. "Sorry to bust into your party," I say as he squeezes me briefly.

"I heard about some crazy shit at work today. You almost got taken out by that serial killer. Dude!" He grips the tops of my arms, stares deep into my eyes. "You could be dead right now. You need a drink."

"I do need a drink," I agree.

"I got some wine for the ladies." He guides me to the fridge with a hand on my lower back. I want to slap the hand away, but I'm here to ask him a favor, so I let it stay.

A tall, lean guy materializes next to Kevin. "Hey, man, you're not gonna introduce me to your friend?"

Kevin is pouring pink wine into a plastic cup. "Jazz, this is A.J. A.J., this is Jazz."

"What's up?" A.J. says to me. "You come alone? You didn't bring your man?"

I look to Kevin for help, and he laughs. "Man, you are barking up the wrong tree. Jazz is the competition, sucker. None of our girls is safe around this one." He crooks an arm around my neck and strangles me in a brotherly half-noogie-hug.

A.J.'s eyes go wide. "No shit. She likes pussy?"

"Can you blame her?"

A.J. looks like it's Christmas morning, which is a reaction I never understand. "I need to talk to you," I tell Kevin. "Do you have a minute?"

A.J. cries out in protest. "Naw, wait—hang on. Let me find you a girl. Let me watch. Please? *Please?*"

"Hard pass."

Kevin laughs. "C'mon, Jazz, we can talk outside." I follow him through the living room, where a few couples are dancing, out through a steel screen door onto a plain concrete patio. Kevin pulls the door shut behind us with a clang, and strains of Wu Tang trickle through it to keep us company. He leads me to two rickety plastic chairs, which sit facing the neat, concrete-fenced yard. Once we're seated, he lifts his bottle, and I clink my cup of pink wine against it. He says, "What do you need, Jazz?"

"I need a favor."

"I figured."

"If you can't do me this favor, I need you to forget I ever asked, okay?"

He cocks his head, sips from his half-empty bottle and nods. "All right."

"The favor is pretty chill. But it's sort of...deceptively chill." I take a sip of the cold wine and wince. It's as sweet as Kool-Aid.

"Go on."

I lean forward with my elbows on my knees. "I wondered if I could crash here tonight and hang out with you for the next day or so." He frowns and opens his mouth to ask a question, but I hold a hand up. "I want you to tell the police later that I never left, that I was here all night and all day tomorrow. But I actually want to go do something for a few hours in the morning, and I don't want the cops to ever find out."

His eyebrows shoot up. He leans back in his chair. His arms cross over his chest, and the diamond in his left ear sparkles in the porch light. "You want an alibi. What are you into, Miss Jasmine?"

"Nothing."

"And you're pretty sure the cops will come knocking on my door and asking where you were because of this nothing."

"Maybe. Possibly. Probably."

He huffs out a breath and looks up at the sky. "That's a motherfucker of a favor to ask, little J."

"I wasn't thinking of it as a favor. I was expecting to have to pay for it."

I have his attention. "How much?" he asks.

"What are you thinking?"

His eyes are reptilian, calculating. "Five grand."

"That's crazy! I could go to anybody with this and they'd do it for less."

"But you came to me because you know I'm gonna come through. And I'm a reliable witness."

"I know a lot of people who are reliable," I argue.

"Then why don't you ask them?"

I look down at my fists, clenched between my knees.

"I know why you don't ask them. Because you and I are not that good of friends for the cops to imagine I'd lie for you. I'm not into any crazy shit. And a lot of other people are going to see you here tonight, so you get a bunch of alibis for the price of one. I understand why you're asking me this. It's smart. But you're gonna have to pay for it."

"Fine. Five thousand. But I have to get it out of the bank later, after the cops have finished looking at me."

He pins me with his eyes. "I'd give you two months to figure it out, but after that..." He spreads his hands, and a diamond glints on his pinkie.

"All right." I feel heavy, like gravity is crushing me.

Kevin scrutinizes me, and I think he sees more than I want him to. At last, he leans forward and clinks his bottle against my cup. "Cool."

I take a deep breath and let it out slowly. This is happening. I'm doing this. "I just need to go home and get a few things. I'll be back in an hour," I say.

"Hey, do what you gotta do," he says. He gets up. Before he goes back inside, he rests a hand on my shoulder. I think he's going to say something, but he just gives me a pat and heads back into the house.

The night sky is high, lit from below by the city. I lean back in my chair and look up at it, but I can't find a single star.

I like being alive. I like my stupid little existence. I want to see Joaquin grow up, break free from the generations of poverty and addiction, and do something big with his one precious chance at life. A tear escapes, and I wipe it away with the heel of my hand.

This is me facing reality. I might die, and soon, and I can't leave Joaquin with Carol if I do. At least in a foster home, they'd give him his insulin and let him go to school. At least in a foster home, he'd have a chance. Right now, he only has a few days left. I'm out of time. I have to do something now.

Tomorrow is Sunday. I have the poison. I have the disguise. I'm going to kill Carol at church tomorrow morning.

23
JAZZ

OUTSIDE MY TRUCK'S dirty windows, the city breathes and blinks in time to my turn signal. It pulses, alive, every car carrying the anonymous potential for violence. For the hundredth time, I check my rearview mirrors. No one is behind me.

A homeless man wheels a stroller across the street in front of my truck. He glowers at me, like my headlights are an attack on him. Another homeless man stationed at the opposite corner watches the stroller's slow, limping progress. This man looks just like Jesus, with a mane of tangled black hair and a thick black beard. His filthy shirt hangs off him in tatters, the sunbaked skin peeking through the rips.

I wonder, when was the last time someone touched him? When was the last time someone touched me, for that matter?

Sofia. Her fingertips were soft, trailing down my arm.

A honk makes me jump. A car has pulled up behind me and is pissed; the light's been green for two whole seconds. I gun it and leave Jesus behind.

I make spontaneous, sudden turns on my way to my apartment, backtracking, but I see no signs that I'm being followed. Still, I don't park right away. I drive through the streets around my neighborhood, scanning all the parked cars and looking for anyone sitting still, anyone who looks like they're watching. I creep past the tent city at the end of my block. It's quiet, everyone tucked away inside their tents for the night. At last, I park around the corner.

I have no weapon with me, unless you count the pair of drumsticks I keep tucked behind the headrest. I grab a stick, wish I had my leather jacket to at least make it harder to poke me with a needle, and let myself out of the truck.

Keys in my left hand, drumstick in my right, I cross the uneven, cracked sidewalk. I catch every detail from the apartment buildings on the way: the couple yelling at each other inside an upstairs unit, the smell of weed drifting out of a downstairs window. A pair of headlights flashes, and I hide behind a bush, but they pass without slowing.

Two stories and small, my building looms humbly in front of me. Most people who live here keep to themselves. The lights are on in a few of the windows, but it's ten o'clock. The families have mostly gone to sleep, and the young people are out partying. I peek around the corner toward the outdoor hallway and the stairwell. There are no planters, nothing to hide behind. I don't see anyone lurking.

I ease around the corner toward the stairs, which are open-air without anywhere for someone to conceal themselves, but anyone could be hiding up on the second-floor landing and I wouldn't see them. I grip the drumstick.

I tiptoe up the steps. I'm about to emerge onto the landing when a dark shape moves, slithering against the shadows in front of my front door.

I jump back, press myself into the stairwell and peek out around the corner.

The figure slips forward. Hands press against my window; the person is looking for me in there, trying to figure out if I'm home.

My heart pounds a hollow, empty beat.

It's a woman. I can see that from the way the figure moves, from how the scant light hits her body. And it doesn't look like she has her syringe out and ready yet, not the way she's pressing both hands to the window. A dark lump against her side must be a purse. That's where she would keep the syringe.

My body takes over for my brain and I bolt forward. I close the distance in two seconds and, as she gasps at the suddenness of my approach, I flip her around and pin her up against the metal screen door, my drumstick slammed across her throat. With my left hand, I yank her purse and send it flying with a rattle of spilled objects. She makes a choking noise. I open my mouth to yell at her, but then adrenaline and shadows clear from my vision and I see her face.

"Sofia," I gasp. I drop the drumstick with a clatter. Her hands fly to her throat and she leans forward, coughing. I cry, "Oh my God, I'm so sorry! What are you doing here?"

She can't talk; she's still coughing. I feel like a monster, like Charles, and I remember the look on her face when he slapped her.

All my fears about the murder club come back to me. "Sofia. I'm sorry, but we need to get inside." I bend to retrieve her purse and slip her wallet and keys back into it. My hand freezes over a shiny palm-sized object that lies on the ground: her flip phone. She lunges for it and grabs it before I can get it.

"I know what that is," I tell her. "I have one, too."

With huge eyes, she says, "Explain what you mean."

"It means I am in the—the—" I gesture wildly. "You know what I mean. The fucking murder club."

She's silent, shocked, for a long moment, and then she just says, "How?"

"You should come inside. They could be watching us." I get the key in the lock and usher her into the apartment. I switch the lights on, slam the door shut behind me and lock the dead bolts. "Stay right here." Drumstick in hand, I check under my bed, in the closet, behind the shower curtain.

"Jazz?" Sofia calls from her post by the door. "Are you okay? What's happening?"

The bathroom is clear. Back in the living room, I recheck the locks on the door. I make sure the curtains and blinds are drawn shut. I check the locks on the windows. I open my closet and check the top shelf. My murder kit is still up there.

Sofia says, "Jazz? You're kind of freaking me out."

I toss the drumstick on the table. "You don't know what happened. Right? You don't know about Trader Joe's?"

"Trader Joe's? What are you talking about?" She looks genuinely confused. One hand rubs at her neck and I feel horribly guilty.

I go to the kitchen and rummage around in the freezer, emerging with a bag of frozen corn. I wrap it in a dish towel and bring it back to the living room. I hand the soft, cold bundle to her. "Put this on your neck. I'm so sorry. I thought you were one of them."

She sits on the sofa and presses the corn to her throat. "What happened at Trader Joe's?"

I sit down next to her. "I messed up my murder, so they put me on the hit list. They tried to kill me at Trader Joe's today."

She drops the corn from her throat. "You messed up? How? They make it so easy."

I gather my thoughts, trying to figure out how to explain things to her, wondering if there's anything I shouldn't say. "They sent me to some shady biker bar to kill this meth dealer and it went real wrong for me."

"A biker bar? Seriously? They sent me to Costco."

We look at each other for a long moment, and then we both start laughing, a grim, almost hysterical sound. "What does that say about me?" she manages to say when she catches her breath. "I'm just this teacher mom. Oh my God."

"What does it say about *me*? They sent me to hang out with meth dealers!"

We dissolve into giggles again, the graveyard humor fueled by fear. At last, she says, "So is that where you hurt your forehead the other day? At the biker bar?"

I wipe eyeliner off my cheeks and decide to be honest. "Well, first Carol beat my ass, and then the bitches at the bar opened the stitches back up."

Her laughter dries up. She looks like she wants to say something reassuring, but I can't open that wound right now. I say, "Anyway. So after the biker bar, they reassigned me. But they assigned me to Charles. I got all the way to his parking garage before I saw him and realized."

"Wait. Back up. They assigned you to *Charles*?" She presses her hands to her forehead. "Did you kill him? I didn't hear anything."

"No. I told them I knew who he was, that I shouldn't be the one to kill him, and I guess they were pissed. Then today they sent someone to my work to kill me. I only barely escaped."

"They'd kill one of their own members? They'd *kill* you? But it wasn't your fault they assigned you to Charles."

"They seemed super pissed that you and I know each other. That's why I haven't called you or anything. I'm worried they'll be mad at you, too."

"How is this our fault? *They* contacted *me*. It's their job to make sure none of us know each other."

"They just missed it, I guess. Or they knew we were connected by Joaquin's school, but look at us. It's not like they'd think we'd become friends."

"You didn't tell any of this to the police?"

"No. I mean, they interviewed me, but I didn't say anything." It's such a mess. I think about Joaquin, about Carol. Am I insane to try to kill her tomorrow? Has this whole thing made me lose my reason? I wish I could get Sofia's opinion. She's so clearheaded and smart. Of course I can't, though. I have to rely on my own judgment. Fucking great.

Sofia asks, "Have you told anyone at work, any friends? No one knows about any of this?"

I smile weakly. "First rule of murder club. Don't talk about murder club."

"Why didn't you just tell the police? They could protect you, put you in witness protection or something."

"Yeah right. More likely they'd blame me for all the murders and be stoked they solved their case. Sofia, do you think they'll come after you next?"

She considers this. "I doubt the… Did you call it a murder club? I doubt they're following either of us right now. If I were them, I'd be keeping my distance until I knew it was safe and there were no cops around. If they come back for you, it's going to be at work or something like that. Somewhere crowded, somewhere unexpected."

"They sent me for Charles in a parking garage. That's not crowded."

"Yeah, but I'm sure they know you well enough by now not to think they could send some random person to overpower you alone in a parking garage. They'd have to take you completely by surprise. You'd have to be distracted—they'd want to sneak up on you. Like at Trader Joe's. Or at one of your shows."

Hmm. That's interesting.

She lowers her voice. "Is Carol why you joined?"

I hesitate, afraid she'll think less of me. It's one thing to want your abusive ex-husband dead. It's another to order the death of a seemingly harmless woman. At last, I say, "She's going to kill Joaquin. I can't let her."

"Oh, Jazz. That's…"

My chest hurts. "Stop. Don't. I can't talk about it."

She stops. I take a few deep breaths. I shove the feelings aside. I'm going to help Joaquin. Tomorrow morning. I'm doing everything I can.

Sofia rests her hand gently on mine. Her fingers are long, the nails painted glossy clear. "I'm sorry," she murmurs.

"Me too. The other night when I came at Charles like that… I didn't know. I didn't understand."

"Not at all. I came here to apologize. I shouldn't have reacted like that."

I shrug. "I fucked up."

"No. It wasn't anything you did. I was just so humiliated. Those goddamn photos. I felt like I would never be able to look at you again. It was so awful. It wasn't that I was mad at you. I just couldn't…" She slumps forward and presses her face into her hands.

I pet her hair, smoothing it over her shoulders. I wish I could take this from her. "How about I make you some tea, and we forget the photos exist? How does that sound?"

She nods into her hands.

I head into the kitchen, fill up the kettle and set it on the electric base. The everyday rhythm of making tea soothes me. I pick out my favorite mug, the one with two owls that Joaquin gave me for Christmas, and use two tea bags to make her chamomile extra strong.

I bring the mug to the couch, where she's still sitting in the same position. "Here you go. Chamomile."

She gives me a weak smile and reaches out for the cup.

I look around the apartment. What's the plan? She needs to get back home. I feel dirty after the long, adrenaline-filled day, and I'd intended to take a shower and change out of these old workout clothes before heading back to Kevin's. I wonder if I still have time. I say, "Here's what I'm thinking. You hang tight and drink your tea. I'm going to take a quick shower and change, and then I'll walk you to your car on my way out. Unless you want me to walk you to your car now, first?"

"No, that's fine. It'll be nice to relax for a minute." She kicks her flip-flops off and curls up with her feet underneath her. "But you don't have to walk me. I don't want you to—"

"Quiet. Don't be stupid." I check the dead bolts again and head for the bathroom.

Alone, I crank the shower on and let it warm up while I pee. Normally I feel guilty for letting the water run, but I'm being hunted by a murder club and the drought can suck it. I shed my clothes, take some ibuprofen from the bottle in the cabinet and get underneath the hot water. It feels like heaven.

I lather my body up and wash my face, trying not to get the stitches wet, and when I wash my hair, I do it with my head leaning back as far as it goes so the soap and water sluice down my back. I'm rinsing the conditioner out when I hear the bathroom door open.

I freeze. I picture a stranger, someone sent to kill me, someone who's already killed Sofia.

"Hello?" I call out, instantly feeling ridiculous, like a dumb girl in a horror movie.

"It's me," Sofia's voice says.

I can breathe again. I go back to rinsing my hair. "You scared the shit out of me. What's up?"

A long pause.

"Sofia? Is everything okay?"

The shower curtain slides aside. Naked, she steps into the shower. One arm is crossed over her chest, holding her boobs up. My head spins with surprise. She pulls the shower curtain shut behind her. The hot water pummels my back.

"You all right?" she asks.

The adrenaline drains from my limbs. "When the door opened, I thought someone had killed you and was coming in here to kill me. I'm losing it."

"That wasn't the reaction I was going for." She takes another step closer. I should say something in return, but I can't. She's beautiful naked. Of course; I knew she would be.

She traces the fingers of her free hand along my collarbones and down my side to my hip. Her eyes follow her hand. She frowns at my stomach and rubs her thumb along a two-inch scar at the very base of my abdomen. "What's this from?"

I can't lie to her. "I usually say I had my appendix out."

"Wrong spot."

"I know."

She looks at me, and I say, "It's from Joaquin. From my C-section." Her eyes go wide. I add, "I wasn't on drugs or anything like that. That's not why they took him. I was just really young. They thought he'd be better off with Carol."

She lets go of her boobs and pulls me forward, wrapping

her arms around my waist. She hugs me tight. It takes me by surprise, but it feels so good, I almost start crying. I wind my arms around her neck and press my face into her steam-soaked hair. Hot water patters against our arms and shoulders. I remember sitting in my car just an hour ago, yearning for someone to touch me. It feels like an answered prayer.

I smooth her hair back from her face and kiss her. Her lips are wet, water running down her face. I'm gentle with her, my palms pressed to her cheeks. She opens her lips and her tongue is soft against mine. It's too much, all her skin slippery wet. Her lips move fast, urgent, and I can barely breathe through the roar of desire in my chest. Water soaks her hair and slips between us. She runs her hands up my spine into my hair, pulls my head back and kisses my neck. Into it, she murmurs, "Please."

24
SOFIA

SOFIA LIES ON the bed, head cradled in her left arm, her right fingers trailing along Jazz's shoulder blades. She shivers lightly, unable to quell the chills that rake themselves up her breasts and arms. Her hair and the sheets are damp from the shower.

"You cold?" Jazz asks, raising her head from Sofia's chest. She rubs Sofia's arm gently. Jazz's hands are always warm.

Sofia says, "I'm okay," but then a whole-body shiver betrays her.

Jazz sits up and detangles the comforter from where it lies crumpled at their feet. She pulls it over them and snuggles underneath it beside Sofia. "You don't have to be macho."

Guilt boils inside Sofia's throat. She swallows it down.

"What's wrong?" Jazz asks.

"I'm worried about you. I don't like sending you back out there."

Jazz props herself onto an elbow and runs a hand through Sofia's hair, combing it back from her forehead. Her eyeliner is smudged and smoky, black hair tangled around her shoulders. "I'll be careful if you will. No crowded places. No parking garages. Do you promise?"

Sofia nods, but she feels sick. She traces the lines of the wings that are tattooed across Jazz's chest. Over her left breast, just under the bottom feathers, the word *Joaquin* is written in loopy script. Jazz asks, "Do the tattoos bother you?"

"No," Sofia says, surprised. "Why would they?"

"I feel like they might look trashy to you. You're so clean and perfect." She loops a tattooed middle finger under the thin gold chain Sofia wears around her neck.

"They look hot to me, if you want to know the truth." Sofia touches the word *Joaquin*.

Jazz drops the chain and rests her hand on Sofia's chest. Her face looks sad. Sofia pulls her closer and kisses her. Her lips are familiar now and bring back all kinds of images. "I feel like you're about to say we need to go," Sofia whispers.

Jazz groans. "I really, really hate to do this, but I have to get back to my friend's house. I told him I'd be gone an hour, and that was, like, three hours ago." Jazz pushes herself up so she's hovering over Sofia, her hair falling down around Sofia's face, making a little cave, and she kisses Sofia's forehead.

Sofia raises her head. "Wait—are you in chaturanga?"

Jazz pushes herself all the way up—goes from chaturanga to a sitting position, just like it's no big deal. "What's chaturanga?" She starts pulling clothes out of the dresser.

"It's a yoga pose. And I hate you." Sofia gets up to retrieve her clothes from the bathroom.

Jazz presses her palms together at her chest and bows. "Namaste."

"Oh my God. Where did you hear that?" Sofia returns with

her clothes in hand and starts sifting through them while Jazz pulls on a fresh pair of jeans.

"Women say that to me at work. They Namaste me at the register."

"No way. You're lying."

"Do you think I would make that up?"

Sofia shimmies into her leggings. "Do you work the cash register a lot? Is that your job?"

"We all do different stuff. Register, stocking, cart runs, whatever."

"I want to come through your line pretending to be a nightmare customer. Demanding kale chips. Would you be mean to me?"

Jazz crooks an eyebrow at Sofia's breasts. "Come through like that and you can have all the kale chips you want."

"Jazz!" Sofia's cheeks flush, and she crosses her arms across her chest.

Jazz laughs as she pulls a T-shirt over her head. "*Now* you're shy?"

"Well, I wasn't a second ago!"

"You bust into my shower butt ass naked begging me to fuck you, but now you're shy."

"*Jazz!*"

"Sofia!"

Sofia transfers her boobs to one arm and raises an index finger. "I did not *bust in*. I *stepped* in very seductively."

Jazz cocks her head at Sofia, eyes scanning her like she's reading words written on Sofia's forehead. She closes the distance between them and picks Sofia's bra up off the bed. She drapes it over Sofia's shoulder and moves around behind her. "I'm sorry I made you self-conscious," she says into Sofia's ear, which sends little shivers down Sofia's spine. Sofia loops her arms through the bra straps and settles it onto her chest, clasping it in the back. "Hand me that brush from the top of the dresser," Jazz says. Sofia grabs it and passes it back over her shoulder. Jazz starts brushing her hair, beginning at the bottom and working her way up to the top, detangling it gently. Sofia can't remember the last time someone brushed her hair. Her mother, maybe, when she was a child.

"Can I ask you a favor?" Jazz murmurs.

Sofia nods. She feels like she's melting.

The brush traces ticklish paths down Sofia's bare back. Jazz says, "If I die, will you look after Joaquin? Make sure he gets his insulin, that he gets to go to the high school he's signed up for, that he gets to have a normal life? DCFS might listen to you."

Oh, God. Sofia feels like she's going to throw up. She blinks back tears. She forces the words out of her mouth. "Yes. I'll make sure."

"Thank you."

Sofia says, "But that's not going to be necessary because nothing is going to happen to you. Because you're smart and you're not someone who's going to die this way."

"This seems like exactly the way I would die—because of some stupid shit I got myself into." From behind, Jazz wraps her arms around Sofia's waist. "Promise me you'll be careful. Don't be stupid like me. Do whatever they tell you. And don't tell them about this. Don't tell them you were ever here."

The guilt is like motion sickness. "I know." Sofia looks down at the hands clasped tight around her stomach and runs her index finger along the knuckles. "Why is there a skull and crossbones tattooed on your ring finger? You don't believe in marriage?"

"I didn't when I was younger. Now I don't know. You?"

"I believed in it when I was younger. Now I don't know."

Jazz gives her one last squeeze, releases her and digs a sweatshirt out of the dresser. Sofia puts her tank top on, and Jazz wraps the zip-up hoodie around Sofia's shoulders. "There. You good?" she asks, her crooked smile tight, her eyes sad.

"I'm good," Sofia lies, putting her arms through the sleeves.

Sofia's car is a couple of blocks away. Jazz checks parked cars on their way, but all the cars are empty, the street quiet.

Jazz herds Sofia into her Camry and gives her the quickest of kisses before closing the car door. "Lock it," she instructs through the window. Sofia makes a show of pushing the button.

Jazz watches her go, and the last thing Sofia sees of her is a slim figure in her rearview mirror. When Jazz is out of sight around a corner, Sofia presses a hand to her mouth. A sob escapes from behind her fingers.

She turns onto Glendale Boulevard and heads north. Tears drip onto the hand that covers her mouth. She wipes them away with impatient fists.

Jazz can take care of herself. She can. She has to.

That feels like a lie. Jazz is just one small, vulnerable person. She can't defend herself against an army of strangers.

The sobs break through. The street blurs in front of her, streetlights and stoplights bleeding into each other like candle wax.

A buzzing sound issues from inside her purse.

Acid roils in her stomach.

She pulls into the parking lot of a closed auto body shop. She pulls the flip phone out of her purse and presses it to her ear. "Hello?"

"Sofia," comes the warm, neutral voice through the disguiser. "We expected to hear back from you earlier. Is everything all right?"

She clears her throat. "Everything's fine. She didn't tell anyone anything."

"She didn't tell the police? Friends?"

She swallows down nausea. "No," she spits out.

Sofia wants to say yes, to tell them that Jazz did tell the police, that they have to leave her alone. But she knows better than to lie to these people. They know everything about her. And they've promised to punish Olive if Sofia does anything wrong.

SUNDAY

25
JAZZ

THE TINY WHITE building sits on a small, forgotten street that abuts the dry concrete bed of the LA River. The church is barely bigger than Carol's house, and its dirt-packed parking lot is crammed full of cars. Next door, a row of abandoned warehouses watch me with broken window eyes. The sun is too bright, even through my sunglasses and my truck's dirty windshield.

I pull into the lot, stirring up dust, and park next to a rusty VW Bug. It's eight forty. Church starts at nine, and small groups of congregants knot together in the parking lot despite the heat and the dust. I should stay in my truck until they start doing music. My old-lady getup isn't going to fool anyone in broad daylight. I adjust the ugly gray wig, which has bangs that hang low over my eyes.

I don't see Carol's Ford, but I don't plan on driving around in circles to look for it. It's fine, though. This is such a small church. It won't be hard to find her inside.

I sit watching the street and the entrance to the parking lot, waiting to see if anyone followed me. I was so careful driving here, but still, I can't relax. I feel like the murder club is right behind me, breathing down my neck, an invisible army with soldiers on every street corner, in every car, in the window of every building.

Last night, after I left Sofia, I came here and parked in almost this exact spot. I sat in the dark, alone, thinking about what I was going to do. I sat here remembering Carol, racking my brain, trying to find some reason not to do this. I tried to think of any other way to get Joaquin safe, to get him his insulin, to get him into the care of a different family.

I came up empty. So here I am.

I pray that Carol's God, if he's real, will have mercy on her soul.

At last, I pull the paper Trader Joe's bag out from under my seat. I check its contents. My hands tremble; the trembling goes all the way up my muumuu-sleeved arms and into my chest. I feel a sudden need to go to the bathroom, but it fades into a shaky queasiness all through my abdomen.

I pull out the Ziploc bag and flip it over to look at the blackbirds-and-flowers design on the back. The blackbirds on the card look like they know things. They have beady little eyes.

I pull a pair of latex gloves out of their Ziploc bag and stretch them onto my hands. My tattoos are faintly visible underneath. I wrap the fanny pack around my waist and place the card inside it. I follow it with the yellow sharps container and the Ziploc of latex gloves.

I review my plan. I've been thinking about this all night as I tried to sleep on Kevin's sticky white leather couch, a pillow over my head to block out the sounds of him banging some chick in his bedroom.

I left both the iPhone and flip phone back at Kevin's in case of GPS tracking. I turned them both off, too, just to make sure no calls came through while I was gone that Kevin would be tempted to answer.

I plan to kill Carol during the worship part of the service. It will be dark and chaotic with loud music and people praying. I'll just sneak up behind her and inject her in the back, then slip out the back door before anyone can see me.

I have clothes on underneath the muumuu; I'll take the outfit off real fast as I'm driving and put all the murder stuff in a Trader Joe's bag, which I'll burn in a trash can by the homeless encampment on Cesar Chavez Avenue. Then I'll head back to Kevin's, where I'll chill out until I hear from the cops. I'm sure they'll call me to check my alibi. And then once I'm clear... will they let me have Joaquin? Maybe. I'm his only relative. It's a long shot, but there's a chance.

The sun suddenly doesn't seem too bright at all.

If they give me Joaquin, I can't take any chances; I can't get caught by the murder club. I have enough savings to stay off the radar for a while. Maybe we can do a road trip and wait to see if the cops catch up with the murder club. What if we left the country? We could live abroad. That'd be fine. Without Carol in the picture, who could stop me?

A small voice in my head asks: What about Sofia? Would she be in danger if I left? Should I offer to take her with me? But then, what about her daughter?

I don't know. First things first. There will be time for thinking and planning later. For now, I need to take care of business.

The ladies in church dresses disperse, heading for the front doors. I watch the group on the small front porch disappear inside and the simple wooden door close behind them. Across the parking lot, another few cars pile in, releasing surprisingly young people in jeans and T-shirts. When the lot has been empty for the longest five minutes of my life, I turn the engine off, get out and stash my keys in the fanny pack.

I check my reflection in the driver's side window. I really do look like a different person. I hunch my shoulders forward to look older, frailer. The muumuu billows out around me like a tent. Sexy.

The church's front door is covered in white construction paper doves, cut with a die cutter and taped to the door like in elementary school. The barred front windows release strains of singing onto the deserted, desert-bright street.

My neck feels tight with anxiety as I trot up the front steps and grip the door handle. I remind myself to move slower, like an older woman.

I take a breath and turn the handle. It's unlocked, and the door swings smoothly open.

I enter a tiny, stuffy lobby. The walls are covered in floral wallpaper, the floor soft with musty, rose-colored carpet. The singing is coming from an open door in front of me, and I press forward through it.

It's a normal, wood-benched sanctuary, and the smell of the room brings back a wave of memories from years ago, of Joaquin on my lap, of Joaquin and me giggling and elbowing each other in the pews. The darkened room is packed full. Most of the congregation is gathered up in front of the stage, in what I would call the pit at a rock show. Their hands are raised, their heads thrown back, lips busy in prayer. Colored spotlights play over the crowd, turning it into a rainbow of grasping hands. A woman at the piano hits the keys with squint-eyed intensity, and the singer and guitarist raise their arms in the air like they want to be called on in class. Behind them, a drummer bangs earnestly on a cheap electronic kit, which freezes me in place as I contemplate the douchebaggery involved in bringing an electronic kit into a church service. "Lord," cries the singer, a good-looking guy in his early twenties, "we come to You in worship, in supplication. We give You all of ourselves!" The congregation cries out in response.

This is different, more modern, than I remember it. The singer is kind of hipster-looking, with shaggy hair and skinny jeans. The congregation is different as well. Some of them are younger than me, and some are Carol's age, but all are moving their lips in quick succession as they reach into the air with searching hands.

Another man, older than the singer but equally handsome and shaggy-haired, trots up to the stage, mic in hand. He lifts his free hand and releases a slew of babbling nonsense words that sound vaguely like Hebrew. Oh, God, this is the speaking-in-tongues thing they do here. I can't with these people. Once Carol told me, "It's my private prayer language that only God can understand, so the devil doesn't know what I'm praying for." I didn't even know where to begin with that one.

"Thank You, God," the dude onstage moans into the mic. "Thank You for Your sacrifice. Thank You, Jesus, for the blood You spilled on the *cross*!" He screams out the last word, and an answering chorus echoes from the crowd. He returns to babbling in fake Hebrew, and babbling rises from the crowd like the chatter of birds.

"Alrighty then," I whisper to myself, and I approach the stage warily, looking for Carol and Joaquin. I press through the crowd, weaving through people, looking for Carol's limp blond hair or Joaquin's emo-style mop while also trying to keep my face down so no one notices I'm not as old as I'm pretending to be.

I'm halfway through, slipping past rapt worshippers chanting to themselves, when the pastor starts talking about "a call to prayer," something about "raising your hands" and "surrendering to the spirit."

He says, "Jesus said that His disciples have authority over unclean spirits, to cast them out, and to heal every disease and every affliction." The crowd roars in agreement. The pastor's hair is sweaty, flopping around his forehead, and he pushes it aside, his expression rapt. "Jesus calls us to heal the sick, raise the dead, cleanse those who have leprosy, drive out demons. Freely you have received; freely give." The music drops dramatically in volume, entering a mellow, hypnotically downtempo song. "Now he that needs healing, let him ask. He that needs healing...let him ask," he chants, sometimes louder, sometimes softer.

I move around the back of the crowd, searching, the lights floating through the throng, confusing my ability to see faces. The hundreds of raised arms float around like the fluorescent tentacles of sea anemones.

A middle-aged woman comes to the stage, her hands lifted, eyes streaming tears. He lays a hand on her forehead and starts chanting. She begins trembling, shaking, and the chanting gets louder. Around her, worshippers reach out to lay their hands on her back, her head, her arms, her waist, and they begin chanting in a hysterical babble of nonsense words. Just as I feel I'm going to scream, the woman cries out and crumples to the floor, her forehead against the carpet, hands pressed to her cheeks.

"Amen," cries the pastor. "She's slain in the spirit. The Holy Spirit is cleansing her body, doing His healing work. Let he who is thirsty come drink! Remember, church, *you* are the blood of Christ—*you* are the resurrection!"

"Amen," cry out worshippers. The music swells. A kid is shoved onto the stage.

It's Joaquin. He looks bored and embarrassed, and when the pastor places his hand on top of his head, he ducks away. Oh, God, they're going to do their pray-away-the-disease thing on him. I feel hot with protective rage. I am absolutely mad enough to kill.

The pastor settles for gripping his shoulder. "Aaaaruuushnaka," he screams, rolling the *R*s.

The lights flash, flickering over the crowd, and I see Carol. She's toward the back of the pit.

Bitch.

Pressed between people with eyes closed and faces raised to the promise of God, I dig around in my fanny pack and get out the sharps container. I pull the syringe out and return the empty container to my fanny pack, which I leave open. I drop my hand to my side with the needle pointed down and slip between people until I'm standing right behind Carol.

I take a deep breath, try to push the pastor's voice out of my head, the incessant chanting, the bad electronic drumbeat. I'm going to do something I can never take back, never undo—

She turns and moves left, slipping away between people. Is she heading for a bathroom?

I follow her to the outskirts of the crowd. She's heading for the left bank of pews. Maybe she left something on her seat.

It's dark over here and separated from the yammering crowd. I clutch the syringe. This is good, better to kill her here. I close the distance between us. I could reach out and touch her.

She spins to face me. She lifts a hand and presses it to my

nose and mouth. It's wet. Wait—her hand's not wet. She's holding a wet towel.

Her face swims into focus, shadowed, pink flashing in her eyes. Her brown eyes—she's not Carol. She's way younger, her skin darker. The hair is a wig. I gasp. The wet cloth smells strong, sweet, a saturated chemical scent that goes straight to my head. I try to back up, holding my breath. She pushes me forward, catches me off guard, presses the wet cloth deep into my nostrils, my mouth. Her face is savage. My head spins. I realize I've toppled back onto the carpet. No one notices. They're all screaming, praying, dropping to the floor themselves.

I grip my syringe. My head is a blur. I can't let myself breathe. I spin sideways, but she's somehow on top of me, the cloth pressed into my face still—I'm breathing it, I'm losing this fight—what is happening? My clutching hand is empty. Where is the syringe?

Get it together, Jazz. Pink and blue lights flash in her eyes. Her other hand comes into view. It holds a yellow syringe.

Adrenaline slams through me. I've lost my arms, my hands. I lunge forward and headbutt her, hard. The wet cloth is gone; the air is warm and clean with no chemical sweetness. She rolls aside, one hand clutching her nose, the other raising the syringe.

I roll out, search the floor frantically for my own needle. My hand closes on it. I scuttle backward, desperate, panicked. I lurch to a standing position and try to run. She grabs me, drags me back. She lifts a hand, gets the syringe up to my neck.

I impale her stomach. She squeals, tries to get her own needle in me. I hear myself sobbing out the words, "Stop it! I don't want to!" She won't. She's hell-bent on poking me with that fucking needle. I depress the plunger. She cries out and falters. I pull the syringe out of her and it falls to the floor.

She crumples to the carpet. Her hand grips her stomach. She looks down at it, her face confused.

My hands are shaking, sweating under the latex gloves. I almost fall, my head like a carnival ride. I push through the crowd. Just a little farther. Got to get outside. Got to get out of here before Joaquin or the real Carol sees me. Can't get caught here. Hurry. Hurry.

26
KELLY

KELLY CRIES OUT when the needle pokes her stomach. Her target's face is desperate. "Stop it! I don't want to!" the woman screams. She's young beneath the gray wig, at least ten years younger than Kelly.

It's kill or be killed. Kelly fights to get her needle in the woman's neck, squirms, writhes, and then the woman depresses the plunger.

Something slides into Kelly's gut, ice-cold. She claps a hand to her stomach. Her knees hit the carpet.

The woman who'd just injected her stares down at her with huge, horrified brown eyes. In the sanctuary's rainbow light, the eyes are beautiful, liquid and long-lashed, the eyes of an angel.

The young woman turns and runs.

No, you don't. Kelly grabs her syringe and lurches to her feet. She doesn't know what the woman injected her with, but it can't be the same poison Kelly has in her syringe. If it were poison, Kelly would already be dead, right? Maybe it's sleeping medication, something to knock her out. The voice on the phone told Kelly this poison kills instantaneously.

The singer onstage calls out, "Thank You, Lord, for the blood that washes all of us clean! We give You all of ourselves. We thank You for trading Your life for ours!" The crowd screams, voices, eyes, hands lifted in prayer.

Kelly pushes through the singing parishioners. A vise grips her stomach and twists. She groans and the vise grinds harder, wrapping around her midsection and squeezing, slow, agonizing.

There! She sees the woman who'd injected her! The flowered dress, the gray hair. She's in the crowd, pretending to pray, trying to blend in.

Kelly pushes herself forward, limping, guts grinding themselves into a pulp. This feels like contractions, like when she thought she could do childbirth without an epidural—before she realized she was totally wrong.

She grips the syringe. She approaches the loose flowered dress, hand clasped to her abdomen. The gray head remains lifted, oblivious to the approach of death. *Bitch, it's your turn now.*

Kelly puts her arm around the woman, and, no hesitation, she slips the syringe into the woman's stomach and pushes the depressor.

I did it!

The woman cries out and grabs at her stomach. Kelly trips back into someone—people—and her vision is suddenly bent, the sanctuary a carnival nightmare. Her lungs pinch shut.

She's on the floor? When did she fall?

She rolls onto her side, grips her knees to her chest, all of her sucked into the band of pain clenching through her ribs.

The kids. Their faces are so close, she could reach out and touch them. Vanessa's pretty pink cheeks; Eli's curly brown hair, so soft to the touch.

The woman she'd injected is on the carpet next to her, writhing in agony just like her own. The woman's face turns toward her, blue eyes wide with fear and horror—

Blue eyes?

"Jesus!" hollers someone near at hand. *Finally someone sees me*, Kelly thinks, desperate, but it's an exultation. Someone places a hand on Kelly's back and cries, "These two are slain in the spirit!" A flurry of incoherence follows as parishioners around her lift their voices in a chorus of tongues.

The gray-haired woman's terrified eyes are wide and full of fireflies. Kelly reaches across the carpet and grips the other woman's hand. "I'm sorry," she whispers, but the woman is past hearing her.

27
NIELSEN

NIELSEN AND PATEL park on the street in front of the tiny church in East LA. They get out of the car and stand in the hot sun, surveying the scene.

Patel says, "They did a good job of blockading the lot. Fat lot of good it does us. They didn't arrive on scene for ten bloody minutes."

"It's going to be a shit ton more admin, all these witnesses," Nielsen complains. "Like we aren't up to our asses already."

"We need to ask for more help with the paperwork."

He gives her shoulder a pat. "Come on, little woman, let's get this over with."

She slaps his hand away and grins. "Don't touch me, twat."

"I love it when you say 'twat.'"

"I know you do."

All the congregants have been brought out into the front yard of the church, where they're contained in a taped-off square, a makeshift fence since the church doesn't have one.

It's a diverse crowd, young and old, different ethnicities, some dressed up, some in jeans.

A pair of uniformed cops led by Gonzalez spots Nielsen and Patel from across the clearing, and Gonzalez waves to them enthusiastically. Nielsen groans.

"Don't be a tosser," Patel says, waving back to Gonzalez.

"She's a terrible cop. You know that."

"She's not terrible. She's learning."

"She's a pain in my ass."

Patel grabs his arm and pulls him to a stop. "You know she lost a child. Why don't you try not to be such an inconceivable prat?"

"She should take more leave. She's not ready to be back."

"She *needs* this."

"This isn't group therapy. You think I haven't lost people? But you don't see me crying about it at work. I leave it at home, and when I'm here, I'm here."

He expects Patel to argue with him, but she nods like she's considering his words. "You know I served, too. Afghanistan."

"Yeah."

She squeezes his bicep. "I'm sorry about those you lost."

The words catch him by surprise. His eyes sting. He wasn't ready for compassion.

She sees his face and does the best thing possible. She makes a joke. "At least no one will ever call you a cheerleader. You'd look bloody horrendous in the uniform."

"I look hot in a miniskirt," he protests, back to normal.

Gonzalez introduces the uniforms as Wilson and Ramos, and they explain that they've kept the band and the preacher in a separate space around back if they want to talk to them first.

"I'm going to need all these folks down at the station," Nielsen says, indicating the churchgoers huddled in the makeshift front yard. "Can you work on transportation? I don't want to lose a single one along the way."

"I'm on it," Gonzalez says.

Nielsen and Patel follow her past the little church, around the side through the parking lot, and up a set of rickety back steps to a back door. This looks more like a house than a church; it can't be more than two thousand square feet, and the neighborhood it's in is all warehouses, recycling centers and scrap yards. Past the parking lot and the railroad tracks, on the embankment to the LA River, a long row of tents stretches off to the horizon.

Patel says, "Why not hit one of the megachurches? This can't hold more than a couple hundred people, and I bet they all know each other. Not an easy place to be anonymous, I wouldn't think."

Nielsen says, "These killings aren't random. Blackbird is studying his victims, planning his kills carefully."

"I'm not convinced of that." She still believes Blackbird picks his victims opportunistically.

"You coming?" Gonzalez asks from the back door.

"Keep your panties on," Nielsen snaps.

They follow her up the creaky wooden stairs and into a claustrophobic hallway that needs a good carpet cleaning. Inside the sanctuary, Forensics has already gotten to work on the bodies.

"How's the crime scene?" Nielsen asks Gonzalez.

"Secure," she replies proudly.

"We'll see." None of the Blackbird crime scenes have been secure.

The sanctuary is as small as Nielsen had imagined, with just ten rows of pews and a tiny stage at the front. In front of the stage is a clearing, which is full of activity. A man in a Dickies jacket with *LAPD* printed on the back squats by a supine shape on the floor. The flash—flash—flash of his camera competes with the dim overhead lighting.

Nielsen and Patel approach the bodies, respecting the boundary marked off by Forensics.

"Two victims," Patel whispers, her tone restrained but excited. There have never been two victims at a single scene.

The victims, two women, are stretched out on the carpet face-to-face, both in a loose fetal position, both with the wide-open, terrified eyes they've come to expect from these killings.

"You think Blackbird positioned them like that?" Patel asks.

"Has to be."

"Or he injected two people side by side and they fell that way."

Gonzalez, suddenly behind them, says, "Take a look at the younger one. Look at her hair."

Nielsen squats down. "It's a wig."

"But *why*?" Patel kneels down so she can get a better look. "She's a brunette. I can see her hairline around the side here under the bangs."

"Do we have IDs?" Nielsen asks Gonzalez.

"On the older woman, yes. Guadalupe Ramirez, seventy-six, from Baldwin Park. Homemaker, six children, seventeen grandchildren. The younger woman with the wig, no."

Nielsen lets his eyes roam over the limp, gaping figure. The woman is probably forty years old with pretty olive skin and deep brown eyes. One of her hands is stretched out to the other woman, like they'd been holding hands before they died.

He does a double take. "Gloves," Nielsen gasps. "Holy shit. She's wearing latex gloves."

"What about the other woman?" Patel asks.

They look. No. Her wrinkled hands are uncovered.

Gonzalez says, "We found a syringe on the ground nearby, and a playing card over there." She points to a spot in the corner of the room by the left bank of pews. "Another syringe was over there, too. Identical to this one."

Patel and Nielsen look at each other, eyes wide.

Patel says, "Suicide? She kills the older lady then herself? Is this our Blackbird Killer? Could Jasmine have been lying about it being a man? No, that's not possible—there were fifty witnesses at Trader Joe's."

The answer explodes in Nielsen's brain like a hydrogen bomb, burning away all his false assumptions, clearing the horizon for one last, standing revelation.

Nielsen says, "We have two killers. That's why the crimes have been inconsistent. One killer is smart, quick, accurate. The other one is an amateur. Maybe our pro got sick of working with an amateur."

Patel casts a sideways glance at Gonzalez, who is deep in conversation with one of the photographers.

Nielsen follows her eyes. "Don't repeat this. We have to work this lead without sending everyone into hysterics."

Gonzalez approaches them and hands Nielsen a clipboard. "There's our list of church attendees," she says.

Patel nudges Gonzalez out of the way and forces Nielsen to hold the clipboard lower so she can see it. Her eyes scan down the list. She points. "That looks familiar."

He squints at the name. Carol Coleman. The name next to it is Joaquin Benavides Coleman, and a little note next to the name says "child—13YO."

"Benavides," Nielsen says. "Is this a relation to Jasmine Benavides?"

Patel gets her notebook out and flips through it. "She was

asking about a brother. I looked it up. Brother is…" She looks up at him. "Joaquin. Yep."

"Call Jasmine," Nielsen says, but Patel already has her phone in hand and is searching for a number.

While Patel tries to get Jasmine on the phone, Nielsen heads for the exit. Gonzalez tails behind him like a puppy. "Show me these two," Nielsen says. "Carol and Joaquin Coleman. I need to speak with them right away."

Gonzalez leads him out to the makeshift pen in which all the parishioners are huddled under the blazing sun. He raises a hand for people's attention and calls out, "Carol Coleman? Carol Coleman, we need to see you, please."

A woman emerges from the crowd. She has a shoulder-length mullet and high-waisted slacks. The slender boy she brings with her is almost pretty, with cheek-length dark brown hair and olive skin.

"Carol?" Patel asks. The woman nods. "We'll need you to come to the station with us right away. We need to ask you some questions."

"About what? I didn't see nothing."

God, she's even worse than her daughter, Nielsen thinks, and then his eyes freeze on the hair. Wait.

"One second," he says to Carol. He grabs Patel and pulls her aside. "Look at the haircut," he whispers.

"What about it?"

"It looks just like the wig on the woman inside!"

Patel's eyes fly to Carol, then back to the door of the church. He can feel the tension radiating off her. They've screwed up this investigation completely. They've gotten it all wrong.

28
JAZZ

THEY'RE HUNTING ME.

My heart pounds a vicious beat all the way up into my neck. I feel hungover from whatever weird shit was in the towel the woman shoved in my face. My hands are unsteady on the steering wheel, but I'm grateful for the job of driving. At least I'm moving. At least I'm safe inside this cocoon of glass and steel. It's everything outside there, in the wild, frenetic world, that I have to be afraid of.

And now I'm something to be feared, too. I've murdered someone. I didn't stick around to see if the shit in my syringe killed that lady, but I know it must have.

Outside my windows, East LA's collection of small businesses flashes past, disconcertingly cheerful: a taco shop; a panaderia; a Laundromat; a frutero under a colorful umbrella; a woman inexplicably selling stuffed animals out of the back of a station wagon. For the first time in my life, I feel disconnected from all of it.

The feeling of pushing the depressor haunts me. I shake my hand out, a shudder passing through my body. I can't believe I did that. And now I'm out of poison and Carol's still alive. And I'm a killer, someone who has taken a human life.

I want to go back and undo it. I can't believe I can't. It seems wrong, that I should be here and not back there again, allowed a second chance at the decision.

But no. That woman is dead. Forever.

I pull the wig off and throw it onto the passenger's seat. The sweat soaking my hair plasters it to my head.

The light turns red, and I stop behind a truck with someone's foot hanging out the passenger window. I'm at the corner of Main Street, almost at Lincoln Park.

How did they know to find me at the church? Were they watching the church, figuring I'd go there since I don't know where Carol and Joaquin are staying? Did they follow me to Kevin's last night and then to the church today? That seems impossible. I was so careful, doing U-turns and taking every side street.

I head west toward downtown. I pass through the ornate gates of Chinatown and turn left to approach downtown from the south. In just a few minutes, I'm surrounded by warehouses, scrap yards and abandoned factories with busted windows. By the time I'm in Skid Row, the sidewalks are lined with tents and shopping carts. I pass two men screaming at each other on a corner and a scattered collection of mothers with babies in strollers marching north through the encampments, their faces slick with sweat in the nuclear sunshine.

On a one-way street with fewer tents and pedestrians, I pull over next to a metal trash can. I lock the door, pocket my keys and slide across the front seat to the passenger's side door. I pull the muumuu off; I have jeans and a tank top on underneath it. I stuff it and the wig into the paper bag that contains the rest of my murder kit gear.

I grab a lighter out of my glove compartment, hop out of the car and place the bag in the trash can. With the lighter, I set fire to the edges of the paper bag. It ignites quickly, and the polyester of the dress and the synthetic hair are quick to catch. Within thirty seconds, the bag is brightly ablaze. The smoke reeks of trash and plastic. I spy a pile of discarded, crumpled newspaper near an abandoned campsite, and I grab it and lay it on top of the fire in the trash can. The paper whorls into flame, and soon the entire contents of the can are engulfed.

I get back into my truck, start the engine and peel away from the curb, putting as much distance between myself and the fire as I can, but I'm not worried about the fire raising much alarm, not down here.

I take side streets all the way to Kevin's house, eyes glued to my mirrors. It's Sunday and traffic is clear. Usually this fills me with exuberance and makes me feel free, like I can go anywhere and do anything. Today, the bright, open city feels hollow and unsafe, like anything could happen to me and no one would be around to see it.

At last, I pull up to Kevin's house. I put the truck in Neutral and engage the e-brake.

I wait. No one else comes driving down the street.

I rest my forehead on the steering wheel, and I start to cry. I grip the sides of the steering wheel, just to have something to hold on to.

All my life, I've worked so hard to not be a certain kind of person, and here I am, so much worse than anything I had imagined. That woman I killed—what if she was in a situation like Sofia, like me? What if I just orphaned some kids?

And what about my own kid, the whole reason I got into

this mess? What should I have done, let her kill me, let Joaquin live his life at the mercy of Carol and DCFS?

I miss Joaquin so much. Where is he?

A small, sick voice in my head says, *He's lost. He's gone.*

At last, I pull myself together, wipe my face and check my reflection in the rearview mirror. I can do this. I can figure this out. First things first, I need to be normal with Kevin, and then I need to get my head together and make a plan. I need to move forward. Because what else is there except putting one foot in front of the other? At the end of the day, that's how life is done.

I get out of the truck. I'm out in the world now.

I cross the street to Kevin's house. I open the screen door and knock a few times. "It's me," I call. I try the doorknob. It turns easily; Kevin had said he'd leave it open for me if he was in the shower.

I let myself in. "Kevin, it's me, man." I close the door behind me and set my purse down on the dining table. The lamp by the TV fills the living room with warm yellow light, casting shadows from the leather couch onto the white tiles. Al Green sings soulfully somewhere nearby.

I reach down by the couch to grab the tote bag in which I'd stashed the phones and some clothes.

It's not where I left it.

Maybe Kevin moved it. It was kind of in the way. I check all sides of the couch. No tote bag.

I hunt around the living room, checking corners. Where did he put it? Maybe in his bedroom?

"Kevin," I call. "You got my bag, dude?"

It occurs to me that the Al Green might mean he's got the girl in his bedroom still. Whoops. But I should let him know

I'm here to avoid an embarrassing moment, and I want to check my phone. I make my way through the living room. "Kevin? Hey, dude, I'm here!" I check the bathroom first. It's empty, and it carries the faint, shampoo-steam smell of a recent shower. Al Green is louder back here, singing about love and happiness. I step farther down the hallway. Kevin's bedroom door is partway open, spilling lamplight into the hallway in a liquid yellow stream. Maybe he doesn't have a girl in there after all. I knock lightly on the door frame. "Hey, dude, you got the bag I left in the living room? It had my phone in it. Can I grab it?"

Silence.

I knock again. "Kevin?" I push the door open.

On the white tile next to the bed, a red puddle glistens.

My heart, a kick drum, pounds a bloody beat.

Kevin is sprawled out sideways on the bed, shirtless, his head hanging half-off the mattress. His beautiful powder-blue eyes stare emptily straight at me. A thin stream of blood has soaked the sheets, trailing from his lips down to meet the puddle on the floor.

I back up until I hit the wall. Someone's talking—it's me. A string of "Oh my God, oh my God, oh my God" is wheezing from my chest.

My foot hits something. I look down.

It's a flip phone.

Stuck to it, a tiny blue Post-it reads *Jasmine*.

I pick it up. It's just like the one from my tote.

What do I do? *What do I do?* I can't think. Not with Kevin's dead eyes staring at a fixed point between him and me. *Get your iPhone and get the fuck out of here*, a voice yells at me, like a conscience, but it sounds like myself.

There's almost no furniture in this room, just a dresser, bed and nightstand. My bag is nowhere.

I back out of the room into the hallway. Al Green sounds warped and melted.

I'm in the living room. I can't tell if I'm breathing too fast or not at all. The air in the house is thick with death.

On shaky legs, I check the kitchen. Nothing. It's not here.

I grab my purse off the table and flee, out the front door, slamming it behind me, down the three steps, out onto the sidewalk.

I'm dizzy. I feel like I'm going to faint. I put my hands on my knees and look down at the sidewalk, at the tiny blades of grass poking out of the cracks.

Dark spots appear on the sun-soaked concrete. They're tears, dripping from my eyes.

How fragile are humans that we can be extinguished so quickly? Two deaths in one day, both my fault.

I straighten up. I wipe my eyes with shaking fingers.

I can run, but I can't hide. I'm a fucking dead man walking.

In my hand, the phone starts buzzing.

29
JAZZ

I THROW THE phone in my purse. I'm in the street. I can't get my key into the door of my truck. My hands are numb. I drop my keys, pick them up from the asphalt. A car driving by honks at me and I scream, cover my head with my hands, but it keeps driving. I finally connect the key with the lock and get behind the wheel.

My purse starts buzzing.

I lock the door. I turn on the engine. I peel out, fly through the stop sign and make a wild left. The phone goes quiet.

At a red light on Adams, it starts buzzing again.

I take the phone out.

Blocked.

My hand is shaking so hard, it slips trying to open the phone, sending it rattling down between my feet. I retrieve it, open it and put it to my ear.

"Jasmine," the warped voice barks. It's the scariest sound, the rage filtered through the disguiser.

I can't talk. I can barely breathe. I push the lock button on my door even though I already locked it.

"Jasmine," the voice repeats.

"What?" My voice is hoarse.

"Who else have you told?"

"Told what?"

"Told about us."

I feel completely blank, like they aren't speaking English. "What are you talking about?"

A weary sigh, and the voice comes at me like a kindergarten teacher. "Apart from the man whose house you were hiding at, who have you told about this organization? Have you told the police? A friend? A neighbor?"

I realize what they're saying, that they killed Kevin because they thought I'd told him about the murder club. "You fucking piece of shit!" I cry. "I didn't tell Kevin anything! I've done everything you've asked!" I dissolve into tears. Through them, I manage to ask, "Why? Why would you do this? Why would you hunt me down like this? Why did you kill Kevin? You're supposed to help people like me. Isn't that what you said you do?"

"I am in the business of trading lives, of determining their worth. You were comfortable with this when your life was on the better end of the trade. You can't argue with logic you supported just because the scales tipped out of your favor."

"But I'm still me! You're still supposed to help me save Joaquin from Carol! You're not supposed to try and kill me!" I sound like a little girl.

"And I am still saving Joaquin from Carol. Or I was, but again, that was your mistake." A distorted sigh. "Do you know why I sent Kelly in dressed like your Carol?"

I've never heard of a Kelly, but I imagine they must be talking about the woman I killed in church. "Why?" I ask.

"So Carol would be blamed for your murder. Carol was on the scene. There would have been witnesses placing the two of you together. Joaquin would have gone to a better foster home, and he would have been spared the trauma of dealing with both of his terrible mothers for the rest of his life. But instead, he went home from church with Carol, and he still doesn't have his insulin. That's your fault. Again. *Your fault*, Jasmine. I'm out of time and energy trying to save your rat of a son from the mess you created. So keep driving. Drive until you run out of gas. We're everywhere. We're everyone. Tick tock, Jasmine."

The line disconnects.

The light turns green. No one is behind me, so I stay put. I don't think I can drive right now.

How did they find me at Kevin's house? How did they find me at the church? I was sure I wasn't followed. Could they have followed me last night and figured out what I was planning? A flash of panic hits me as I realize they could be using the GPS on my phone to track me, but then I remember that I didn't take my phone to the church, either last night or today. What else could it—

My truck?

Could they have put a GPS tracker on my truck?

I know you can buy those. I remember Joaquin talking about them once, about how parents are using them to keep track of teenagers. He was outraged, of course, but I remember thinking it wasn't a bad idea if he ever went through a rebellious stage.

I throw the truck in Reverse and back up to the curb. I straighten out into some semblance of a parking job. I turn off the engine, flip the hood release under the dashboard and grab the flashlight out of the glove compartment.

I get out and open the hood. I don't know much about cars. The only thing I've ever done is change my oil and jump it when the battery died. I shine the flashlight around in the engine, but I don't think I'd recognize anything out of place.

I have to hurry.

I get down on the asphalt and shine the light up around the undercarriage. Nothing looks out of place. I get up, go around to the back and get down on my back to look at the underside of the truck bed.

Something reflective catches my eye on the inside of my passenger's side tire well. I shine the flashlight at it.

A silver-and-white box the size of a pack of cigarettes is attached to the corroded black metal.

I'm afraid to touch it and leave my fingerprints on it. I rack my brain. I have no spare clothes anymore, and I'm not wearing a sweater. At last I pull a sneaker off, yank off my sock and use it as a glove to try to pull the silver-and-white box off the tire well.

It's slick and shiny and is really stuck on there. I pull harder, grunting, and then I shine the light right on it to see how it's attached.

"Damn," I whisper. It seems to be bolted onto two slim metal straps that wrap around it and are secured to the tire well. I'm not getting it off without a wrench.

I put my sock and shoe back on and get up. This means they know exactly where I am. They could be sending someone my way right now.

I get in the truck, turn it on and go right at the light, heading east for downtown.

It takes all my willpower not to break the speed limit, but I manage to make it back to Skid Row without getting pulled over. There's a street I remember from a Google Maps detour to Little Tokyo that's full of car stereo shops and scrap yards with plastic-covered chain-link fences.

I pull the truck over in front of an abandoned warehouse with broken window eyes. I leave it unlocked with the key in the ignition. I take my house keys with me.

So now I have to walk through Skid Row alone, which isn't great. I transfer my driver's license, credit cards and house keys into my bra. Just in case.

I walk fast, purse clutched to my side, eyes straight ahead. No one bothers me as I pass the tents, but a few drunk-looking dudes hanging around the bus stop at the corner holler at me. I ignore them, but my steps slow as I pass the corner. My eyes are fixed on a grate, which I know leads down into another drainage channel. I squat down by it, pull the new flip phone out of my pocket and wipe it off on my shirt to get rid of any fingerprints.

I hesitate.

Whatever else the murder club has done, they know where Joaquin is. They could lead me to him.

This is my last connection to Joaquin.

They're not going to help me, I scream at myself. And it's a piece of forensic evidence that could maybe link me to Kevin's murder. What if it has trace amounts of his blood on it?

This is too much. I need to tell the police. I can't keep running from this on my own. But I need something, some form of evidence, anything, to link even just one of the other murder club members to the crimes. The thought, juxtaposed against the former worry about trace amounts of blood, brings my memory rushing back to the night at Villains when I got the first flip phone.

I remember the guy pushing his way through the crowd,

desperate to get out of there. I'd read his expression as hostility, but it was panic, right? He'd just committed his murder and he was running, and there I was, blocking his way, attacking him, making him drop his flip phone, punching him in the face...

Punching him in the face. Giving him a bloody nose.

I have his blood. At home. On my clothes from that night. They're buried in the bottom of the hamper.

I wipe the phone off one last time and throw it into the drainage channel.

Behind me, a bus makes a limping path down the potholed street. It screeches to a stop at my corner, and the doors hiss open to admit the three drunk guys.

Across the street, a new Jeep approaches, shiny and out of place on this broken-down street. It comes to a stop by my truck. The front door opens, and a woman steps out. She bends down to peer into my truck's driver's side window.

Oh, shit.

I hop up onto the curb and run to the bus stop. Just as the doors begin to swing shut, I push them open and jump inside. Outside the scratched, dirty window, I see the woman outside my truck pull a flip phone out of her pocket and start to dial.

30
NIELSEN

THE WOMAN WHO sits across from Nielsen in Interview Room 3 is skinny, birdlike and obviously unhappy to be here. It's a different vibe than he got from Jasmine, though. Jasmine's suspicion felt related to police, or maybe authority in general, where this woman feels…sketchy. Manic.

Next to him, Patel scribbles in her little notebook like she always does. Nielsen elbows Patel and gives her a meaningful look. It means she should lead the interview; it's their standard protocol with women and children.

"Don't I need a lawyer or something?" the woman, Carol, asks. Her voice is rough, like she's been smoking cigarettes since she came out of the womb.

Patel plasters a smile on her tired face. "Not at all. You're a witness. We're here to help you."

"Where's my son?"

"He's just on the other side of that wall, and he's being taken care of by my colleague. I believe she's spoiling him with some hot chocolate and cookies."

Nielsen almost says something. This is bullshit; there's no hot chocolate or cookies anywhere in here. He'd have eaten them if there were. But Patel shoots him a tiny look that tells him to be quiet.

Carol hesitates. "You shouldn't feed him that stuff. He's got diabetes."

Patel scribbles something in her notebook. "I'm sorry to hear that. Is his diabetes quite serious?" Her British accent is stronger when she's being solicitous.

"Are you a Christian?" Carol asks.

Patel blinks, and Nielsen almost laughs at her face as she tries to make sense of this response. "Why do you ask?"

"'For I will restore health to you, and your wounds I will heal, declares the Lord.' Nothing is beyond His ability to heal. Nothing. Not diabetes, not cancer, nothing."

Patel says, "So Joaquin has been healed of his diabetes, then?"

The forehead scrunches into a frown. "He's in the process." Into the silence that follows, she says, "'Is anyone among you sick? Let him call for the elders of the church, and let them pray over him, anointing him with oil in the name of the Lord. And the prayer of faith will save the one who is sick, and the Lord will raise him up.'" The skinny chin lifts, which tumbles the mullet into the stretched collar of the oversized pink blouse. "He who has ears, let him hear."

Wow.

Patel taps her index finger on the table. It's the signal to switch interviewers; in other words, he's up.

Nielsen smiles at Carol, deferential. "Did you know your

daughter was almost killed by the serial killer who's been in the news?"

"I don't have a daughter. I have a son."

"Your foster daughter? Jasmine Benavides?"

"We don't speak." She raises her hands to make air quotes. "'They have given themselves over to all kinds of evil pleasures.'"

Jesus. Nielsen thought his own mom was religious—Irish Catholic—but this woman takes the cake.

Patel leans forward. "Did you see anything at the church? Anything unusual, particularly a woman who looked like you?"

Carol raises her eyebrows. "Looked like me?"

"The woman who was killed—one of them—was wearing an outfit and a wig that looked very similar to your own hair and clothes. Can you think why that would be?"

She looks baffled. At last, she says, "No."

"I see."

"So you think she was killed on accident? That I was really supposed to be the one who got killed?"

"That's what we're trying to ascertain."

It's interesting, the idea that Blackbird would want to take out an entire family, and even more interesting to consider why someone was at that church wearing what appears to be a disguise meant intentionally to look like Carol. This case isn't just a mess; it's a convoluted steaming pile of shit.

Nielsen asks, "Have you had any unusual experiences lately? Anything strange at home, anyone hanging around your house, anything you can think of that seems out of place, no matter how small…"

"We're not staying at home. We're staying with friends."

"Why?" asks Patel.

"Family reasons. I wanted to surround Joaquin with the Word."

Nielsen scribbles the words "psych evaluation?" in his notebook and passes it to Patel.

She writes, "Can't psych eval someone for being religious unless you want to get sued."

He heaves a sigh. Of course she's right. He writes, "Checking on the kid," and she nods. He gets up, casts a last disgusted look at Carol and heads for the door.

He closes it lightly behind him and lets himself into Interview Room 2. It's empty except for a plastic cup. He retreats down the corridor and catches Gonzalez at the desk, buried in paperwork on a computer from the Dark Ages. "Where's the kid from Interview Room 2?"

She barely glances up. "Bathroom."

Nielsen goes to the men's room, which is just around the corner, and pokes his head in. "Joaquin?" he calls. A few cops are in front of the urinals, but the stalls are all open, unoccupied.

He hurries back to the desk. "Gonzalez. Where the fuck is the kid?"

"He's in the bathroom, last I checked."

"He's not in there," Nielsen says, his voice warming up with anger.

Her eyes go wide. She jumps up from her desk.

Yeah, now she's in a hurry. *Goddammit*, Nielsen curses, as they run to check the security footage. "Patel," he calls as he passes Room 3. She bursts out of the room. "Kid's missing," he says. She runs behind him, down the hall to the security room. They're holding their breaths, waiting for the video to play, when a suited man with gray hair and a beer belly pops into the darkened room behind them. It's Marcus, one of the detectives on the Blackbird team.

"Got another one," he says, out of breath.

Patel and Nielsen whirl around. "Where? Who?" Patel asks.

"Kevin Stanley, down on Adams and La Brea. Guess where he works."

"Where?" Nielsen asks.

"Trader Joe's, Third and La Brea."

"Motherfucker," says Nielsen. Patel closes her eyes and pinches the bridge of her nose.

Marcus goes on, "And he had a houseguest yesterday. Guess who."

Nielsen says, "Jasmine Benavides."

"Yup."

"She's not there now?" asks Patel.

"Nope. And we found her truck in a scrap yard south of downtown. Dried blood all over the front seat."

Nielsen's stomach drops. Jasmine is dead. He knows it. They've been trying to reach her for twenty-four hours with no luck, and Blackbird leaves no survivors. To Patel, he says, "You find the kid. I'll go work this lead." She nods. Her face is pale. He can see she's thinking the same thing he is.

31

JAZZ

THE STREET OUTSIDE my apartment is quiet when I drive by. I'm in the rental Hyundai I paid for with my new prepaid Visa debit card. I'm totally off the grid now, with an Android burner phone I can barely figure out how to use. I can't think of a single way they could be tracking me now.

But after all that trouble to be untraceable, I'm coming back to my apartment, where they might be waiting for me. This is dumb. I know it. But I need to get those clothes out of my hamper.

It's dark but not late, only eight thirty, and the sidewalks are cheerfully bustling with moms pushing strollers, men pushing elote and paleta carts, and tired-looking people trickling off the bus from long, hard workdays. I drive by slowly, examining every pedestrian, checking every parked car. My building looks small and haphazard, some windows yellow and curtained, some slatted with blinds.

I find a parking spot pretty close to my apartment. I turn

off the engine and power on the Android phone so I'll have a way to call 911 just in case. As the phone lights up in my hand, I wonder if I should call Sofia, and then I realize I don't have her number memorized. It's in my iPhone that the murder club stole. It's probably better this way. I should stay away from her. I just want to know she's safe, and I want to tell her about Kevin. Maybe I could call her at work tomorrow. That's probably safest.

Someone tall and slender lopes across the street. They slip between parked cars and trot up into my apartment building. It looks like they're wearing a hoodie with the hood pulled up.

I rack my brain, remembering all the occupants of the other seven units in my building. There's the family downstairs with the mom who always gives me a bag of her bomb Christmas tamales. There's the old man who lives alone, the young couple who has sex really loud, the roommates who fight, the single musician guy who always needs a drummer...

I can't think of anyone in my building who looks like this. Maybe it's a friend of someone who lives here.

Should I get out? Should I wait?

Before I can make up my mind, the hooded figure exits my building, trots across the street and gets into a gray Honda Accord three cars in front of me.

That's weird. Why would someone come and go so fast?

The answer is obvious. It's someone from the murder club, someone looking for me.

The taillights go red and the headlights flicker on.

Maybe I could point the cops toward this guy. With the blood, that would give them two members of the club. And I bet this person still has their murder kit, their flip phone. I start the engine but keep the headlights off.

The Honda takes a few tries to get out of its parking spot before speeding up the street. I wait a beat and follow it.

I tail the car east through Echo Park and onto the 2 freeway. It heads north to the 5, then west to the 134 toward the Valley. The 134 turns into the 101, and my stomach starts to gnaw as we enter Studio City, which is where Sofia lives.

The car gets into the right lane to exit at Laurel Canyon.

"What the hell," I mutter to myself. This is Sofia's exit. I don't like that. I don't like it at all.

"Turn left, turn left," I whisper, willing the Honda to head south, away from Sofia and toward Hollywood.

It turns right. "No," I groan. It flips around to park on the street, a block away from Sofia's building. I don't want to flip a U-turn, which would make it pretty obvious that I'm tailing them, so I pull over on the opposite side of the boulevard.

What do I do?

Should I call the cops? Maybe they can catch this person in the act?

The gray Honda's headlights turn off, and the car goes dark. The driver's side door opens, letting the hooded figure out onto the street. Quick and lithe, the silhouette slips along the sidewalk, back bulging as though with a backpack. The figure bypasses the front entry and lopes around the corner, where I know there is a metal gate opening to the underground parking garage.

Oh, shit. No time to waste. I jump out of the car, wait for a few cars to pass, and run across the five lanes and along the sidewalk to the front gate. My hands are shaking as I find Sofia in the directory. It starts ringing. "Come on come on," I whisper.

"Hello?" Her voice fills me with a warm wave of relief.

"Sofia, it's Jazz. Is your door locked?"

"Jazz! Are you downstairs?"

"Is your door locked? Just answer. It's important."

A pause. "Yeah. Why?"

"Your windows? Are they locked?"

"I think so. Why?"

"Go check them right now. Don't answer the door for anyone. Promise. No one."

"O…kay."

"Buzz me in."

The gate buzzes and I slip in, making sure it closes behind me. I don't want to head to the elevator alcove, which takes me close to the parking garage, so I turn right down a hallway and look for a stairwell. Sure enough, I find the door to the stairs at the northern corner of the building, on the opposite side of the apartment building from Sofia's unit. I poke my head in, imagining a syringe-wielding old person leaping out at me from behind one of the darkened staircases. It's nowhere near as creepy as the stairs in my building; it's well lit, the stairs carpeted and the walls clean white. I close the door behind me and jog silently up to the second floor.

I keep myself pressed to walls as I hurry past peaceful front doors. *Don't forget to breathe*, Apartment 201 instructs me.

I stop at the intersection of corridors that leads to Sofia's apartment. I slip across the hallway and peer around the corner.

There's a man crouched down by her door, doing something to the doormat or maybe shoving something under the door.

I'm about to jump out and start yelling when he lifts his face.

It's Charles. He's putting more pictures on Sofia's door.

Motherfucker.

He examines one, and I hate the proprietary way his eyes look at the image of her naked body. He snaps a piece of tape off a roll and attaches the picture to her door, obsessive in his placement of the image next to another one just like it.

I want to launch out into the hallway. I want to call the cops and catch his stalker ass in the act. But I remember Sofia's frantic begging. She doesn't want the police knowing about this, not now when she's in the murder club.

Charles tapes another flyer to the door. He's deep into the task, a spiteful smirk twisting his lips into a smile.

Inspiration strikes. I get the Android phone out and poke at the home screen until I find the camera app. I set it to video and push the record button. I focus on Charles and record him at work.

It's like he can feel me watching him. His head snaps up and he looks right at me. "Hey! Who's there?"

What am I going to do, turn and run? I round the corner, still recording. He jumps guiltily to his feet, and the stack of unused photos falls from his hands.

"What's up, dickwad? Doing another stalker collage? You are *such* a loser." I turn the camera on the door, then back on him, capturing his handiwork and his stupid, caught-in-the-act face.

"It's a felony to record someone without their permission," he says, his voice pinched and livid.

What a wiener. "Why don't you call the cops, then?"

He fumes silently.

"Oh right. Because you're being a psycho stalker and you don't want them to know."

"Give me that." He lunges at me, hands outstretched. I snap the phone behind my back and slither out of his grip. He throws his arms around me, tries to pin my arms against my sides. I spin out from the hold and shove the phone in my back pocket. He rams himself at me, using his size and no skill at all, and pins me to the wall, trying to get his hands in my pockets. His chest heaves against mine. His breath is hot and smells like day-old coffee. He leans real close to my cheek and says, "You think you can fight like a man, little dyke?"

I squirm, hoping to get a leg free and knee him in the groin, but he's too close, pinning me to the wall. I can't free my arms enough to hit him, but I get my hands up inside the prison of his chest, pinch his little man-boobs and twist them hard in opposite directions. He makes an injured rhinoceros noise and flecks of spit spray my cheek. I twist harder, my stomach roiling with revulsion.

A door opens three doors down, and an older man steps into the hallway, a canvas grocery bag on his shoulder. He sees us and stops midexit.

"Everything all right?" he asks.

Charles backs off me. He runs his hands down the front of his sweater, smoothing it out where I'd stretched it. He can't fix his face, which is a mask of petulant fury. He shoots me one last glare and strides off down the hall in the opposite direction.

"You okay?" the older man asks me.

I put my hands up as though to push his kindness away. With Charles gone, I suddenly feel his weight on me, a delayed reaction.

"I'm fine," I manage to answer. "It's all good."

The man is obviously torn between not wanting to be nosy and wanting to stick around and make sure I'm taken care of. It's sweet.

"Honestly. I'm totally cool," I say.

"Okay," he says, and at last he turns to the elevator alcove and walks away.

I return to Sofia's door and scoop all the papers up, trying not to look at them. I take them down to the trash by the stairwell, rip them into a thousand tiny pieces and put them inside the can. I realize Charles's nasty spit must still be on my face, and suddenly, I'm sure I'm going to be sick. I lean over the trash can and wait for the vomit to come up, but my stomach settles. I spit into the trash can. My breathing slows. *I'm okay. He's gone. It's okay.*

I keep a flyer out and bring it back with me to Sofia's door. I knock on the door and call, "It's me."

The door opens a little, and I note with approval that the chain lock is still on. I force a smile at her through the opening. "It's okay, I think. It must have been Charles. I found this on the floor outside your door." I pass the photograph to her through the opening.

She closes the door, disengages the chain lock and opens the door again. She's wearing boxer shorts and a loose T-shirt, her hair curly and wet like she just got out of the shower. She looks behind me at the empty hallway. Barely audible, she whispers, "You can't be here."

"Why?"

"We can't talk here. Tomorrow morning meet me at the Starbucks at Laurel and Riverside. In the bathroom at six thirty."

"Okay."

She raises her voice. "I told you not to come here. I don't care what you think Charles is doing. I don't want to see you anymore."

It stings, but then I realize—she thinks we're being watched, overheard. I don't know from where or by whom; we're the only people in this hallway. But I go along with it and say, "Okay," and pull her front door shut in front of me.

My body feels creepy-crawly with the idea that someone

can see me. I let my eyes roam around the hallway—casually, I hope—but I don't see anything out of place. I guess I'll find out what she's talking about tomorrow morning.

I make my way back through the maze of hallways, using the stairs instead of the elevator in case Charles is still hanging around. Outside, I cross the street to the rental car and am behind the wheel, buckling my seat belt, when my eyes land on the car parked across the street.

The gray Honda. It hasn't moved.

That's weird. Is Charles still here?

Wait.

Two things click: Charles doesn't drive a Honda. He drives a Lexus. The second click: Charles wasn't wearing a hoodie. He was wearing a sweater.

Headlights flash to life a few cars in front of the Honda, and I recognize the car as Charles's Lexus. It pulls away from the curb and heads south on Laurel, and the Honda pulls out of its spot and follows the Lexus, headlights off.

What the hell? Is this the murder club after all? Are they on their way to kill Charles?

If it is one of the murder club members, I can follow them home afterward. Maybe I can even get their murder kit if they throw it in a dumpster or something without burning it. If they kill him, his DNA will be on the needle. That's evidence I can take to the police; this could be the break I need.

I start the car and flip a bitch, pissing off a lady in an SUV, and try to catch the Honda at Ventura Boulevard. I make it to the light as the car is turning right, and I follow it west. I'm pretty sure we're headed to Charles's apartment.

Sure enough, the Honda pulls up to the curb as Charles enters the parking garage. I pass both of them to go around the corner. The first floor of the parking garage is half-subterranean, and the sidewalk and flower beds abut the metal-barred, glass-less windows that provide glimpses of the fluorescent-lit garage. Headlights flash around a corner, and I catch a glimpse of the Lexus's taillights as it turns toward the parking spot I myself had staked out not so long ago.

I'm having second thoughts. *Should* I let them kill Charles? If he dies, could Sofia be implicated when I go to the police?

Even if it does implicate her, would she rather take her chances on the police investigation than on Charles staying alive? How could they really pin any murder on her anyway? They won't have her fingerprints, nothing like that, not the way the murder club has this organized.

I should let it happen. I should let him die. I *want* him to die.

And it's what Sofia wants. She'll get her daughter back. I can't ruin that for her. I can't let that man raise her child. I won't.

It's strange, knowing someone's going to die, someone I was just fighting with minutes ago. I can still feel his skin on my fist, his disgusting spit spraying my cheek—

Oh no.

We were just fighting. My DNA is all over him, and his is all over me. I'm sleeping with his ex-wife. I'm already con-nected to two other Blackbird crime scenes. If Charles dies here, these murders get pinned on me.

I've already wasted so much time. I get out of the rental car and shut the door behind me. I run along the clean, well-lit sidewalk to the Honda. I walk right up to the passenger's window and peer inside. The car is empty. I step back and take a picture of the license plate.

I run across the sidewalk. I squash a bunch of flowers tramp-ing through the bed to peer through a barred window down into the garage.

There's Charles. He's walking through the wide, half-empty garage, his face dark, glowering like an angry toddler. He's headed for the elevators.

A flash of movement catches my eye, someone in a black hoodie leaping from behind one parked car to the other, closing in on Charles.

It's a woman, her face half-hidden under her hood, and she's going to catch Charles in the elevator.

I open my mouth to warn Charles, but I don't want to be seen by this murder club lady. I flounder, panicked. My eyes land on the decorative stones that border the flower bed. I grab one, aim for a nearby Benz and heave the rock through the bars into the tinted window.

The glass splinters with a crack, and the car's alarm wails to life. Charles jumps and searches for the sound. I pick up another rock, aim for a Toyota and hurl it through the bars. Another alarm squeals.

The woman in the hoodie has disappeared. Charles covers his ears and runs for the elevators like he's being shot at. What a pansy. He jabs at the call button and the doors ding open like the elevator was already on this floor. He jumps in and the doors close behind him. I wish I could throw a rock at *him*.

The black-hooded woman emerges from behind a car on the opposite side of the garage and runs for the exit.

I turn and sprint around the corner, back toward my rental car. I need to follow this lady, but her car peels out before I can even get my key into the ignition.

Fuck.

I just ruined Sofia's second chance at freedom. I can't imagine she'll ever forgive me.

32

JOAQUIN

IT FEELS SO good to be free. He doesn't care that he got lost and had to backtrack all the way through downtown. He doesn't care that he doesn't have a phone. The outside world is a wonderful, wide-open place.

Downtown is a little scary at night. He shakes that off. Imagine trying to tell his friends that he crossed to the other side of the street because some lady pushing a shopping cart was talking to herself.

He shoves his hands deep in his pockets and walks faster, past a group of high school girls who ignore him completely, past a bus stop bench with a dude sleeping on it, up the hill north of downtown. He's starving because he hasn't eaten since breakfast, and his head feels weird and woozy. That's probably not good.

It's okay. Jazz will take care of it. The idea fills him with warm, soothing relief. Jazz will take him to the clinic and make them give him a bunch of blood tests—ugh—but then she'll buy him something, she always does, and maybe he can spend the night at her apartment tonight.

He can't go back to that creepy house where Carol has been keeping him. That old lady who owns the house is weird, and so is her daughter, the one Carol got to be friends with at the snake charmer church. All those cats—those weird lace doilies—the Bibles—he can't go back. He'd rather be homeless or in a foster home. All those hands on him, praying for him, the voices raised up around him in fake languages... He's done with all of it.

He passes through the Financial District, which is filled with homeless people stumbling around like a zombie apocalypse, and hurries north across one of the bridges over the 110. The railing is too low, only hip-height, and it's easy to picture tripping and falling, splattering brains and gore onto the freeway below. He hurries past a high school, and finally, he turns right onto Jazz's street.

The smoky aroma of barbecued meat crosses his path, and his stomach growls. He'd kill for some carne asada right now. Maybe Jazz can cook something for him real quick before she launches into Diabetes Protection Mode.

He turns left onto the outdoor path that leads to Jazz's small building and climbs the stairs to the second floor, his heart beating fast with excitement. He stops outside Jazz's door, runs a hand through his hair and takes a deep breath. He reaches through the bars and knocks on the front window.

He stops being excited when he realizes the apartment is dark. Maybe she's not home.

He knocks again, louder. She might just be sleeping. *Wakey wakey.* He remembers how she used to get him up in the morning when he was in elementary school. She'd make a show of blasting open his curtains. "Rise and shine, little angel," she'd croon in a high, teasing voice. "The birds are singing. The sun is shining!"

"The birds are dead," he'd moan into his pillow.

He knocks again, louder. *Come on, Jazz, be home.* He doesn't have a phone. What's he going to do if she isn't here?

If she were home, she'd have answered the door by now. Now what?

A set of footsteps makes him look hopefully at the stairwell. It's not Jazz, though; it's a middle-aged woman with chin-length brown hair wearing office clothes. She's got keys in her hand and is about to open the neighboring door when she spots him. "Are you all right?" she asks. She has a faint Southern accent.

"I'm fine. Just waiting for my sister." He points at Jazz's closed screen door.

She walks toward him. "Well, you shouldn't wait out here alone. It's not safe."

"I'm fine. She'll be back soon."

She has mom eyes, and she pierces him with them. "You know what time she'll be home?"

"Any minute. She's just running a little late. I'm fine." He wonders what age he'll have to be for all the adults to leave him alone. He's not a baby.

"Okay, then," she says. She goes to put her key in the door, and then she turns back around. "You know, this isn't the best neighborhood, and I'm not trying to be a worrywart, but I'm not sure your sister would like you having to wait out here. Her name is Jasmine, right?"

"You know her?"

"Sure. We've been neighbors for, gosh, two years now." She smiles, which crinkles lines around her eyes. "Why don't you come wait at my place? I can make you a sandwich or something. You can watch TV. It'll be safer than waiting out here."

Joaquin almost laughs. He's so sure he's gonna go into some strange lady's apartment. He wonders how long this lady's been in LA. Not long, obviously, if she thinks bringing random teenagers into her home is a good idea. He doesn't want to be mean, though, so he just says, "No thanks. I'm good."

"Well then, how 'bout this? I'm goin' to get us a couple of chairs, and a couple of Cokes, and I'm goin' to sit out here and wait right next to you till she gets back. Sound good?"

Oh, God. He casts a desperate look around—*Jazz, where are you?*—and says, "Okay. But I can't drink Coke. I'm diabetic."

"Lucky for you, I'm on a diet. All I got is Coke Zero. It's pretty good, though." She jiggles her key in the door. "Well, shit." She glances at him guiltily. "I mean shoot. Sorry. Do you mind holding this?" She hands him her purse and the tote bag she's carrying. The bag is heavy, and he glances inside it. Books. Of course. He bets this lady is a teacher. She fights with her key again, but she can't get it to turn. "Well, drat it, you know, maybe I will be stuck out here with you whether I like it or not. Here, you want to give it a try?"

They trade keys for bags, and Joaquin tries to get the little silver key into the door handle of the metal screen door. He flips it over, but it won't go in. He tries it the original way, flat side down, but no luck.

He examines it in the dim lighting. "You sure this is the right key? It doesn't even really fit."

A pinch in his side—a burning, cold sensation. He cries out and drops the keys.

The woman is holding a syringe in latex-gloved hands. Her expression has changed. It looks dangerous.

He opens his mouth to yell, tries to get his legs to turn and run, but he slips and topples down to the ground. He tries to scream, but she drops down by his side, and a piece of duct tape is suddenly covering his mouth.

He tries to push himself up. *Be strong, fight.*

"Nighty night," she says, and the Southern accent is gone.

33
NIELSEN

THE STREETLIGHT FLICKERS a sickly orange onto the eight-foot-high, tarp-covered chain-link fence. Circles of barbed wire loop around the top of the fence, and a single open gate reveals piles of car parts within. Four squad cars train spotlights on the gate, illuminating the junk with a fluorescent glow, like Jesus himself is going to step out of the scrap yard and welcome them all to heaven.

A detective Nielsen's never seen before greets him when he pulls up in his car. Nielsen gets out and gives her a nod. "I'm Nielsen. I'm lead on this case."

"Chen. Yeah, they told me to expect you." They shake hands—she has a tough, manly handshake to go with the buzz cut—and she leads him through the open gate. "A call came through about a blue Toyota truck getting stripped in here, so we sent uniforms to check it out. And it's the truck you're looking for, correct plates, everything."

"Forensics?"

"On their way."

"Where are the owners of this shop?" He looks around for anyone who seems to work here.

She grins. "Yeah right. Entire block's dead silent. Everyone dematerialized when the squad cars showed up." She leads him past a pile of parts, an old El Camino and a skeleton of a Honda Civic to a blue Toyota truck minus the doors and tires.

She points to the driver's side door, which hangs ajar. "Confirmed VIN. They haven't even had time to file that off yet."

"Don't let anyone near this until Forensics arrives." He peers inside the truck, careful not to touch anything. There's the dried blood Marcus told him about, smeared all over the driver's seat.

He circles the truck, arms crossed, deep in thought. The police spotlights cast evanescing shadows around the scrap yard. He tries to piece together the chronology.

Jasmine left the station yesterday afternoon. Apparently, she went to Kevin Stanley's house and spent the night there. Gonzalez is interviewing witnesses and says at least a dozen people place her there. One girl, a casual romantic partner of Kevin Stanley's, even confirmed Jasmine was there all night.

And then what?

Well, she must have left in the morning at some point. And Blackbird must have arrived and found his bird flown. He would have been pissed about having missed her again, and he killed Kevin and tried to track her down. Maybe that's what sent him to the church; maybe he was hoping to find her there.

Oh, shit. Maybe it worked. Maybe she did go to the church. Here's her truck, and she's gone. He tries to frame the church scene in that context, and he can't make it fit, but he feels like he's getting closer.

Here's the million-dollar question. Forget everything else.

How did Blackbird find Jasmine at Kevin's house in the first place?

An idea hits Nielsen, fast and hot.

He drops to his knees, pulls a pair of latex gloves out of his pocket and starts feeling around under the truck. Chen asks what he's looking for, but he ignores her. He crawls around until his hand encounters exactly what he expected. He lies down on his back. "Flashlight," he yells at Chen. He holds his hand out and a flashlight is shoved into it. He flicks it on and gets a look up under the car.

There it is.

He laughs, an abrupt, triumphant sound.

Chen crouches by his side. "What is it?"

"A tracking device." Nielsen grins. *I'm on you now, fucker.* "Get me a wrench, pliers, something. This thing is bolted onto the tire well."

Chen hustles off. He goes back to his car for evidence bags. They return to the truck at the same time, Chen with a set of rusty-looking pliers. "Got them from over there," she says, nodding to a makeshift workbench.

Nielsen works carefully, not wanting to disturb fingerprints, and at last twists the bolts out so the box comes free. He bags it separately from the bolts and jumps up. "Keep an eye on Forensics," he tells Chen. "I gotta get this down to the station. Make sure they pay attention to the whole undercarriage. Prints, DNA, everything."

"Will do."

He hops into his car and starts the engine. He pulls his phone out and dials Patel. When she picks up, he asks, "You got the kid?"

"We've got teams searching for him now. He doesn't have a phone or anything else for us to track, so we're looking for a Hispanic teenager in LA. I need coffee. Or a drink. And maybe soon, I'll need a new job. I hear Walmart is hiring security guards."

"Here's some good news. I got a tracking device off Jasmine's truck."

"Are you serious?" she gasps.

"Bringing it in now. Say goodbye, little Blackbird." Nielsen pulls away from the curb, waves at the row of uniforms and makes a U-turn. "I'll get coffee if you get IT ready to receive this. I want info on this fucker tonight."

"Yes! Where are you coming from? I want the real stuff. Hipster coffee, nitro cold brew."

"Well, it's ten p.m., so you're getting Starbucks. I'll hit up the one north of Central and be there in twenty." He hangs up. The little silver box rests peacefully on the seat next to him in the clear plastic evidence bag.

Gonna get you, Blackbird. Your time is almost up.

Starbucks is a ghost town, only a few cops and party kids in line for coffee at this time of night. He gets Patel a venti cold brew and himself a venti red eye. He almost has to flash his badge to get the creamer pitcher away from a tweaked-out college kid with blue hair who's taken up residence at the condiment stand, but he's back at the station in exactly twenty minutes just like he'd promised.

Patel is waiting for him in the conference room, typing rapidly on her laptop. When he hurries through the door, she flashes him a grateful smile. "You're the best secretary a guy could ever ask for," she says, and he tries to give her a smack on the head, which she ducks away from. She grabs her coffee and takes a long sip. He chugs his own bitter brew and sets the little silver box on the conference table, on top of a pile of witness statements from the church. She raises her eyebrows at it. "How'd you know to look for it? That was smart thinking."

"I was trying to figure out how Blackbird has known everywhere Jasmine has gone or would go." He feels proud; Patel doesn't give praise easily. He sprawls out in a rolling chair, takes another long sip of coffee. It tastes especially bitter, like it's been sitting for too long, but it warms him up from the inside out. "How's the team? Where is everybody?"

"Gonzalez has taken over kid duty. She's going door to door to Joaquin's friends' houses. No luck so far. They've got a couple of people on phones, working with uniforms. We just sent someone over to Jasmine's apartment to canvass the neighborhood in case he headed there. Everyone's on top of it, but we've got nothing yet."

That's how this case has been. Everyone working at top speed but nothing happening.

"We're going to get something off the GPS. I can feel it," he says. He's flushed with excitement, hot on the trail.

She sets her coffee down with a grimace. "Ugh. I need to eat something. My stomach feels like bloody shite and this tastes terrible."

He checks his watch and takes another deep swig of coffee. "Where the fuck is IT?"

"They should be here any minute. I told them to get their asses down here. I can call them again." She presses her hands to her face and wipes her eyes.

"What's up with religious nut mom?"

"She's still here. Threatening to call lawyers and senators and the newspaper and whatever head of the bloody denomination."

They laugh together, a dark, grim sound. The kid could be dead. They both know it.

He drains the last of his coffee and tosses the empty cup in the trash can by the door. It topples out of the can and tumbles to the floor.

"There's no future for you in basketball," Patel says. Her voice is thick, and she wipes at her eyes again. "I'm so tired. It just hit me. Maybe I should grab a nap on one of the cots."

"Now? You don't want to see what IT says about the tracking device?"

"Right," she slurs, like she'd forgotten. She sounds drunk with exhaustion.

"Look at you." His own voice sounds foggy.

"What about me?"

"You're a mess. This is why the draft should never include women. You're lost without a good night's sleep." He gets out of his chair to fetch the coffee cup from the floor. The room tilts, and he drops to his knees. His stomach roils; he's going to throw up. He crawls toward the trash can, but the floor tosses him like the rodeo, and he collapses on his side.

"Dave?" Patel asks, from across the universe, using his first name, which she never does. "Dave—" and then a thud as Patel hits the ground.

He tries to push himself up. His hand fumbles for his belt, for his cell phone.

Across the room, Patel croaks out a scream of pain.

MONDAY

34
JAZZ

I'M SHIVERING EVEN though I have the heater on. Through the windshield, the dark city is coming slowly to life. The windows of Starbucks glow golden as employees arrive and turn the lights on. I'm parked right out front, in a spot that becomes illegal at seven o'clock. I've been here for hours.

I wrap my arms around myself. I'm cold.

The Starbucks is open now, and two women go inside and order drinks. I watch them, waiting for some sign that they're from the murder club, but they get their coffee and leave. Two cars pull up, one in front of me and one behind, releasing their occupants into the lightening gray dawn.

I feel like a bug in a spiderweb. I can struggle, but I'm about to be wrapped up and devoured.

I check the time on the console. It's six o'clock. Another handful of people arrives, one after the other. I watch them, anxious, wishing I could see where they all parked. I count them obsessively, one after the other. They all leave with their drinks. None of them stays to hang around.

And suddenly Sofia is here, dressed for work in slacks and a button-down with a zip-up sweatshirt on top, her high-heeled steps brisk on the sidewalk. She glances around and lets herself in through the glass door. How is she so put-together at six in the morning? When I work early shifts at Trader Joe's, I look like an orphan in a Christmas movie.

I get out of the car, check around me for anything suspicious and enter the Starbucks a minute behind her. A couple of women are ordering drinks at the register. Neither of them looks at me. I make my way past them, past the condiment stand, to the bathroom at the back of the store. I knock on the door a few times.

"Jazz?" Her voice is muffled.

"Yeah."

The lock clicks and the door swings open. She looks tired and pale under her makeup, like she hasn't slept. I slide inside and lock the door behind me.

"Hey," I say. I move forward to give her a hug, but she steps back and takes my hands, pins them in front of me. Her grip is hard enough to hurt, and she squeezes my fingers a few times, fast. I look down in confusion. Written on her hand in black pen, at an angle so I can read it, are the words *They're watching us.*

What the fuck. There's a camera in here?

"Are you okay?" she asks. Her voice has an anxious edge.

"I'm fine." I sound guarded.

"Good. I'm so glad you're okay." She gives me a quick hug, pulls away and squeezes my hands again. "Where have you been?"

I hesitate, not sure what the murder club is looking for. Why is Sofia doing this? Are they making her? What do they want? At last, I say, "I've just been here and there. How are you?"

"I'm fine." She takes a breath but doesn't release my hands. I can feel hers getting sweaty. "Jazz, have you told anyone about any of this? Have you spoken to the police or friends or anything?" Sofia squeezes my hands hard a few times, and I glance down. She's turned her hand over so I can read something written on her palm. *Say no.*

Duh, Sofia, I'm not an idiot.

This is what they want. They want to find out who else I've told so they can murder them. I want to rage, to rush out of this room and go...go what?

"No, of course not," I tell her. "Who am I gonna tell? The cops? Why, so they can pin the murders on me?"

"I thought maybe you'd told some friends or your bandmates or something."

"I haven't told anyone," I snap, and it's fear in my voice now. "I haven't told my bandmates. I haven't talked to them at all. I don't even have my iPhone, so I don't have anyone's phone numbers." As I'm saying it, I realize this is probably why they took it. Fuckers.

She nods. Her face is scared, and mine probably is, too. I know this isn't her fault, but I'm mad at her, hurt by her saying these words on their behalf.

A little puff shoots out from a wall-mounted air freshener, and we jump.

She unzips her sweatshirt. "This is yours. I accidentally stole it."

"It's fine. Keep it," I protest, but she puts it around my shoulders and I slide my arms in. It does feel amazing. She's wearing a long-sleeved white button-down under the sweatshirt, so she probably isn't as cold as I am in my tank top.

She looks at the door. "I have to go. I'm going to an all-day training that starts at eight, and I have to get on the road." She kisses me lightly on the cheek. Her hair is soft and smells delicious. She pulls the door open, steps through it and looks back at me. Silently, she shows me the palm of her hand that has no writing on it. She slides it into the pocket of her pants. Her face is intense, like this means something.

She's doing this outside the bathroom. That must mean they have a camera in the bathroom, and she's showing me something she doesn't want them to see.

She pantomimes putting something in her pocket again, nods at me and lets the bathroom door swing shut. I'm alone.

I have to act like I don't know there's a camera in here. I go to the sink and look at myself in the mirror. I look haggard and drawn, like I need to eat a meal and take a shower. I wash my hands and leave the bathroom. On my way out, I stop at the counter to buy a cup of coffee. I carry it to the rental car and am behind the wheel, about to take a sip, when I think—how do I know they didn't poison this?

I stare at the white lid of the cup, and then I pull it off, open the door and dump the coffee out on the pavement.

I start the engine and remember Sofia, putting her hand in her pocket. Why did she do that? Did she slip something in my jeans pocket when I wasn't looking? I check my pockets, front and back, and then I remember the sweatshirt. I put my hands in the pockets and encounter a hard, slim rectangle. I'm about to pull it out when I remember this car was sitting here on the street for at least ten minutes while I was inside. What if they got in here and left a recording device? What if they put another tracking device on this car?

I groan internally.

I hate them.

So now what? I have to get a new rental car?

I leave whatever it is in the sweatshirt pocket and pull away from the curb. I head north on Laurel Canyon toward the Burbank Airport. Assholes. If they want to make me switch out my rental car every day, so be it.

It's not until half an hour later, when I have a new rental car from a totally different provider and am behind the wheel of a Kia, that I pull onto a small suburban street near the airport and take the rectangular object out of my pocket.

It's a laminated ID badge with a little clip attached, the kind you wear at work. Sofia's picture looks back at me. She's smiling her professional work smile, her high, sculpted cheekbones beautiful against her wavy caramel hair. Above her picture, the logo for LAUSD is printed on the white plastic, and below her picture it says *Sofia Russo*.

A thin stack of Post-its is stuck to the back of the badge. I pull the stack off and read the words printed in tiny, neat handwriting.

They said they'd kill my daughter if I don't help them get their hands on you. I need to talk to you away from them, where they can't see or hear us. They want to make sure you haven't told anyone else about them, and then I think they're planning to kill you.

Ya think?

The next Post-it reads, *Meet me downtown at the LAUSD Central Office building. It's got tight security; we can talk there. Make sure you aren't followed. Be there at 8am. That's when I told them my training starts.*

What follows is a series of directions to a parking garage downtown and a set of instructions like "Use the badge to get into the parking garage" and "Walk across the bridge to the door with the keycard entry."

I get the new phone out, ready to program the address into

the navigation, and then cough out a dry laugh. It doesn't have navigation.

The address is on Beaudry. I know that street; it's close to my apartment. I check the time. It's seven fifteen. I need to hurry.

A plane roars overhead, so loud I think it's crashing. I look out the windshield and see the underside as it flies south and gains altitude. My ears ring in the silence it leaves behind.

I take the 5 and make pretty good time. By seven forty-five, I'm off the freeway and cruising up and down Beaudry, starting where it intersects Sunset and heads toward downtown. It's hard to read the building numbers; most of the structures on this street are under construction, boarded up or have been turned into charter schools. All the homeless people are starting to wake up, and I pass one old dude who already has himself a 40 in a paper bag and is drinking it happily on a bus stop bench. He's having a way better morning than I am.

The address sneaks up on me. It's a massive triangular skyscraper that towers over the 110 freeway on a hill just north of the Financial District. It backs up to a high school with a track I run on sometimes.

I swing into the adjacent parking structure. There's a little keypad that controls a security entrance with a swinging gate arm. I search for a ticket dispenser but can't find one. In the next lane, a lady beeps herself in with a rectangular badge, and the gate arm rises to let her through. I grab Sofia's badge and use it to beep the keypad, and the gate arm swings open.

The parking garage is ten stories high and must fit thousands of cars. I follow signs for LAUSD and find a spot on the third floor. The only other people I see are two tired-looking women lugging tote bags to the elevators.

I take the elevator to the eighth floor. I follow the ladies through rows of cars out an exterior door, and suddenly I'm on a bridge. It stretches above a street from one building to the next, and I can't help but pause in the middle of it to admire the downtown skyline. The sky is golden around the edges, and the city feels fresh and clean in the cold morning air.

As I watch, a red-tailed hawk plucks a pigeon from the sky, wings flapping in an aerial dance of death. I've watched this happen before, but today I have to look away. I don't ever want to see death again.

Am I stupid for coming here? Am I sure I can trust Sofia?

I don't know what else to do, so I take a breath and head for the building.

I beep a glass door open with Sofia's badge, and I'm in a large tiled hallway with security guards and hordes of business-people bustling around. Sofia's instructions tell me to follow this hallway to a stairwell door at the end. I continue on, past a window in the wall that says *Building Management* and into a door marked *Stairwell B*. I let the door close heavily behind me.

A set of lights flickers on. I'm in a dank, concrete stairwell with metal stairs stretching up above me. The note tells me to meet her on level nine.

I walk slowly up the stairs. I don't like this. I feel like this is an A+ place to murder someone. A door opens on the fourth floor, scaring the shit out of me, and a man pops into the stairwell. He nods politely and walks ahead of me up to the fifth floor, where he lets himself out of the stairwell by beeping his little badge on a keypad next to the door.

The ninth floor is a sort of landing. The walls are lined with pipes and valves, and Sofia is standing in the corner, out of sight from both the stairwell leading up and the stairwell leading down.

I stop when I see her. I feel wary.

She pushes off the wall. "Hey."

"Let me see your hands."

She puts them in front of her, palms up. "Why?"

I approach her slowly. She doesn't have a bag that I can see, nothing to conceal a syringe. I can't imagine how I could find a little tiny camera or anything in the vents and pipes. Maybe that's on purpose. Maybe Sofia brought me to this floor because there'd be so many places to hide a camera.

I say, "Come on. We're going to somewhere I pick, not you." I take her by the hand and pull her toward the stairs going up. She has to work to keep up with me in her heels.

"Why are we going up?" she asks.

"Because I don't know if I can trust you." That shuts her up. I drag her up three flights of stairs to floor twelve. The landing here is small, just a turn in the staircase, with no hidden corners or crevices. I spin around. "Where's your purse?"

"I didn't bring it. Just my keys. I was worried they might have put something in it."

"Show me your keys."

She pulls them out of her pocket and I snatch them from her. I scrutinize every single one. Nothing on here looks suspicious. I hand them back to her and examine what she's wearing. I search her skinny belt for a camera. Her button-down shirt is white. I can't imagine she's wearing anything underneath it, but I'm not sure how wires work; I'm not a cop. I feel like I've seen people hide wires under T-shirts in TV shows. "Unbutton your blouse," I say. "Please."

Her eyes go to the nearby door, the one marked *Floor 12*. I press my hand on the door to keep it from opening, and she quickly untucks her blouse and unbuttons it. She's not wearing anything under it except a beige bra that matches her skin.

"Turn around," I say.

She turns. I pull her shirt up to look at her back. Nothing is on her.

"Okay," I say. "I'm sorry."

She buttons her shirt up. I watch her, one eye on the stairwell. She tucks her shirt into her slacks and pulls the sleeves straight. She looks up at me and stops. "Why are you looking at me like that?"

"Like what?"

She reaches for me, but I take a step back.

"Jazz?"

I feel torn up inside. I don't want her to touch me. I want to run away from her.

"What's wrong?" she asks.

"Why did you ask me to come here?"

"I want to talk to you. This is too much. I think they're just using me for now, but if they're this determined to kill you and I know about it, I have to imagine they're coming for me as soon as they get you."

I nod. If she's telling me the truth, this is probably right.

"So I think we should go to the police, and I wanted to know if you'd go with me. Maybe if both of us talked to them, they'd listen."

I hesitate, afraid to say anything.

"Why are you looking at me like that?" she cries.

"Because I don't know if you're you or if you're them! Is this Sofia asking or is it the murder club speaking through you?"

She makes a wordless whimpering sound and presses her hands to her face.

A door opens somewhere in the stairwell. Footsteps echo below us. We freeze, waiting. Another door opens and the footsteps fade into silence.

In unison, we peer over the railing. The stairs spiral down floor after floor, empty.

She pulls me into the corner near the door, away from potential echoes. "I don't *want* to tell the police. I want Charles to die. I really, really want him dead. But if he dies, that'll implicate me, so we need to make a decision before they send someone after him. Do you understand? With Charles alive, I can say I was invited to join but never got as far as doing my assignment—would you please stop looking at me like that?" Her eyes sparkle with tears. "Your Carol is still alive, right? We can still go to the police. It's not too late. It might be a good idea to go to a lawyer first, though. We shouldn't go in there without representation. I'm sure they'll do all kinds of things to get us to mess up our stories."

Sometimes you do just have to trust someone. Sometimes there aren't a lot of other choices.

I swallow. "I was thinking the same thing, except you're right about the lawyer. I hadn't thought about that. I have the license plate number off one of their members' cars. And I have some other evidence in my apartment. I just need to get to it. We should bring those things with us."

"What evidence?"

"Remember the Villains murder? I was there playing a show. That was how I got my flip phone in the first place. I also got the killer's blood on me. It's on a T-shirt and a pair of jeans at the bottom of my hamper."

"How did you get his blood on you?"

"He was being a dick, so I gave him a bloody nose. That's why he dropped his phone."

She laughs. "Of course you did. Okay, well, you can't go back to your apartment. They're watching it." She leans on the wall next to me so our shoulders are touching. "You know how they're so worried about you having told someone?"

I nod.

"What if I tell them I saw something in your apartment, something that looked like… I don't know. A letter or something. I bet they'll let me go in and check it out."

"Sofia, that's really dangerous."

"This whole thing is dangerous!"

We stand there, both of us heavy with the weight of it.

She says, "You have to go keep an eye on Charles. Make sure no one kills him."

"Great."

"Try not to hit him."

"No promises." She still doesn't know about my little fight with him. I think I'll tell her some other time. Or not.

I turn toward her and rest my hands on her waist. "You're so tall in your heels."

She runs her fingers through my bangs, straightening them. "I wish I had met you at a different time."

"You wouldn't have liked me if you weren't in such a dark place."

She frowns. "That's not true."

I smile, and the smile feels sad. "Yes, it is. But I don't care. Pathetic, right?"

"Hey. Stop it. What's your deal? Don't create problems where there are no problems. Don't we have enough to worry about?" I raise my eyebrows at this clapback, and she says, "Did I offend you?"

"No." I wrap my arms around her waist and pull her close. I can't explain to her how much she didn't offend me, how comforting it is to be told the exact and immediate truth. Her arms encircle my shoulders, and we stand there with our faces buried in each other's necks.

"It's really not true," she whispers. It's a nice thing for her to say. I can almost believe it.

I take a deep breath. Her throat smells sweet. "Let's think about what we'll do once we get through all this," I say, my lips brushing the soft skin.

She squeezes me tighter. "Like what?"

"Something totally normal. Like taking the kids to the zoo or something."

"Olive loves the zoo." Her voice is so small and sad, it's going to break me.

I nod, my nose rubbing against the collar of her shirt. "That's perfect, then. We'll make Joaquin ride the carousel. He'll be so embarrassed."

She giggles, just once, like a hiccup.

I pull back. "Okay. I'm going to go protect your terrible ex-husband."

She looks like she feels sick. "Let me give you his work address. He works from nine to six usually, but he occasionally stays late."

I pull my new Android phone out and have her program her number into it, and then I call her so she'll have this number in her phone. She texts me the information about Charles, her lips set in a grim line. I pull my house keys out of my purse and hand them to her.

Hers is the only number I have in the contacts list. A faint, frightened voice inside my head wonders if I'm being foolish by trusting her.

I make a note to myself: when I get back in the car, I'm going to take the business cards Nielsen gave me and program the detectives' phone numbers in, too, just in case.

35

BELINDA

BELINDA WAITS IMPATIENTLY, fingertips drumming on the steering wheel. She's parked outside Jazz's apartment, watching Sofia.

She checks her watch. 6:15 p.m. The daylight is starting to darken into evening. The sky is turning orange around the geometric silhouettes of apartment buildings, palm trees and telephone wires. She takes a sip of the stale coffee, grimaces and puts it back in the center console. There's not enough coffee in the world to make her feel right.

The iPhone on her lap buzzes. Eager, she picks up the mobile and scans the screen for the text from the answering service. She nods in recognition—good, good—and goes into Contacts to dial the corresponding number. She activates the voice disguiser app and puts the phone to her ear.

It only rings once. "Hello?" comes the voice from the receiver.

Belinda closes her eyes to center herself. "Good evening," she says calmly. "Are you alone?"

"I'm in the car. No one can hear me. I drove around the corner."

"Good! And how did everything go?"

Amy's now-familiar voice stammers, "It didn't work. I'm so sorry."

Belinda closes her eyes, grabs on to the first thing she can find—the steering wheel—and squeezes it hard. "Can you elaborate? Take a deep breath and tell me what happened."

Belinda can hear the intake of air. Amy is a professional woman who works in a high-stress corporate environment. Surely she should have been able to take Charles by surprise. She should have been perfect.

Amy sounds calmer now. "So I went to the office building just like you said."

"Good."

"And I saw the man. The one in the picture you sent me. He was getting on the elevator."

"All right."

"But this woman was in the lobby, kind of hiding around a corner, and the second she saw me she started following me, watching me. I felt like she knew what I was going to do. Do you think the wig was too obviously fake? But why would— You should have seen her. It was downright rude, the way she was staring at me. I said to her, 'Excuse me. Can I help you?' and she said, 'I don't know—can you?' And then she kept following me everywhere I went! Are you sure no one knows? What if the police—"

"It's not the police." Belinda prays for patience. "Can you describe the woman?"

"Young, black hair, light skin. Not an office worker. She

was dressed more casual. Jeans and a sweatshirt. Her hair was straight, with bangs, in a ponytail."

"Go home, pack your kit up and keep it hidden. I'll follow up later with more instructions." Belinda disconnects the call. Her limbs are full of heat.

What is Jasmine doing? Protecting Charles? Why?

This is the third time Belinda has tried to finish Charles's assignment. She needs him dead. He's like a cockroach that you step on over and over again, but it still keeps squirming.

She starts the car and peels away from the curb. Outside, Sofia is walking down the sidewalk, her face turned toward Belinda's car as it screeches away. Belinda can't care. She's out of patience. And she's eager to squash the cockroach herself. She's been behind the camera for long enough; sometimes the director has to make a cameo.

If you want something done right, you have to do it yourself.

36
JAZZ

"FUCKING CHARLES," I mutter to myself, following his stupid Lexus off the freeway. I think I saved him from a woman in the office building, this anxious-looking lady following him whose hair was clearly a wig.

Here I am, guardian angel, making sure Douchebag gets into his apartment all safe and sound. Why does it seem like the worst dudes always have guardian angels?

It's rush hour, so Charles and I enjoy a leisurely drive from Woodland Hills to Sherman Oaks on the 101 accompanied by eleventy billion of our closest friends. Charles has no idea I'm behind him. He spends the drive on his phone. I wonder what he's talking about. Contracts. Papers. I bet he's talking to someone named Chad. *The numbers don't add up, Chad!* I snort a little laugh to myself.

He gets off on Sepulveda and I follow him south toward the hill. By the time night descends, we're on his quiet, up-scale street with the flower beds and the streetlights that don't flicker. Charles pulls into the underground parking garage and I park my rental car half in a red zone, banking on suburban meter maids being off duty by now. I lock the door and walk down the sidewalk to Charles's building. I'm not sure how I'm going to get in, but as I hesitate in the driveway, an SUV swings in, almost hitting me, and opens the sliding gate. I slip through the gate as it closes and jog to Charles's parking spot. His car is empty.

I contemplate leaving. I already stopped that woman in the lobby of his office building. But I should see him up to his apartment, right? Just make sure he gets tucked in all safe and sound. Fucker.

I follow the exit to a stairwell. Charles lives in apartment 204 on the second floor. Shouldn't be too hard to find.

I trot up the stairs. I spent all day waiting in that horrible office building, keeping myself hidden from security guards, and my stomach aches with hunger. I let myself out on the second floor and hurry down the main hallway. This building is a dead ringer for Sofia's, all fancy carpet, crown molding and personalized front doors. I can never get over how quiet these expensive buildings are, like hotels. Everywhere I've ever lived, you can hear your neighbors' music, their arguments, their car alarms and dogs barking and sex.

I turn right and stop. At the opposite end of the hallway, a blonde woman in jeans and a black sweater is walking toward me. Is it bad for me to be seen?

The Android phone buzzes in my pocket. I back up around the corner and pull it out. The screen says *Sofia*.

I answer it. "Hello?" I whisper.

"Jazz, I did it! I did it!" Her voice is wild with excitement. "I got the clothes. But more importantly, I think I saw someone from the, you know, the murder club. Like maybe someone who runs it, or works for it or something! Maybe it's the person from the phone calls! She was watching me go to your apartment, and then she peeled out when she saw me. And I got her license plate number!"

I peek around the corner. The apartment numbers are written on the doors. I can't see the number on the door the woman stops in front of, but across the hall, the door is marked 203. The blonde woman has her head down and is fiddling with something by her side.

"What did she look like?" I whisper into the phone.

"She's blonde, maybe in her thirties or forties. Her hair is cut in a collar-length bob."

I take another careful look. The woman is knocking on Charles's apartment door. "What was she wearing?"

"I couldn't really see. Something dark. A black shirt, maybe. Do you think it's enough to bring to the police?"

Knock-knock-knock-knock.

What do I do?

"I'll call you back," I whisper. I hang up the phone and put it in my pocket.

Should I say something? Yell? Run out? This might be the same lady Sofia's describing. Or it could be a totally normal person, in which case Charles would know I'm stalking him.

The door handle turns and Charles's door opens inward. A long, rigid shape swings up to the woman's shoulder. A sharp sound—

Chht chht—

I freeze.

BOOM. Blood sprays red around the door frame.

The shape—a shotgun—swings down by the knocker's side.

The blonde turns and runs, away from me down the hall in the opposite direction. I hesitate—do I run, do I try to help?

I don't want to get shot. But no, it's a shotgun. It has to be re-loaded. She can't just turn and shoot me right away. I push off from the wall, run toward the open apartment door, where Charles is sprawled out on the tile floor, a gaping, bloody hole in the center of his chest. A small, heavyset woman kneels over him, crying and screaming in frantic Spanish.

He's dead. This must be the nanny.

"Hey!" I yell at the woman. "Where's the baby?"

A trembling hand points back into the apartment.

"Don't let her see this! Call the police! Lock the door!"

She nods. Tears stutter down her cheeks.

I run in the direction the shooter went. A door slams at the end of the hall—another stairwell. I throw myself through the door down the stairs, following the woman's echoing footsteps.

I leap down the last five steps and burst through the exterior door onto the side walkway. Ahead of me, the woman fumbles with the shotgun, swings it up and turns it on me. I dive back into the stairwell just as the boom of another shot deafens me. The door shakes with the blast. Stucco dust rains from the wall. A car alarm goes off. I check myself, looking for gunshot wounds. Nothing. I'm fine.

I push the door open slowly. The woman is just making a left onto the sidewalk. I race out after her, get to the sidewalk and look left, right.

Faint, shadowy motion. The woman slinks around the corner. I run across the street to my rental car, fumble the keys out of my pocket with shaking fingers and get in.

A parking ticket is tucked behind my windshield wipers.

I almost laugh at the ridiculousness of it. I open the door, reach out to wrestle the ticket from the wiper and slam the car into first gear. I gun the engine and pull away from the curb.

A set of headlights flashes and the car they belong to swings drunkenly onto the street in front of me.

It's an old-person car, a beige Chevy sedan from the early aughts. I follow it onto Ventura Boulevard. She's driving too fast and almost hops a curb as she turns right. I pull my phone from my pocket and search through the contacts. It's easy; there are only three. Sofia, Nielsen and Patel. I debate for a split second and decide women are better in a crisis, so I press the button to dial Patel.

The line picks up after two rings. "Detective Patel." Her voice is rough and tired, like she just smoked a pack and a half of cigarettes and stayed out all night drinking.

"Hi, it's Jasmine Benavides. I don't know if you remember me, but I was just in there the other day and—"

"Jasmine! I'm glad to hear from you. We've been trying to reach you. We found your truck."

"Are you okay? You sound terrible." Maybe I should have called Nielsen. I follow the beige Chevy onto Moorpark.

"I'm fine. I've…" She pauses. "You may as well hear it from me—you'll be seeing it on television tomorrow morning. Detective Nielsen is dead. We were both poisoned, presumably by the killer we're investigating, but I'm fine. Or, I will be fine. Jasmine, it's urgent that we get you into protective custody. Where have you been?"

The beige sedan flies right onto the 101 South on-ramp. I ignore the light that mandates one car every green and floor it. The rental car's tiny engine whines in protest. "Patel, I'm sorry to interrupt you, but I think I'm tailing the Blackbird murderer in my car. I just watched her shoot a guy with a shotgun, my friend's ex-husband, Charles, so I decided to chase her, and I'm following her car, but I don't know—"

"Where are you now?" Her voice is hard, her British accent sharper than usual.

Traffic comes to a screeching halt, and I slam the brakes, almost rear-ending an Audi. The beige Chevy is a few cars ahead of me. With cars all around, I almost worry the woman will get out and come shoot me through the window.

To Patel, I say, "I'm on the 101 South. I just passed the Woodman exit. Traffic's really slow." As soon as I say it, traffic picks up. The beige car changes lanes, gets one lane farther to the left.

"One moment." It sounds like she puts her hand over the phone's receiver and yells orders at someone. Then she says, "Do you have a make, model or license plate number of the car you're following?"

"It's a beige Chevy, kind of older... I can't see the license plate. Do you want me to get closer? She might see me. Or shoot me."

"No, do *not* do that. Four-door or two-door?"

"It's a four-door."

"One moment. Putting you on a brief hold." The line goes silent.

The beige car changes lanes again, getting in the far left lane like she plans to head downtown.

Patel comes back. "I have units getting on the 101 at Normandie," she says. "I want you to get off at Western and park in the Pier 1 lot on Hollywood Boulevard. Do you know where that is?"

"Yeah, but what if she gets away?"

"We've got her, don't worry. But you are not the person to apprehend an armed killer. Can we agree to that?"

"When you put it that way."

"I'm going to meet you at that parking lot myself, and I

want you to be very careful. If anything seems strange, or if a suspicious car enters the lot, go ahead and take off. Keep your car on while you're parked. Do you hear me?"

"Got it."

"I'll have a red police light on top of my car. If you do not see the light, pull out of the parking lot and call me."

"Got it." I get into the right lane. "I'll be at the parking lot in a minute."

"I'll see you there." The phone disconnects.

It takes twenty minutes to get to the Western exit. I take a wrong turn off the freeway and have to backtrack down Hollywood Boulevard. I pass Thai restaurants, gas stations, and I only see Pier 1 at the very last minute. I turn hard into the empty parking lot and park in the back corner facing out so I can see any cars that enter. I slump down in the seat, pull my purse onto my lap and wait.

It feels like forever.

At last, a set of headlights bumps up the driveway into the parking lot. My heart stutters, but then I see the red flashing light, and relief floods me like a drug. It's almost over. Thank God. Maybe the police will help me find Joaquin since I helped them catch their Blackbird Killer. I turn the car off, put the keys in my purse and get out of the car.

The car pulls to a stop right in front of me. The driver's side window rolls down, and Patel waves to me from behind the wheel. "Get in. You can sit up front."

I hurry to the passenger's side and slide into the seat. Shutting the door feels amazing, like closing myself off from danger and fear.

"Are you all right?" Patel asks. "Get your seat belt on. I'll take you back to the station."

I reach for the seat belt. As I twist to my right, a hard, painful pinch in my left side makes me gasp. I think I've pinched myself in the space between the console and the seat. Patel looks me in the eye. She withdraws a little clear syringe from my side, and the pain stops. I open my mouth to say something. The car swirls around me. It's an ocean. I'm underwater, being tumbled by a wave.

I reach for the door. My hand fumbles for the handle and falls to the armrest.

"It's locked anyway," she says. Her voice sounds far away.

I try to turn and look at her, but my face is stuck staring out the window. The car is moving. Pier 1's blue-and-white sign swims lazily by, acid trails connecting it to the horizon.

37

JAZZ

IT'S A HEAVY ascent back to consciousness. I'm being jostled, like I'm on a bus.

I want to go back to sleep. My whole body drags me back into unconsciousness, down into a deep, dark river.

I try to roll over. My arms don't obey. They're dead.

I panic, try to retract my arms. I can't; they're above me, pinned by something. I struggle, trying to pull them free. They won't come loose. The world bumps again.

Patel.

I gasp. My eyes fly open.

Blurry. Dark. Flying lights with phosphorescent trails—jellyfish in a midnight aquarium.

I stare at the jellyfish. They swim closer, get sharper, come into focus. A car. A street sign. A gas station.

My forehead is pressed to the tinted glass of a back seat car window. We're stopped at an intersection. I try to free my arms, banging my elbows on the window.

"Stop. You're handcuffed," a voice says nearby. It's husky and more familiar than my own.

Joaquin.

He's next to me in the back seat. His hands are raised like he's stretching, but then I see that he's handcuffed to the grab handle above the left window. I look up at my own hands—I'm shackled in the same way. I'm behind the passenger's seat, which is separated from the back seat by a tinted window like in a limo, and Joaquin is behind the driver's seat.

"You okay?" Joaquin asks.

I try to clear my head. My legs feel heavy. I try to move them, but they feel stuck together somehow.

"They're tied up," he says. He squirms a little to show me his own feet, which are wrapped around over and over with thin, synthetic blue rope.

"Patel," I start to say, but I can't talk. I thrash, panicked, thinking my tongue has been cut out, and then I realize my mouth is duct-taped shut.

Joaquin smiles at me ruefully. "I got carsick and almost died inhaling my own puke, so she let me take the tape off. It hurt. I was just starting to grow a mustache, too."

"What's going on? Why are you here?" I ask, but it just comes out as humming.

"I don't know who she is." He nods to the invisible driver. The car slows down, and outside the tinted rear windows, the shadowy shapes of cars slow to a stop. I try to elbow the window and get someone's attention, but I'm too close to it to get enough force into the blow. I curl my knees and try to bring my feet up to kick out the window. I can't. There isn't enough space.

"I already tried that," says Joaquin. His hair is tangled over his right eye, but he looks wonderful, beautiful, skin glowing in the filtered city light, brown eyes huge and gleaming. "Hey, you know what this car reminds me of? It reminds me of Carol's car."

I don't know what he's talking about. It is an old American sedan, sure, but why—

He looks frustrated. He looks up at my hands, tied to the grab handle. He makes a point of looking intensely at them, like this is supposed to mean something to me.

He sighs. He slumps back against the seat.

"Hey. I love you," I hum through the tape. It's four syllables: "Hm hm hm hm."

He gets it. One side of his mouth crinkles in a crooked smile just like mine. "Love you, too."

A crackle, like feedback, and then a voice blares out of the speakers behind us. "Jasmine, please hold still. You don't want to distract a driver." It's Patel's voice but not; she's faking a Southern accent. The speaker goes quiet.

Joaquin says, "I left the police station—someone got murdered at church when I was there with Carol—and I went to your house to see you. And she was there, pretending to be your neighbor. Do you know who she is?"

I nod frantically.

"Do I know her?"

I shake my head.

"Does she work at Trader Joe's?"

I shake my head. My ponytail is loose and flops around behind me.

The speakers crackle to life. "I hope you're happy to see Joaquin. He's been keeping me company today. I've been taking real good care of him. I gave him his insulin. Can't have him fainting dead away." She laughs lightly, a fake, stupid sound.

I know this voice. Even with the fake accent, I recognize

the way it sounds through the speaker. This is the voice on the flip phone.

It's so much worse than I'd imagined. Patel is in charge of the investigation into the same killings she's organizing. Even if I got Joaquin out of this car right now, we are so, *so* fucked. I'm so terrified of what she has planned for us that I feel like I might actually shit myself.

She says, "Let's talk about our little field trip. Joaquin here's gonna help us with a few things. Joaquin, you wanna be a real big helper?"

He says, "I'm cool. Thanks, though. If you could just let us off at the next stop, that would be great."

"Joaquin, you're funny like your mama. It's endearing how much y'all have in common. You look alike, too, with those big brown eyes and those pretty crooked smiles. Lady-killer smiles, right? Your mama could teach you a few things about that, couldn't she?"

Joaquin's face is blank. My heart is dead with panic.

He looks at me, confusion in his eyes. "How does she know our bio mom?"

I shake my head. I feel my eyes welling up with tears. I hate Patel. I fucking *hate* her.

The car pulls to a stop on a side street. Outside the window I see a bank of planters and a backlit apartment sign. The speaker crackles. "So, Joaquin, here's the thing. Your mama's in some trouble. And she owes me. You're going to help dig her out of the hole she's gotten herself into."

Joaquin's face is changing. He's starting to understand. "Jazz, what—is—she—talking about?"

I beg for his forgiveness with my eyes. I will him to be able to read my mind.

"Oh my God." He doubles forward as far as his pinned-up arms will allow, his face contorted into a grimace of pain.

I've pictured this moment a hundred times, but nothing could have prepared me for this. I try to tell him things through the tape that covers my mouth. His eyes are squinched shut, and in profile against the night, a single fat, glimmering tear drips off the point of his nose.

The car shudders into silence; she shut off the engine. "Don't be mad at her, Joaquin. She was a kid. Can't you see she's tried to make it up to you?"

He blinks his eyes hard to clear them of tears, a gesture that tweaks my heart. At last he looks at me. No kid's face should look this old, this pained. "You should have told me."

I nod. I know. He's right.

"Why didn't you *tell me?*" His voice cracks.

I force myself not to look away. In the streetlights, his irises are liquid and beautiful. I say the only thing I have for him. "I love you." *Mm mm mm.*

Patel says, "So, Joaquin, your mama has created a mess for me, and you're going to help me clean it up. You're going to be my little child soldier. How does that sound?"

"Child *soldier?*"

"You're going to tie up a loose end. Jasmine, you know where we are."

I look out the window again. Through the tint, I see flowers, a side street… We're on a small side street off a major boulevard.

We're in front of Sofia's apartment building.

I shake my head frantically at Joaquin. I don't know what Patel has planned, but it isn't good.

The smoky glass divider rolls down. A silver cylinder pokes in through the widening gap. It's a gun with a long barrel—a silencer, I think, from what I've seen on TV—and it's pointed at me. Behind the gun, I almost don't recognize Patel; she's wearing a blond, shoulder-length wig and makeup that changes her facial contours and skin tone completely. She looks white, with bright red lips and smoky black eye shadow under black-rimmed glasses.

Is she going to kill me in front of Joaquin? *Please no.*

Patel says, "Joaquin, I'm interested in your thoughts on something. Would you kill a stranger to save your mom?"

His big, scared eyes are fixed on the gun. He stammers, "I don't know."

"You have to choose."

"I mean, yeah. If it was to save Jazz, I'd kill a stranger. Wouldn't anybody?"

"Would you kill someone you knew? Not a stranger, but an acquaintance? A teacher, a doctor?"

"I—I don't know. I mean, I'd kill anyone to save Jazz. She's the only family I have."

"Good! So let's get going, my little child soldier." She withdraws the gun and gets out of the car.

As she's coming around to open his door, he whispers, "Carol's car! Don't you remember?"

The back door opens. She unlocks his handcuffs and pulls him out of the car. She leaves the car door open, so I hear her giving him instructions. "Put this over your neck," she says, followed by a pause. "I can hear and see everything you do. You understand? Do not remove this. If you remove it, Jasmine dies. If you disobey my instructions even a little, she dies."

A long silence, and then Joaquin says, "What's that for?"

"It's for you. I hear you're good with needles."

38

JOAQUIN

JOAQUIN LOOKS DOWN at the pendant the woman fastens around his neck. It looks like a gold Aztec coin on a silver chain. "What is it?" he asks.

"It's a camera. I'm going to be watching and listening. You understand? If you remove it, Jasmine dies. If you disobey my instructions even a little, she dies." She pulls on a pair of latex gloves and gets an oblong plastic container out of the bag she's carrying. The gun is stuffed into the waistband of her jeans like a cop. He wonders if he could grab it.

She pulls a yellow syringe out of the plastic container. "What's that for?" he asks.

"It's for you. I hear you're good with needles. You inject your own insulin, right?"

He nods, uncertain. This is a big syringe, and he doesn't like the look of the yellow fluid inside it.

"You're going to put your money where your mouth is.

You're going to get rid of someone and trade a life for your mama's. You ready?"

"Wait—with *that*?"

She nods. Her deranged smile is like something out of a horror movie.

"What am I supposed to do with it?"

"You're supposed to inject it. You want to get it in the torso, not the arms or legs. You want to do it when she's not looking. Quick and simple. She's going to know what this is when she sees it, so you'll need to get her to turn her back and do it when she's not looking. This is important. Do you understand?"

"I understand, but wait. Who is she? I'm supposed to inject this into a girl? A stranger?"

"Not a stranger." Her smile is mean. "You'll see when she opens the door. It'll be a fun surprise."

"But…" He tries to gather his thoughts. When she turns the syringe over, it has a poison symbol on it, a skull and cross-bones like the one on Jazz's ring finger. "But *why*?"

"You don't get to know why. You trust me that there's a good reason why, and you rest easy that that part of the decision isn't on your shoulders."

"Then why don't you do your own murder? Wouldn't that be way easier than all this?"

"You don't worry about that, either. You just make your choice. Your mom or this woman."

He jumps from idea to idea. Run away right now. No, Jazz is in the car. Take the syringe and use it on this lady. No, she has a gun. Grab the gun? Try to wrestle it away from her?

Like she's reading his mind, she gets the gun out of her waistband and points it into the car at Jasmine. She holds the syringe out with the other hand. "Choose."

He takes the syringe from her. It's clammy on his bare fingers. He puts it into the pocket of his hoodie. "Where am I going?"

"Apartment 215. Here's a key to the gate, but you'll have to knock on the apartment door when you get there."

He accepts the key. He takes a deep breath and decides to make one last attempt. He looks her in the eyes. They're brown behind the glasses. He says, "I don't understand why you're doing this. Can't you just stop? Can't you let us go? We haven't done anything to you."

"You haven't, but your mama has. Now off you go."

"So I just… I just kill whoever answers the door?"

"You got it."

"Apartment 215?" he checks. "You're sure?"

She smiles. "I'm sure."

Joaquin turns. He walks away. His knees are shaking. His head feels light.

He casts a last glance back. He can't see Jazz through the tinted window. Him looking back seems to piss the woman off. She points the gun into the back seat, and for a second, he thinks she's going to shoot Jazz right now.

He spins around and hurries up the sidewalk toward the front gate of the apartment building.

Come on, Jazz. Figure it out.

39
JAZZ

PATEL GETS BACK in the car. She picks up an iPad off the front seat and props it up on the dashboard. She presses the home screen and navigates to an app I don't recognize. She presses a yellow icon and enters a password, and the screen lights up to show a grainy black-and-white view of the front gate of Sofia's apartment building. It's from Joaquin's perspective; his hands are visible, fumbling with the gate lock. *Please, Joaquin. Please don't do it.*

He might do it. He might think he has to.

"He's nervous," she says. "Poor little guy."

I cuss her out through the tape, telling her she better hope and pray I don't get out of these cuffs.

She casts a careless glance back at me. "Oh, I'm sorry. I forgot." She turns back to rip the duct tape off my mouth. It takes some skin with it.

As soon as it's off, I'm talking. "Don't ask him to kill Sofia. Don't do it. Please. Please, I'm begging you."

She returns her eyes to the iPad. "I hate improvising, but this time I think I've done well. I've decided your brother is going to be the Blackbird Killer we've been looking for. He'll be the youngest active serial killer in Los Angeles history. Like it?"

"You're framing him? You can't do that. He's just a kid."

"I'm in charge of the investigation now. So, yeah. I can." On screen, Joaquin is in the elevator. "And the way Carol has been keeping him holed up at home, he doesn't have an alibi for any of the murders. I've already created a psychological profile for him, a child acting out of stress after imprisonment and abuse at the hands of his adoptive mother. It's textbook. The injection of poison stems from his lifelong issue with needles as a result of his diabetes. It's trauma and psychopathy. The media will love it, trust me."

"But *why*?" The words come out as a wail. "Kevin was innocent. Joaquin is innocent. You're supposed to help people like us. Why do you even do the murder club if you're going to kill the people you're supposed to be helping?"

She looks at me in the rearview mirror. Her dark eyes are fringed in long, pretty lashes. "I learned long ago not to be sentimental. When you're weighing the value of lives, and you set your rules, you can't make exceptions. Those are the rules of war."

"This isn't a war, you fucking bitch! This is my son you're sending in to kill an unarmed woman!"

She smiles sadly. "That's what war *is*, Jasmine. Any soldier can tell you that. Now be quiet and let me concentrate." Her eyes disappear from the mirror, and she leans in to study the iPad.

My hands have gone past numb into painful tingle-stabbing, and the burn in my shoulders is becoming impossible to ignore.

I wiggle my fingers, try to get some mobility back. The grab handle squeaks a little under my handcuffs. It brings Joaquin's words back to me, about Carol's car.

I know what he meant.

It was five years ago. I was doing pull-ups on the back seat grab handle to make Joaquin laugh, and it broke off, sending Carol into a rage. I had to buy a new one and fix it for her, but she still never forgave me. This grab handle is just like that one. It's not one of the hinged ones that swings forward and back; it's stationary and looks deceptively like it's made of one plastic piece. It's not, though. It's made of three pieces. The middle piece is attached to the sidepieces, which are screwed into the car ceiling. I'd broken the middle piece, which is just plastic and only held on to the sidepieces with clips.

God, that kid is smart. I love him so much. Gently, so as not to alert Patel, I slide the handcuffs forward a couple of inches so the chain that connects them slips into the seam where the centerpiece connects to the side bracket. That should be the weakest part of the mechanism. I grip the handcuffs by the chain to take some of the stress off my wrists and pull, hard.

On the iPad screen, the elevator doors open in front of Joaquin, and he walks through them.

My muscles are weak from being suspended for so long, but pull-ups are such an automatic thing. The grab handle creaks. I pull harder, muscles trembling with exertion.

40

JOAQUIN

HE STANDS IN front of the door marked 215. The hallway stretches out on either side, silent and empty.

The syringe is a strange oblong shape in his pocket. He has his right hand wrapped around it to ensure the needle doesn't stab him. With his left hand, he knocks on the door. His stomach is doing somersaults.

What does it feel like to die from poison? Do you just fall asleep?

There are so many doors in this hallway. What if one of them opened? What if he asked someone for help? Or he could just start yelling right now. Would that work?

But then he thinks of Jazz, in the car at gunpoint.

He has to be a hero. He has to man up. This is what you do in a crisis situation: you look out for your sister. Mom. Whatever. The thought hurts, a new ache in his stomach.

He looks down at the necklace. The eye of the camera is a small black pearl in the center of the fake Aztec coin. He can't see a place for a microphone, though. It's a smooth gold coin, no holes anywhere, just the shiny lens of the miniature camera. He pinches it between two fingers and pulls it a few inches away from his body to look at the back face of the coin. There's no hole for a microphone back there, either. That's weird. He's sure the lady said she could hear him.

The door handle clicks. The door cracks open, fastened with a chain on the inside. A pair of brown eyes in a tanned face look out at him. "Joaquin?" The door shuts, the chain rattles, and the door swings open.

Ms. Russo stands before him, in leggings and a stretchy tank top. She is such a surprise, he stares at her silently like an idiot.

"Joaquin! What are you doing here? Are you all right?"

"Ms. Russo?" he asks, just to confirm he's still in reality and hasn't wandered down some Alice in Wonderland rabbit hole.

She checks the hallway behind him. "Joaquin, what's going on? Where's Jazz?"

He shakes his head, stricken with stupidity. How does she know Jazz?

"Where is she? How did you get here?"

He grips the syringe. He needs to pull it together. The coin on his chest is watching, listening. "Can I come inside?"

"Of course. Come in, come in." She pulls him in with a hand on his back, almost a hug, which is weird; he barely knows her.

What alternate reality has he wandered into? What is happening? Why is his AP hugging him? Why is he even at her apartment? And how did he never notice her boobs before?

She closes the door behind him. It's a rich-person apartment, with shiny wood floors and a kitchen full of fancy appliances visible to the left.

Inspiration strikes. "Hey, I'm sorry, Ms. Russo, but with

my diabetes, I get kind of shaky. Do you have a glass of milk or something?"

"Of course!" She leads the way to the kitchen.

Now is when he should inject her. His hand tightens on the syringe.

Jazz wouldn't want him to. But Jazz doesn't get to decide. He's lived his whole life thinking his biological mother abandoned him. To know there is no such person, that it's been Jazz this whole time—

Ms. Russo opens the fridge and peers inside. "Jazz would laugh at me, but all I have is LaCroix and coconut water. How about I make you some hot tea?"

Jazz would laugh at her? She knows Jazz well enough to know what Jazz would laugh at? How do they know each other? Is he in trouble at school and no one told him?

Ms. Russo puts a mug in the microwave and pushes a few buttons. She says, "Now tell me what's going on. Where's Carol?"

He remembers Jazz's face in the car. She doesn't want him to do it. She'd kill him if he did this.

The decision happens without his approval. It's just a click in his head, a relaxing of the muscles in the hand that holds the needle in his pocket.

He can't do it.

The realization breaks his heart. This means Jazz might die. Because of him. Because he can't. It's not in him. It's not who he is, and it's not who Jazz would want him to become.

So now he has to find a way out.

41

JAZZ

DON'T DO IT, *Joaquin.* I'm thinking it at him like he can read my mind, begging him, pleading with him.

If Patel looks behind her, she's going to see that I'm almost in a full chin-up, muscles shaking.

The grab handle creaks. I pull harder.

Come on, Joaquin. Don't do it. No kid's morals should ever be put to the test like his are right now, but I've learned life is fucked up like that. *Should* and *shouldn't* are nothing in this world.

On the iPad, Sofia is putting a mug into a microwave. Patel grumbles to herself. She seems annoyed by how long it's taking Joaquin to kill her.

Don't do it.

I pull my knees into my chest to get all my weight off the seat, to make myself as heavy as I can.

The handle snaps. I tumble forward, bashing my face into the cloth seat.

Patel spins around. The gun points at me. It fires—a hiss—there's a silencer.

I fling myself behind the driver's seat. I push myself up behind her and whip my handcuffed hands around her neck, choking her out from behind. Her gun hand flies up. She tries to aim it at me behind her, but she can't get her hand positioned right.

In her ear, I growl, "Do you think it's gonna be that easy? I have fought for every breath my son has taken."

42

JOAQUIN

MS. RUSSO STIRS the tea. He's sweating. His brain reminds him that she is still wearing the tight tank top. *Shut up, brain, please.*

Her phone is on the counter. It's dark and silent. If he could just call 911 without alerting Ms. Russo, so she doesn't ask questions the horrible lady in the car will hear...

He turns his back to the phone so it's not visible to the camera. He reaches out for it.

Ms. Russo turns around and hands him the mug. "Give that a try." She steps past him and picks her phone up. "Let me call Jazz. Does she know you're here?" She unlocks the screen and searches for a contact.

I've got to get her away from her phone.

He drops the mug onto the floor, a little harder than would be natural. It cracks into pieces, and boiling hot tea goes splashing all over the floor and his shoes. "I'm so sorry," he cries. He's a terrible actor. It sounds so fake.

"Oh, it's fine. I'll get the broom and a towel. Hang on."

Rather than put her phone on the counter, she tucks it into the strap of her tank top. *Fuck!* She hurries out of the room, leaving him standing there in a puddle of tea. The kitchen light catches the coin. He can see every little crevice.

There's no microphone hole. For sure. For *sure*.

That lady lied. He's pretty sure she can see him, but she can't hear him. She just didn't want him saying anything to Ms. Russo. *Ha!*

Ms. Russo returns, a broom and a towel in her hands. He turns his back on her so the camera is facing the opposite direction.

"Ms. Russo, listen to me." His voice is shaky. "I have a camera around my neck and a needle full of poison in my pocket. I've been sent up here to kill you. I know this sounds totally crazy. But there's a lady holding Jazz hostage down in the car. She wants to see me kill you or she'll kill Jazz. Can you call 911 from your phone real fast?"

Ms. Russo is quiet for a moment. He holds his breath. She's not going to believe him. She's an assistant principal. She's going to think he's playing some weird prank on her. She's going to—

Then she says, "Here's what we're going to do. I want you to go downstairs and hide in the closet of the pool house. My keys are on the little table by the front door. I'm going to wear the camera necklace, and I'm going to call the police and explain the situation. What kind of car is she in?"

"It's like…a four-door old American car. Beige or gray. Parked on the small street to the side of your building."

"Perfect. You're doing great." She's in full teacher mode now, in control. He feels her fiddling with the catch of the necklace. "We're going to take this off you and put it on me.

I'll move around so it looks like you're just waiting in the kitchen."

The catch releases. He ducks down out of the necklace, and he steps aside. Ms. Russo puts the chain around her own neck and fastens the catch. She has her phone in her hand, and she's starting to dial. He casts his eyes around the kitchen. A knife block.

She looks up at him. "Go. Now. Pool house. Hide."

He reaches a sneaky hand out and pulls a paring knife out of the knife block. On his way out of the kitchen, he passes a wine rack filled with dark bottles. He grabs two of them and runs for the front door of the apartment.

He's not going to the pool house. No way. He's going outside to help Jazz, because he knows who he is.

43

JAZZ

I'M CHOKING PATEL so hard my arms are cramping up. She flails, wild. The gun goes off, fires into the ceiling.

Outside the windshield, a flash of movement. A small body—Joaquin—and then a crash as something hits the windshield. The glass cracks in a web. The windshield is covered in blood? No—

Wine? He threw a wine bottle.

Another bottle smashes into the windshield with a massive crack. More wine coats the glass.

Patel twists out of my grip and raises her gun to aim at Joaquin. The wine and cracked glass make it impossible to see. I scream and try to get my handcuffs around her neck again, but she's too fast. She fires through the windshield, sending more cracks through the tempered glass. I try the door handle—of course it's child locked—and Patel points the gun back at me. I drop down fast. A bullet slices through the back seat with a thunk.

The door beside me opens, and Joaquin beckons me out. I jump out and fall on my face on the asphalt, cuffed hands in front of me. My ankles are tied. Joaquin crouches by my feet. He saws at the knots with a little kitchen knife.

The driver's door opens, and the gun precedes Patel out. It kicks back and a chip of asphalt splinters violently off the ground next to my hand. I grab the door with both hands and slam it into Patel's face. She drops back, squeezing the trigger as she goes, shooting the palm fronds above us and sending little bits of tree tumbling down.

I kick the ropes off my feet and Joaquin and I sprint away from the car, closing the distance to the apartment gate, and tuck ourselves behind the trunk of the palm tree. Our breath is fast and ragged in the quiet suburban night.

To Joaquin, I say, "Go up to Sofia's apartment. Use the side gate. That's a short fence—you can hop it."

"I have a gate key."

"Good! Perfect."

"Ms. Russo is calling the police. So they should be here soon."

"You're awesome." I peek out sideways from the tree. Patel is hiding behind the car, the gun aimed at me over the trunk. To Joaquin, I say, "Get behind the concrete wall that surrounds the planter, and stay behind it the whole way in case she starts shooting at you. If she makes a run toward you, I'll tackle her."

"Are you going to be okay?"

"Of course. I'll keep her busy till the cops get here." With my tethered hands, I grab some of the white decorative rocks. "Go!" I say.

I reach back and hurl the handful of rocks at Patel's car. She shoots at the motion, and Joaquin takes off in the other direction, vaulting over the concrete wall and ducking behind it into the planter. He's fast, his hoodie and jeans dark on dark in the shadows. He's strong and he's fast because he's *my son*. The thought fills me with explosive pride, and fear is a distant memory as I imagine ripping Patel limb from limb.

I yell in the direction of the car, "The cops are on their way. You can say hi to your friends when they get here and tell them what you've been up to."

A bullet hits something nearby. I sprint across the sidewalk to the front gate entry and duck inside the nook where the keypad is, which shelters me from being shot, but now I can't see Patel. I try to catch my breath.

"Come on, bitch," I call out. "What are you waiting for? Come and get me."

Silence.

I sidle back around the corner and peek between the bars of the gate.

She's not at the car. She's gone.

44

SOFIA

SOFIA KEEPS HER phone down by her side, out of view of the camera. She dials 911. She brings it to her ear.

It rings. Three times. Four times.

She can't just stand here. But if she doesn't make it look like Joaquin is still up here, that could mean Jazz's life.

Six times. Seven. *Come on*, she screams internally.

Nine rings. Ten.

Her phone cracks to life. "Nine-one-one, what is your emergency?"

"I need you to send the police. 12774 Laurel Canyon Boulevard. Someone has a gun. Someone is trying to kill someone in the front of my apartment building. You need to send the police. Please. Now!" She forces herself to hold still, to keep the necklace steady.

"Ma'am, I need you to take a deep breath and repeat yourself. What is the nature of your emergency?"

Years of training bring Sofia's panic to a screeching halt.

She's been through lockdowns. She knows how to handle an active shooter situation. Steady and calm, she says, "There is someone with a gun holding someone hostage in a car. I need the police to come to 12774 Laurel Canyon Boulevard."

"Ma'am, are you in the car that is being threatened?"

"No, I'm upstairs in my apartment. Someone just told me they saw it happening."

"One moment. I'm going to transfer this to LAPD. Stay on the line."

It's pure torture to hold still, but she does, and in the silence, she hears gunshots.

Jazz.

She can't just sit here.

She puts the phone on speaker and sets it on the counter. Carefully, she unlatches the necklace and, keeping out of view of the camera, hangs it on a fridge magnet shaped like California, from a long-ago vacation. The camera has a view of the oven. It's not ideal, but it's at chest level, at least.

She grabs the phone and runs for the door. She sprints down the hallway just as the woman comes back onto the line. "Ma'am, I'm connecting you with LAPD. Officer Ramos."

She yanks open the stairwell door and hurries down the steps. "You need to hurry. I hear gunshots. Do you have someone on the way?"

"Ma'am, I need you to calm down. I can't understand you— it sounds like you're running. I thought you were inside your apartment."

Sofia leaps down the last two stairs and almost runs into the exterior door. She turns the handle and pulls it open.

A woman steps through the door. In the harsh fluorescent light, her blond wig gleams white.

45

JAZZ

I STEP AWAY from the front gate, back toward the sidewalk. This seems wrong, the quiet. Patel must be just outside, waiting.

I take another step, clinging to the gate, hiding behind bushes.

Nothing happens. The silence creeps into my gut like poison.

I keep low and hide behind the same wall Joaquin used for shelter. I make my way along the building and raise my head when I'm nearer to the side street.

The car is quiet and dark. The street is empty. Unless she's hiding behind one of the parked cars or palm tree trunks, she's not here.

I feel like I'm walking into a trap, but I don't know what to do except continue forward. I don't want to do my usual thing, where I barrel into situations without thinking. I want to be smart and clearheaded. Joaquin's life might depend on it.

I strain my ears for sirens. Nothing. Where are the police? I don't like this. I need to check on Joaquin.

I run the direction Joaquin went, toward the side gate. I climb the six-foot fence awkwardly with the handcuffs and drop onto the other side. I throw myself into the planter and hunch over, keeping in the bushes down the deserted, narrow walkway until I make it to a fork. To the right, the sidewalk leads to a door that takes you up into the stairwell; straight ahead lies a side entrance to the parking garage. I take the right path and pause outside the stairwell door.

All is quiet.

My heart pounds, thuds, a maniacal drum line inside my chest. I push at the stairwell door, but it's blocked.

I stoop down, lower than she'd probably shoot, and peek around the door.

At first, I just register a body, and then it comes into focus, and my stomach plummets into the floor beneath my feet.

It's Sofia. Blood. Soaking through her shirt. Just under her collarbone.

This moment has no thought. My breath and my brain and all of myself are wrapped up in the horrifying images before me.

Her eyes, staring at the ceiling. Blinking. Lips trying weakly to form words.

Chest, catching visibly with each breath.

The moment sucks back into my chest, and my brain whirs to life. My eyes fly around the empty stairwell. Patel is nowhere to be seen.

I drop down by Sofia's side. She's on her back, legs tucked under her in an unnatural position. I'm whispering, a broken stream of "no no no no no." I don't know what I'm supposed to do. Put pressure on the wound? But won't that push the bullet farther inside her?

"Sofia, do you have your phone on you, honey?" I search her body with my cuffed, shaky hands, but there's nowhere on her leggings or tank top to conceal a phone or anything else. Her face is slack, eyes closed now like she's dreaming.

The wound is far away from her heart, all the way at the top of her chest. There's not that much blood. She'll be okay. I pat her cheek. "Hey. Come on. Wake up. Let's get you to a safe place. We need to find a phone."

Dead silence. No sirens in the night.

I don't think she called the cops. They'd have been here by now.

I can feel the danger to Joaquin pulling me away from her. Panicked gasps escape my lips. I want to scream, beg anyone to help me, but this is a closed, soundproof stairwell. Screaming isn't going to do shit.

Sofia coughs, the sound wet and thick. Blood splatters onto my chest and beards her chin in red.

"Oh, holy shit," I hear myself say. "Sofia, honey, I gotta get to a phone and call 911." I roll her onto her side so she can cough without choking on the blood. I don't think she knows I'm here, but then one of her hands seizes mine, shockingly tight. She coughs again, spewing blood into the carpet.

I squeeze her hand and press my lips to her forehead. I'm not helping her by staying here. I need to go. I need to *move*. "I gotta get a phone. Sweetie. I have to—" I'm losing it. I need to pull it together. I need to be a soldier.

So now I do the unthinkable. I do the inhuman, the inhumane. I pull my hand out of her grip.

She clings on tight, and I hear myself sobbing as I wrench my hand away from hers. I put her hands together, baby elephant style, to give her something to hold on to.

I stand up. I almost can't. I double over in pain like I've been punched.

I want to throw up. I swallow it down. I try to breathe. I turn toward the stairs.

I put my feet on the stairs. I push down with my muscles, force my feet to move. Sofia's presence, like a psychic tether, weakens as I get farther away from her.

On the second-floor landing, I straighten up and square my shoulders. The door is in front of me. I have to walk through it.

I know this place. This is the place past fear, past pain, where you've been beaten bloody and lost everything you ever had to lose. This is the place where blood runs cold and real decisions are made.

I reach for the handle, turn it and pull the door open. The silent hall stretches ahead of me, the front doors decorated cheerfully. *Don't forget to breathe.*

I'm done playing Patel's game. I'm tired of her baiting me like an animal. If she wants me, she can come and fucking get me.

I grab the vase off a table and hurl it at the door across the hall. It explodes in a crash. "Get the fuck out here," I yell. My voice is muffled by the low hallway ceiling and the hotel-style carpeting. I seize the small table and bash it on the door it belongs to, bang it over and over, making a huge racket, until the leg comes off in my hand. I brandish the table leg like a baseball bat and stride to the next door. I ring the doorbell, bang on the door with the stick. "Hello! Come on out, everybody. Let's call the fucking cops." I run down the hallway. I turn the corner that leads to Sofia's apartment. "Come out, bitch," I scream. I bang on another door, ring the doorbell.

Sofia's door cracks open. I flatten myself against the wall just as the barrel of the gun sneaks around the edge of the door frame and spits at me. The bullet whizzes past my face—I can feel it slice the air like water. I bend down, run forward in a squat and leap around the corner, swinging the stick like the bat Carol uses on me. I hit something—a grunt—I fling myself into Sofia's apartment, stick swinging blindly.

Patel is down, the gun on the tile at her side. It looks like I struck her in the hand; she's scooting backward on her butt and wringing it out. I kick the gun away, swing the stick as she tries to retrieve it and connect with her ribs, knocking her down. The blond wig loosens, revealing a slice of shiny black hair underneath.

"Where is he?" I roar, an animal, ready to rip her limb from limb. I pull off her wig, toss it aside and grab her hair in fists, pull her head back, hands tearing hair from roots. "Where *is he*?"

From the hallway at the back of the living room, Joaquin steps through the door. "I'm here. I'm fine," he says. I open my mouth to tell him to go find a phone.

Patel pulls a small gun from the waistband of her slacks. I draw in my breath to yell, but her hand lashes sideways and cracks off a silencer-muffled shot that hits Joaquin in the thigh and spins him sideways to the ground. He screams, his puberty-cracked voice shrill.

A knock on the half-open front door. "Hello? Everything okay in there?" A middle-aged woman with a bathrobe drawn around pajamas steps through the doorway.

Quick as a snake, Patel snaps her arm left and fires a shot at the woman. The woman goes down hard, a hand clamped to her chest.

I grab for Patel's gun hand. The woman by the door is making gurgling, screeching, wailing sounds, and Patel whips the gun toward her and snaps off two more shots in quick succession. The woman goes quiet.

I tackle Patel from behind. My hands are cuffed; I can't easily pin down the gun hand while keeping her immobilized.

She bucks and thrashes. I hear my own voice, like a child's, hissing curse words that sound like prayers. I'm fighting to keep her down, and then the gun swings up and reality sucks in to the black hole in the barrel.

It snaps. A crack of fire spits into my shoulder. I topple back and she climbs on top of me, gun pointed at my face. Her hair is messy, a disheveled bun sticking up from the side of her head. Her chest heaves. She's ugly with fury, and she parts her lips, pressing the gun to my chest.

She swallows, catches her breath. My shoulder flares into pain like it's been set on fire.

I wait for the shot.

"Joaquin," I hear myself whimper. I can't do this to him. I can't die and leave him here.

She digs the gun into my breastbone. I try to struggle, try to thrash aside, but she's got my wrists pinned with her knees.

God, please, let Joaquin be okay. Let him be okay. Let him be okay.

"I tried," she says. "I tried to make you one of my black-birds." Her tone fills with rage. "And you messed everything up. Like you screw up everything you touch, right, Jasmine? Everything you touch, you turn to shit."

Tears fill my eyes and blind me. I wait for her to pull the trigger.

Movement behind her. A shape, shadowy and limping.

Joaquin.

His face is white with pain. He lifts his hand. He's clutching an object that glints translucent yellow in the light from the open front door.

The syringe.

Patel turns her head to see what I'm looking at. I take the opportunity, grab her gun hand and pull it up so it points over my shoulder at the floor. She fires reflexively. Joaquin darts his hand into the space between her neck and shoulder.

The silver needle pokes into her neck. He pushes his thumb down on the depressor, and the yellow liquid vanishes.

She stiffens, freezes.

He's fast. He has practice.

Joaquin pulls his hand back and drops the syringe to the floor. He clamps his hands to his bleeding thigh. Patel goes rigid on top of me. I buck her off, sending her tumbling onto the floor. I shake the gun out of her hand and throw it far away, out past the dead woman into the hallway.

She curls into the fetal position. She turns her face to me. Her eyes are wide, like she sees more light than exists in this darkened apartment. On the floor next to me, the syringe lies discarded and empty.

"You did good," I tell Joaquin. "Let's get you out of here. We need an ambulance."

"Don't leave," she whispers.

"Fuck you."

I push myself into a sitting position. I forgot about my shoulder, and now it flares to life with pain. It's dripping blood warm and sticky down my arm and onto my hand. I can't tell if the bullet is still lodged in there, buried in my deltoid, or if it passed through; it feels like I'm being stabbed with every heartbeat. Joaquin's looking sleepy, slumped sideways onto the carpet.

"Come on come on," I tell him. I push myself up and close the distance between us.

Patel groans, a low, guttural sound of pure misery. Her body stretches suddenly, feet flexed. She clutches at her stomach, and then she heaves, spewing a small stream of blood onto the carpet beneath her.

I kneel by Joaquin, who has his leg clutched in his hands.

His face is twisted into a childlike expression of pain. Through my own agony, I say, "Sweetie, can you hop? Let's get out of here. Let's find a phone. Sofia's been shot, too. We gotta get an ambulance."

He lifts his hands for me to help him up, just like I used to when he was a kid. I take his hand and pull him to his feet. He moans, and I say, "You're going to hop. Don't put any weight on that leg."

We're almost out the door, and I'm trying to figure out how to get Joaquin around the dead woman who lies prostrate across the doorway with terrible, wide-lidded eyes that stare straight into my soul. "Don't look," I tell Joaquin. He hops around her. Now that Joaquin is safe and Patel is taken care of, my need to check on Sofia burns worse than my shoulder, worse than my worry about Joaquin's leg. I pray she's okay. I pray with everything inside me.

From behind us comes a rustling sound. I turn. Patel has rolled onto her back and is fumbling with her ankle, under the leg of her jeans. She lifts something—another gun. A small one.

I cry out and shove Joaquin toward the door. He stumbles and turns to face me in protest.

She raises the little gun in a two-handed cop grip and fires.

The bullet hits Joaquin in the chest and launches him back into the hallway.

She aims at me. I brace myself.

When she opens her mouth to speak, a trickle of blood leaks out.

"It's worse to let you live," she whispers. She drops the gun and collapses.

46
JAZZ

WHEN JOAQUIN WAS born, I was allowed to hold him in my arms for a day and a night. In the hospital, with another new mother in the neighboring bed, I pressed him to my bare chest and squeezed my love into him through sheer force of will. His skin was my skin. His blood was my blood.

He loved me, from the first time I held him, fresh with the warmth of me, my insides laid out and cradled in my arms. Is it weird to say I could feel his love when he looked at me? He was just a tiny baby, but he *loved me.*

I loved him more. That first day, and every day after.

I chose the name Joaquin. It means *uplifted by God.* Carol approved of the Biblical connotations, but she didn't know I held that name in my heart for a decade. When my biological mother was pregnant with the little brother I never got a chance to know, I begged her to name him Joaquin. I thought it was the most beautiful name. I clutched it like a talisman.

Joaquin. Lifted up by God. Favored. Joaquin. Safe. Special. Eternal.

I had expected to feel shame when holding my baby. I expected to find him pitiful, this pathetic victim of my own stupidity, destined to continue the cycle of poverty and abuse—

But it didn't feel like that at all.

I felt hope. I saw the future in him—pure, untapped potential. I saw it in his bright little eyes, in the swoop of his thick dark hair. I saw it in the softness of his tiny bicep, in the grip of his itty-bitty fingers around mine.

He wasn't here to perpetuate the cycle. He was here to break it. He was here to redeem me, to make the best of me. He would never bring me shame. He would be my forever pride and joy, from that moment until—

Until—

I had always thought it would be until my last breath.

My last breath.

Mine.

47
JAZZ

THE LIGHT IS too bright in here. The swinging doors stay shut no matter how hard I stare at them. Every time they do open, a nurse walks through and I rise, but the nurse turns left or right, and it's never my turn.

A police officer stands on duty by a painting of a woman doing ballet. Next to the chair I occupy with the very edges of my butt cheeks, a stack of magazines blares rudely. *Keep Your Waist Tight for Summer*, suggests *Fit Woman*.

What a thing to look at while I wait on death.

I lean forward to rest my elbows on my knees, but my shoulder screams in protest. I have a bandage there to match the one on my forehead. "You're going to have a scar," the nurse had said disapprovingly when she learned the stitches had been ripped out three times. I wanted to swear at her. But I didn't. It didn't matter. Nothing matters, nothing except what's happening behind the swinging doors.

The hallway door the cop is guarding opens and a blonde

woman hurries through, her face red with tears. She runs to the nurses' station and gasps out incoherent words I can't quite hear. The nurses approach her with matching expressions of careful concern.

I watch the woman with half interest. She's in her late fifties or early sixties and wears yoga pants and a sweatshirt. It's the middle of the night. Maybe she was roused from sleep.

She turns toward me, the motion robotic, and approaches the seating area. Her face is melted into an expression of blank, cold horror.

She stares at a chair, like she's deciding if she should sit down. She spins slowly, as though she's forgotten how to do it. She lowers her ass, but halfway down her legs give out and she slips. Her butt hits the floor. I jump to catch her, but I'm too late, and I end up with a handful of her sweatshirt as she sprawls sloppily on the tile.

The cop rushes forward. "You all right, ma'am?" He's younger than me, a handsome man with beautiful clear brown eyes.

She shakes his hands off her and shrieks unintelligibly. I tell him, "Back off. She wants space."

The woman draws her knees up to her chest and presses her face into them. Her hair is messy, like a child's.

I sit on the floor beside her and rest my back on the chair legs. I wonder if she has a relative behind the swinging doors, too.

An old man enters the waiting area. He checks in with the nurses and sits in a nearby chair. Another person enters behind him, a woman with a small child in tow. They take a pair of seats by the cop, who has returned to his post by the door. They shoot the woman and me a strange look. They can suck it. We can sit wherever we want.

The woman pulls her face out of her knees and wipes her hands across her cheeks, which are dripping with tears. In doing so, she jostles my shoulder, and I hiss with pain.

"I'm sorry," she says.

"It's fine."

"What am I doing?" she asks, and her voice breaks into tears again.

A plainclothes detective enters the waiting room and approaches me. She's the same detective I spoke to when I arrived here, the one I gave my statement to in the ER as they were stitching me up. I forget her name. She's a fair-skinned, freckle-faced woman with a blond ponytail and hairsprayed bangs.

I get up off the floor. "Any news?" I ask her.

"No, not yet. I'm actually..." She scans the room and her eyes land on the woman at our feet. "Did she just arrive?"

"A few minutes ago. Do you know her?"

She squats down next to the woman, whose head is buried in her knees again. She touches the woman's shoulder. "Mrs. Russo? I'm Detective Gonzalez. We spoke on the phone."

Russo?

The woman snaps her face up. "Do you have news?"

"No, ma'am. I just wanted to check on you. May I help you up?" Gonzalez offers her hands.

"You're Sofia's mother," I say. Oh my God.

She looks at me as though for the first time. "You know my daughter?"

"I was with her," I manage in a pathetic squeak that doesn't sound like me at all.

Her eyes are so hungry, so filled with the need to grab at me and devour everything inside my brain, that I have to look away.

Gonzalez helps her onto a chair. I sit beside her, and Gonzalez squats down in front of us. "They've been keeping you both updated?"

I nod. "They're still in surgery."

"Still in surgery," Mrs. Russo echoes weakly.

Gonzalez says more words to us. We stare at her blankly. We have no words to give back. She retreats to have a quiet conversation with the officer by the door. The other people in the waiting room stare at us out of the corners of their eyes.

After a few minutes, Mrs. Russo says, "Did you see what happened?"

"No. I just...found her after."

A choked sob escapes from her mouth. "Did you do it to her? Just tell me. Did you shoot her?"

"Me? No. Of course not. My son is in there with her."

She grabs my hand. "I'm sorry. That was ridiculous. If you did it, you wouldn't be here in the waiting room. They'd have you in jail. Right? Is that how it works?"

"I guess."

She nods.

A moment passes.

"How old is your son?" she whispers.

"Thirteen."

She spits out a curse word and covers her face with her other hand.

"He's her student," I say uselessly.

She opens her mouth to ask something else, but the swinging doors open.

My heart explodes.

A doctor walks out. He's got female nurses on either side of him and a lady in a skirt suit behind him with a clipboard.

It's going to be bad news. I know it. Why else would there be so many people with him?

Everyone in the waiting room stares at these new people. I can feel the collective holding of breaths.

I've been wishing so hard for them to call me, but now I pray they're calling anyone else. Let that lady with the toddler get the bad news. The old man. Anyone else. Not me. Not Joaquin.

"Mrs. Russo?" the doctor calls.

She waves her left hand weakly. It shakes so hard I can see it. She grips my hand hard with her right.

The group approaches us. The doctor clears his throat. "You're Sofia Russo's mother?"

She nods. Her face is dead white.

"We're sorry," he says.

More words follow, but they're drowned out by the awful, howling wail that erupts from Sofia's mother's chest. My own grief for Sofia stops in its tracks, overpowered by the raw agony of the woman who clutches my hand almost hard enough to break it.

And horribly, unforgivably, disgustingly, underneath the pain that racks my body is a cold, bloodless relief.

There's still a chance for Joaquin.

48
ALICIA

ALICIA GONZALEZ WATCHES the blonde woman receive the news.

Alicia knows the feeling. It never gets better, either. You just get colder on the inside. You detach from the starry-eyed person you were before your child was dead. *Welcome to the rest of your life.*

She glances sideways at Officer Washington. His eyes are red, and he passes a hand under his nose. "You need a minute?" she asks roughly.

He squares his shoulders. "No, ma'am. I'm fine."

They wait in silence. The doctor takes Mrs. Russo by the arm, and the clipboard-bearing woman accompanies them along a hallway to the left. That's the grief counselor's office, Alicia remembers from other visits to St. Joseph. This is a nice hospital, a hell of a lot nicer than Kaiser.

Another doctor pushes through the swinging doors, a small Asian woman with tired eyes. "Miss Benavides?" she calls into the waiting room.

Jasmine stares at the woman. It looks like she's too shaken up to answer. Alicia steps forward and waves down the doctor. "Right here." She sits in the chair next to Jasmine, whose entire body seems to be quivering.

The doctor says, "I'm Dr. Lee, and we just finished working on your...son?" She casts a questioning look at Alicia. Jasmine is clearly too young to have a teenage son, but Alicia nods.

"And?" Jasmine says.

"He suffered damage to his right lung, a fractured rib. He's got a fracture to his left—"

"Is he going to live or not?" Jasmine barks.

"Oh, he's going to live. You might be looking at long-term PT, and we'll have to continuously reevaluate that lung for a while to make sure it doesn't collapse. It's made more complicated by his diabetes, so we'll need to keep him in hospital for at least—"

Jasmine isn't listening. Alicia watches as she presses her hands to her face and folds forward onto her knees.

The doctor gives Alicia a frustrated look. "I'm needed on another floor. I'm going to pass this along to Dr. Stein, who arrives in thirty minutes. In the meantime, Joaquin is being moved to Room 1502, and the nurses will let you know when he's up for a visit."

As the doctor walks away, Alicia remembers her own ER waiting room horror last year. Her ex-husband hit her infant daughter in a rage during one of his visitations, sending her into a coma from which she never woke. Isabella. That was her daughter's name. It's tattooed on her shoulder. Isabella.

She should be happy Joaquin will live. She can't muster it up, though, because Joaquin living means Belinda Patel is dead. Belinda was her only friend, the only one who understood her buried grief. And now Belinda is gone.

Jasmine sits up. She wipes her face. "Sofia is dead," she says. "Dead. Dead and gone." Her teeth chatter, extending the last word into a sigh.

This is your own fault. If you had followed instructions, everything would be fine. Belinda and Sofia would be alive, and thirty more people would be getting the justice they deserve.

She can't bear the thought of the project going unfinished. It's horrible to think of all those people waiting by their phones for a call that will never come. Belinda would never have wanted that.

EIGHT WEEKS LATER

49
JAZZ

JOAQUIN REACHES FOR the doorbell because I'm too nervous.

I stop his hand. "Don't."

He's paler than usual from all the time indoors, but he looks good. His hair flops over his eye as he raises an eyebrow at me. "Jazz. We can't stand out here all day."

I pull him into a hug and squeeze him tight, almost tight enough to hurt him. I feel his ribs and the muscles of his back and the wonderful warmth of the blood inside him. I nuzzle my face into his shoulder and inhale the clean scent of his shirt that smells like mine because I washed them together. I had a serious moment at the Laundromat, pulling his clothes out of the canvas laundry bag. I held his shirt clutched tight, tears welling up in my eyes.

I release Joaquin. "I should have changed my clothes."

"Why?"

"I should have dressed more proper." I gesture around me at the expansive front yard, the Spanish-tiled roof.

"You're fine," he says.

"I'm sorry," I blurt out.

"Sorry for what?"

"I'm sorry I lied to you for all those years about being your sister. I wish I had told you the truth from the beginning."

He takes a deep breath. We've talked about this, but it was overshadowed by our relief to be alive and my grief about Sofia. He blinks a few times, fast, and turns his pretty, long-lashed eyes on me. "I wish you would have told me, too."

"I thought you'd be ashamed to have me as a mother." That's the cold hard truth, and I spit it out, but it tastes awful and I have to look away from him when I say it.

"Why would I be ashamed? That doesn't make sense."

"Because I'm so young. And so stupid. And so..." I shrug. "It doesn't matter. I was wrong. You should have always known the truth about your own life story."

"You're right. I should have."

He gets this from me, this bluntness, and I love him for it.

"Can you forgive me?" I ask.

He rings the doorbell. "I *guess.*"

A set of footsteps approaches, and the door swings open to reveal the exact kind of hallway I'd expected from the way the house looks from the outside: dark wood floors, a chandelier hanging from the high ceiling and fresh flowers on the entry table.

Mrs. Russo—Rachel—presses her lips together into an attempted smile. "Hi," she says, the syllable flat and sharp. She's thinner, her cheeks sunken, eyes blazing blue from rings of darkness.

I try to smile back. "Hey."

"Is this your son?"

"Yes. Joaquin."

"Nice to meet you," he says. He holds out a hand to shake. It makes me proud, the straightness of his back and shoulders.

She takes the hand but holds it gently instead of shaking it. "You look well. Are you better?"

"I still have to go to physical therapy. But I feel good."

Her chest rises and falls, and I recognize the gesture as something Sofia did, a brief yoga breath meant to calm herself.

I can't be here. I have to run.

"Come on in," she says. Joaquin pulls me forward. Rachel leads us past a dining room with a fancy table and a kitchen with granite countertops. She brings us to a living room. Joaquin stays on her heels and enters the room, but I stop in the doorway.

On the floor, surrounded by toys, sits a beautiful toddler. She looks up at Joaquin, then me. Her hair falls like streaky caramel around her shoulders, and her deep brown eyes peer up at us with curiosity.

I stumble back a step. I turn the corner and press my back to the wall. I try to breathe.

A framed picture of Sofia in a blue cap and gown smiles brightly at me.

She's so pretty.

Was.

Was so pretty.

Through the din inside my skull, I hear voices. "I'll go," says a woman's voice, and then Rachel is leaning on the wall next to me.

I can't take my eyes off Sofia's face. Her smile.

At last, Rachel whispers, "This was taken when she got her bachelor's degree."

My face is hot. "She looks happy," I manage.

"She was so funny. She wouldn't let me throw her a graduation party."

"Why not?"

"She wasn't done with college yet. She wanted to finish her master's before we celebrated. She didn't want to get cocky."

I try to smile, but I can't. I didn't have time to get to know everything about Sofia. I wish I'd had time to know these pieces of her.

"Olive looks so much like her," I say, which breaks my voice and my heart.

"She does." After a pause, she says, "I'm so angry. I wish that detective was alive so they could send her to prison and give her the death penalty so I could watch her die myself. I can't believe the way the media has been behaving. It makes me sick."

I'm pretty sure there's no execution any state would dole out that would be more painful than the poisoning death I know Patel suffered, but I don't say anything. I know what Rachel means. She wants to see the murderer of her daughter suffer with her own eyes. She wishes she could kill her daughter's killer with her own hands. I understand.

I peek around the doorjamb. Joaquin and Olive are silently collaborating on a complex structure made of Legos and crayons.

She's watching over my shoulder. "I'm happy he's all right."

"You are?"

"Yes."

"I thought you might…" I trail off.

"I know. I did. But not anymore. Sofia wanted him to be all right. That's how she was. That's how I want to be." She takes a deep, audible breath. "You said you wanted to meet Olive. So let's do it."

I push off the wall and step toward the kids. I drop to the floor, cross-legged, and force myself to take a good look at Olive.

She's beautiful. Joaquin hands her a green crayon, and she sets it atop a tower of Legos in a very exacting way.

"She only places them horizontally," he murmurs out of the side of his mouth. "It's smart. It makes for more solid construction with the way the Lego holes are angled."

I shoot him a look that is supposed to make fun of him for being a dork, but instead it gets filled up with mush. "Oh yeah? Is that so?"

Rachel settles onto the carpet across from me and rests a hand on Olive's back.

I say to her, "I want to help."

She frowns. "What do you mean?"

"She's going to be a handful. Lots of energy. When you need a day off, I want to…" I fumble for the words. "I could take her to the park, the zoo. Or I could go to the store for you, or drive her to lessons…anything you want. I want to be someone you can call for help. I would have been that for Sofia, and I…I still want to be that for her." I can't talk anymore. This is too hard. But it's harder for Sofia's mom, so I need to suck it the hell up.

She says nothing.

I grip my hands together in my lap. Baby elephant.

Joaquin reaches out and takes one.

Olive reaches for me, too. She touches the skull and crossbones, the roses around my wrist, the letters scripted into the sides of my fingers. "Paintings!" she says in a small, adorable voice.

I laugh, the sound tearful. "Yeah, honey. I painted myself."

"I paint myself," she mimics, returning to her Legos. She

places a crayon carefully between the holes in the Legos, just like Joaquin had said.

"All right," Rachel says to me. "I'll call you."

50
ALICIA

THE BROWN-HAIRED WOMAN waves at her.

Alicia looks up from the purple flowers and waves back with a gloved hand. She has to pretend she belongs here.

The woman hurries to her car, yoga mat rolled under her arm, as Alicia returns to her plants.

She adjusts her gray wig and brushes dirt off her muu-muu. She's seen that woman a few times. She wonders who the woman thinks she is. It's hilarious, actually, that you can plant flowers in any apartment's planter you like. The tenants will think you're another resident or someone related to the landlord. The landlord will think you're someone related to a tenant. And no one is ever bothered by a beautiful scattering of flowers in their planter.

Satisfied that her babies are doing well, and careful not to let them touch her skin, she leaves and walks down La Cienega to her next guerrilla garden, which is what she calls the patches of the purple-flowered plants she's tucked into planters all over the city. When she sees the next flower bed on her route, she lets out a frustrated sigh. This apartment's automatic irrigation system is on the fritz, and it looks like she's going to lose this batch.

It's all right. She has forty-seven other guerrilla gardens planted from Santa Monica to Pasadena, and all her other plants are doing well.

While she's out here, she always thinks about Belinda. Since Belinda had no family, there was no one to claim her ashes. Alicia had taken them, offering to scatter them overseas, to the coroner's relief. Instead, she added them to the soil in these guerrilla gardens. It's perfect, poetic, and exactly what Belinda would have wanted.

Belinda was a great woman. Alicia made sure she got all the credit for the Blackbird Killings. She helped the higher-ups find Belinda's keys to the apartment and storage unit she used, which contained all the flip phones and the syringes.

The police are still looking for Belinda's list of participants, but they'll never find it, because Alicia took it. The Blackbirds will remain anonymous, which is as it should be.

Alicia made sure to paint an accurate picture of Belinda for the media: a powerful woman driven to extremes in her desire to protect the types of innocents she was never able to save as a soldier or a police officer. Every true crime podcast has done a piece on Belinda. Netflix is developing an eight-part documentary series around her life and her activities as the Blackbird Killer. People don't hate Belinda. They love her. They admire her. Just the other day, Alicia read an opinion piece in the *Guardian* about how Belinda should be regarded as a vigilante hero. She's a martyr, a voice for the voiceless. Her legacy will live on for decades.

Satisfied with her work, Alicia takes the gardening gloves

off, revealing latex gloves underneath. She pulls these off as well and wads them into a ball, careful not to touch the surface of either pair of gloves with her bare hands.

She has a degree in organic chemistry from MIT. No one ever pays attention to that. They notice her blond ponytail and her perky demeanor, but they always forget how smart she is.

It's okay. That's the best way to hide: in plain sight.

51

JAZZ

THE COURTHOUSE LOOMS above me, its sharp corners correctional against the too-clear, too-bright blue sky. I don't like it. I feel like I'm going to walk into this building and never walk out. They'll wrench him out of my arms just like they always have.

"Jazz." Joaquin nudges me. "You stopped walking." To his point, a family almost collides with us, and they funnel their way around us impatiently.

I look at my feet. They're encased in new, unfamiliar ankle boots. I miss my Docs. "Do you think I'm too dressed up?" I ask.

"No. You look like an actual grown adult." His face is suddenly serious. "I want us to win. I want to go home tonight and be done with this."

"I know, little man. Me too."

He looks scared. I pull him into a hug that he doesn't resist. I bury my face in his slim shoulder and wind my arms around his back. "You are safe, and you are mine," I whisper.

He makes dramatic choking noises until I release him. I smooth the front of my long-sleeved button-down shirt. "I look so gay," I say, just as Joaquin says, "You look *so gay*."

"Shut up, Marco Polo." He hates this polo shirt more than anything. I lace my arm through his and pull him toward the stairs.

"Marco Polo," he mutters. "Dumbest joke ever."

"Oh okay, I didn't realize you were the king of comedy." I pull the door open and usher him inside.

My lawyer, Sarah, is waiting for us. She greets us with a broad smile and hugs me first. She's a statuesque woman at least eight inches taller than me. She looks me up and down, clutching my shoulders. "Look at you, so sharp."

Joaquin opens his mouth to mock me, but then she turns her hug on him and his face gets lost in her bosom. I press my lips together to keep from laughing. When she releases him, he combs his bangs out like a cat straightening its fur.

She says, "We're in Room 202. How are you holding up?"

"We're a little nervous," Joaquin replies.

"I get it. But does it make you feel better knowing your mom's done literally everything a human can do to make sure this goes your way?"

He nods, but he looks unconvinced.

We get in line for the metal detectors, emptying our pockets and putting our bags on the conveyor belt. I get scanned by the security guard's little metal detector wand, as does Sarah—although of course she's much more cheerful about it than I am—and she leads us to the courtroom. On the way, she keeps us distracted with a string of chatter about the weather, her dogs and her little girl, who is apparently quite a spitfire, and before I know it, I'm entering Room 202. She guides us to a table on the left facing the podium where the judge will sit. I slump into a wooden chair and place my hands on the slick wooden table in front of me.

The walls of the courtroom are wood. So are the witness stands, the judge's podium, the low walls separating the seating areas, the chairs…

Joaquin sinks into the chair next to me. We watch Sarah unload a bunch of files and papers from her briefcase onto the table.

I say, "Whoever decorated this place loves wood."

"That's what she said."

I blink at him. "What?"

"Get it? Wood?" He elbows me and smiles, and in this moment, I know I'm forgiven.

The door opens, and Sarah's eyes fly to the back of the courtroom. She stands up, back stick-straight, face converting into a mask of fierce professionalism.

Carol is here.

She follows her lawyer in, and suddenly I notice there are other people in the courtroom with us. Random people are sitting in the seats—waiting their turn, maybe, since we're the first case of the day. Uniformed officers are at the door, or maybe they're bailiffs. Carol's lawyer is a pinched-looking gray-haired man I'm assuming she got from her church.

Carol and her lawyer take the table to our right, and only when she's seated, with her lawyer digging papers out of his briefcase, does she look over at me.

Her eyes are ice.

I want to look down. I want to avert my eyes both from the pitiful hollowness of her eyes and her skeletal, radioactive fury.

But I don't.

How did I let Carol control me for so long?

Sarah says I could have kept him. If I had reported the

things Carol did to me right when they began, I could have asked to be moved to a different foster home together with Joaquin until I turned eighteen, and then we'd have been free to live our lives. This whole time, he could have been with me. I've lost ten years with him. That's my fault. No one can carry the burden of that guilt for me.

Carol's lawyer leans in to show her a piece of paper. Beside me, Joaquin is a kid-shaped statue, his hands clasped in his lap.

The judge enters, her black robe billowy around her. She looks tired. We learn that her name is Judge Luu. I'm relieved the judge is a woman.

I put my hand over Joaquin's in his lap. I lean toward him and whisper in his ear, "It's really going to be okay."

He laces his fingers through mine, which he hasn't done for years. I don't listen to what the judge says, some sort of introduction that she seems to have memorized. It's not until Sarah stands up that my focus swings in and Joaquin squeezes my hand so hard it hurts.

Sarah begins to explain why we're here, and Carol's lawyer joins in with section numbers and penal codes, and they begin negotiating the plan for the proceedings. I feel Joaquin lean in toward me, and I tilt my head so I can hear the words he whispers in my ear. "I'm scared."

I swallow my own fear and turn my expression into a smile. "Almost over," I murmur. "This won't take that long."

The judge asks each side to explain what they want. It's actually pretty simple. It seems like the judge is there to find a middle ground. However, our situation is not an easy one to mediate. I'm requesting full custody with no visitation for Carol. Carol is requesting full custody with no visitation for me. Between us is an ocean of paperwork.

Sarah presents information on the civil suit I'm filing against

Carol for assault, and then the info on the criminal case that's under way against her for assault on me and criminal negligence of Joaquin. Carol's lawyer argues that she has a right to withhold medical treatment for religious reasons, and Sarah gets riled up talking about cases where children died and their parents were charged with murder. Carol's lawyer argues that those parents weren't convicted. Sarah argues that I saved Joaquin from certain death, and then they have to talk about the Blackbird case and debate what evidence should be allowed into these proceedings. Sarah wants to present everything the prosecutor has entered into evidence in the assault case against Carol, and I'm overwhelmed by the rapid-fire back-and-forth, my own fear of losing Joaquin buzzing in my head like a swarm of bees.

Judge Luu asks about the child abuse charges against Carol, and Carol's attorney immediately protests. His client is out on bail, and those criminal charges can't be entered into this custody hearing until the evidence has been officially entered and the material reviewed by the DA. Sarah argues back furiously—"How can you suggest that we not present this court evidence of criminal neglect and endangerment when your client is seeking to retain custody of a minor child she has been keeping locked in a bedroom and denying his lifesaving medication?"

The judge holds her hands up, and both lawyers shut their mouths.

"What is the first thing you would like to enter into evidence?" she asks Sarah. "I've familiarized myself with the pending charges against Ms. Coleman, so you may need to present less than you've anticipated."

"I'd like to start with photographs of Joaquin's bedroom," Sarah says calmly.

The judge looks at Carol's lawyer. "Would that be a problem?"

"It's not relevant to this case. Unless you want to see photographs of the tiny studio apartment Ms. Benavides plans on keeping him in so you can get an accurate comparison."

The judge looks at Sarah. "Does that sound fair? Photographs of both living situations?"

"Not only fair, Your Honor, but I have brought photographs taken at that apartment just this morning." So that's why Sarah asked me to text her photos of my place this morning.

Sarah brings her phone and a stack of photographs to the judge's podium, and the judge flips through them. "This is his room at Ms. Coleman's house?"

"Yes, Your Honor. Please note the window."

The judge's eyebrows shoot up. She flips the photograph around and shows it to Carol. "You want to try and explain why you would board up a child's window?"

Carol's attorney says, "Ms. Coleman is a single woman living alone. She was afraid of the constant intrusion of Ms. Benavides, who regularly broke into the house and stole from them."

Sarah says, "Your Honor, if you flip to the next photograph, you'll note that Joaquin's window is fitted with bars on the outside. The purpose of boarding up the window was to keep Ms. Benavides from slipping him his insulin through the bars, which was something she commonly did when Ms. Coleman would not permit him to take the medication. There was no theft."

"I see." Judge Luu puts the photographs down. She flips through the pictures on Sarah's phone and looks at me. "How long have you been living in this apartment, Ms. Benavides?"

Everyone is suddenly looking at me. I clear my throat. "Five years," I say.

"I see you like Miley Cyrus."

I feel my cheeks heat up. "That's Joaquin, actually. He's… a fan."

The judge looks at both of us with a tiny twinkle in her eyes. "I thought as much." She puts the phone down. "I'd like to ask some questions now. Jasmine," she says, turning her eyes on me. "I've seen your medical records. You've visited the urgent care and ER a dozen times in the last twelve years. That's one injury a year. I see burns, a broken collarbone, a broken wrist, broken ribs. I see blood evidence and Ms. Coleman's fingerprints on the bat used to assault you. Why are you just now pressing these charges?"

I feel Sarah's hand on my back. I try to think clearly. "I thought if Carol went to jail, they'd take Joaquin to some other foster home and split us up. She didn't physically assault him like she did me, so I thought I could make everything okay for him if I could just get him his meds. We worked around her."

"And did you try to sneak Joaquin his medication through the bars in his window? Did you break into the house?"

"Yes. I always tried to sneak him his meds if Carol wouldn't let him take them. I'd do it any way I could. Through his school, through the window, anything. He almost died once, when he was younger, and I…" I hold my hands up. It's too much. I miss Sofia. If she were here, she would have helped me prepare for this. This seems like exactly the kind of thing she'd be good at. But she's gone, and I have to be the person Joaquin has to rely on. I take a breath and lift my chin so I can look Judge Luu in the eyes. "I should have gone to the police much sooner. I had a few lawyers tell me I didn't have a lot of options for custody, but I could have still called the police when she assaulted me. I shouldn't have let it go this long. To be honest, I was afraid I would not be taken seriously, and I was afraid of Joaquin getting taken to some foster home that would be even worse. I've been in ones that were a lot worse. At least if I took the beatings, it got that energy off of him and onto me. And it let him focus on school and be a normal kid. That's all I wanted for him. All I *want* for him."

She's been listening to me intently. She turns to Joaquin. "Would you prefer to answer questions in private? I'd be happy to speak with you in my chambers."

Joaquin shakes his head. "I'd rather just answer them here."

She shuffles through the photos and holds one up. It's a picture of his bedroom door. "I want you to tell me about this."

It's a sliding lock that locks his bedroom from the outside. I hadn't noticed it when I went to the house.

I spin toward Carol. "You locked him in there?"

Sarah grabs my arm and holds me in my seat. My head is red with fury. I should have murdered Carol while I had a chance. I want to tear her limb from limb.

"I'm sorry, Your Honor," Sarah says.

"Are you okay?" the judge asks Joaquin.

He nods. "Yeah, she locked me in there sometimes. I'm sorry, Jazz. I thought you knew."

"I didn't know. I'm so sorry."

Judge Luu says, "Joaquin, you've given this info to the police?"

"They asked me about it when they interviewed me, yeah."

"Well, good. And happy birthday, by the way. You turned fourteen last week, didn't you?" She smiles at him warmly.

He nods. He looks too nervous to smile back at her. I shove my own feelings aside and put my hand over his on the table. *It's all right*, I want to tell him.

"Did you have a party?" she asks.

"Jazz took me and two of my friends to Universal Studios."

"That sounds like fun."

He nods again.

"Well, I'm not sure if you know this, but at fourteen, you get to be a bigger participant in these proceedings. You get to have more of a say over what you'd like to see happen. So why don't you tell me what your ideal scenario would be? Forget what your adoptive or biological mother would like. And again, if you feel more comfortable talking to me in private, that will be fine."

"I just want to be normal."

"And what does normal look like for you?"

"I want to go to school." He shoots Carol a furious look. "I don't want to get homeschooled by someone who didn't even graduate high school herself. I already picked out the high school I want to go to, this STEM magnet downtown."

"That sounds very reasonable."

"And I want to have a normal life. I want to have friends. I want to go out on the weekends, do normal things. I don't want to be locked up like an animal." He takes a deep breath. "And obviously I want my insulin. I don't want any more drama about it. Jesus isn't going to heal me. It's ridiculous. This whole thing is… It's not normal."

"I agree. So we have two choices for you. We can place you in a foster home close to school, and we can make sure you're taken care of medically by your new foster parents. That's one option."

I feel like I've been slapped. Stabbed. Set on fire. This is everything I was afraid of.

"Another option is to live with your biological mother.

I'm not sure how experienced she is at taking care of your diabetes—"

"She's the *only* one who's taken care of it. She's done all the doctor's appointments, filled all my prescriptions. She's the one who got me into the lottery for the STEM school. She does everything."

"So that's your second choice. Keep in mind that your biological mother does work a full-time job, and she does have a small apartment. It won't always be a comfortable situation."

Carol's lawyer pipes up. "Your Honor, I'd like you to at least consider a joint custody arrangement with my client—"

"Your client has forfeited her right to joint custody or visitation by locking this child in an empty room, denying him his insulin and beating his biological mother into a bloody pulp for the last twelve years," Judge Luu snaps.

Joaquin says, "The second choice. Please. The second one. I want to live with Jazz."

"All right. That's what we'll do, then." To me, she says, "You need to remember that this could have happened sooner if you'd learned to advocate for yourself as insistently as you've advocated for your son. I'm going to mandate weekly trauma counseling for both of you—separately—as a stipulation to this custody arrangement." I feel like it hurts her to look at me, like she understands the whole thing way too well. She goes on, "He's clearly an exceptional young man. Despite his taste in music." She twinkles her eyes at him, and I feel the breath whoosh out of me in a huge gush of relief. Somehow, I register that Sarah has her hand on my back again, but the only thing I care about is the overwhelming peace that makes me feel like I could float away. I can't remember a moment of my life where I wasn't worried about Joaquin. Is this what the rest of the people in this world feel like? Is this what it feels like to just…be?

52

CAROL

THE SUN IS setting when Carol pulls her car into her driveway. Her body is vibrating with anger.

Jasmine finally did it. This has been her plan this whole time, to steal Joaquin. No one sees how manipulative, how conniving Jasmine really is, poisoning Joaquin against her over all those years until this was the only possible outcome.

Carol lets herself out of the car, slams the door and crunches through dead grass to the front door. A pretty gift basket is set in front of the metal screen, a baby blue ribbon looped through the cellophane wrapping. Carol pulls the card out of the ribbon and opens it.

It's a pink card with the words *Jesus is always with you* written in calligraphy next to a white dove.

She opens it. In elegant cursive, a message reads, *We're all with you in the Spirit. Stay strong. Where two or more agree, there also is He.* It's signed, *Your brothers and sisters in Christ.*

Tears well up in Carol's eyes. Without her church family, she doesn't know how she would have survived the years of spiritual assault from Jasmine. It's been a supernatural battle between good and evil, and evil has won for now. She can feel the Enemy rejoicing.

Carol unlocks the door and brings the gift basket inside. She unties the bow and pulls apart the cellophane. Inside is an assortment of goodies: See's candy, a bottle of sparkling nonalcoholic apple cider, bright red pomegranates, scented candles, a new travel Bible in light pink and, her very favorite treat, Reese's Peanut Butter Cups.

She opens the wrapper and sits to enjoy the candy. She's hungry after a long day, and she polishes off each peanut butter cup in two bites while reading random passages in the Bible. It's a New Living translation, which is a little strange, since everyone at her church agrees the New King James Version is the only accurate translation. Maybe they delegated the Bible-buying to someone new.

She uncorks the cider. She pours herself a glass and takes it to the television. She sits in her armchair and whispers, "Thank You, Jesus, that I do not have to worry. Thank You that today brings enough problems of its own." Ain't that the truth. Her stomach growls uncomfortably. She winces. Chocolate for dinner may have been a bad idea. She recalls her attention back to her prayer. She whispers the verse: "'Do not be anxious about anything, but in everything by prayer and supplication with thanksgiving let your requests be made known to God. And the peace of God, which surpasses all understanding, will guard your hearts and your minds.' Shhraaam hararrra calaaaa—"

Her prayer is interrupted by her stomach lurching in a horribly familiar way. She jumps off the chair and runs for the bathroom, where she barely makes it to the toilet. She groans and clutches her stomach as she relieves herself.

She's washing her hands when the sink and soap go blurry. She grips the edge of the sink. She's exhausted. She needs to sleep.

She heads for her bedroom. It's too far. She collapses on the hallway carpet.

She vomits on the carpet in front of her. She almost can't breathe—she's going to choke—and then her throat clears of vomit. Now she can't breathe for some other reason. Her airways are closing. She clutches at her neck and tries to make her lungs expand.

And suddenly she's not alone. A pair of shoes stretches into legs above her. The shoes are covered in clear thin plastic booties. She tries to look up through her wheezing, tries to see the person above her.

It's a woman with a blond ponytail tucked into a plastic shower cap. The woman is watching her dispassionately.

"Help me," Carol squeaks through a throat that closes tighter with each passing moment. Her vision spins and darkens around the edges.

The woman squats down beside her. Her entire body is clothed in a coverall made of the same plastic material. Why isn't she calling an ambulance?

The woman smiles. "This is better than I was expecting. I knew it would take under an hour, but this is impressive. Especially for my first time. I haven't done this type of chemical extraction since college."

Carol closes her eyes. She needs to rest for a minute. Then she'll get up.

Something soft and fluffy touches Carol's face. She tries to understand the cotton that rains down around her.

They're flowers. Fresh purple flowers.

The room goes dark. The purple flowers cover her face.

53
JAZZ

WE HAVE TO get a bigger apartment.

I pull the comforter up to my chest and stare at the slats on the underneath of Joaquin's bunk. Of course he took the top bunk.

I pick numbers apart in my brain. If I stop saving up for Joaquin's college tuition, I can probably get us a two-bedroom. But is it financially responsible? We need more space, though, and he deserves privacy.

I turn onto my side and try to shut my brain off. I need to stop worrying. It won't do me any good. Besides, money worries feel so petty.

And they're distracting me from thinking about Sofia.

I play the courtroom scene in my head again. I remember Sofia's battle for custody of her daughter, and I feel so much guilt that she'll never get a victory like that. Look at the cost of Joaquin's life: Olive has to live as an orphan, just like me. It's a horrible, awful tragedy.

And now the images come.

Sofia on her side, coughing up blood, clinging to my hand. Me, pressing her hands together like a baby elephant, leaving her alone to die.

I did that. I left her.

I pull the pillow over my face and cry into it. This is the only time I can mourn her. I can't show any of this to Joaquin. I don't want to burden him or make him feel like I regret saving him. I don't. I'd do it the same way again, and Sofia would tell me to do it that way.

But here in the dark, I can remember that I would have loved her. I would have helped her with Olive. I would have been kind to her. I wanted to be those things.

Imagine if we had both gotten our kids back. My brain constructs the image without my permission: Us, sharing an apartment with both our kids. Oh, God, it'd have to be a three-bedroom, and even with Sofia's and my combined income, we might not have been able to afford that.

I laugh-sob into the wet pillowcase. What a stupid thing to think about.

The bed creaks. I freeze. I think Joaquin's rolling over in his sleep, but then the ladder squeaks and he topples into bed beside me. He stretches out next to me and pats my arm.

"You have school tomorrow," I whisper. "You should go to sleep. I'm sorry to wake you up."

"Shut up." He snuggles into my blanket and puts a hand on my shoulder. "You thinking about Ms. Russo?"

"How do you do that? You're such a creepy little psychic." I wipe my eyes on the pillowcase.

"Because I know you." He rolls onto his back and rests his head in his arm. "I'm sorry. It's not fair."

"It's not." My voice cracks.

We're silent.

At last he says, "Come on. Go to sleep. Olive isn't alone. She has her grandma. That's a lot more than you had."

I swallow a sob and nod.

"She's little. She's not going to remember anything bad. She's going to be okay. She's in a nice safe place with a grandma who loves her." He rubs my back like I used to rub his when he was little and had a bad dream. The tears stream hot and angry down my cheeks, but then eventually, worn out by the emotions of the day, I fall into a restless sleep filled with nightmares about syringes, vacant eyes, and beautiful, special women coughing up blood.

"Hurry—the fuck—up!" I yell at Joaquin, who's molding his hair into a fine art sculpture in the bathroom. I pull on my Trader Joe's shirt and gulp down the rest of my coffee.

"I'm coming!" he yells back. "I've only been in here for, like, two minutes!"

"Yeah right," I mutter. I shove my feet into my new Docs. He's been extra popular since he got shot by the famous Blackbird Killer, which has led to some serious before-school primping I have exactly zero patience for.

Joaquin comes trotting out of the bathroom, his hair looking exactly like it always does. "I'm ready."

"And I have no makeup on," I complain.

Suddenly, he has no idea where his phone is, even though I just reminded him ten minutes ago to make sure it was charged. We have a last-minute scramble to unearth it from his piles of clothes all over my formerly clean apartment. I find it in the pants he was wearing yesterday and give him shit about not having taken it out of the pocket, and what if it went through the washing machine, and now we can finally leave. I'm right behind him on the doorstep with my keys in hand when he tosses an Amazon box back into the apartment. It must have been delivered yesterday after we got home. I'm lucky it didn't get stolen. I think it's the new pair of Vans I ordered him.

I stop. I turn to look at the box. It rests just inside the front door on the "vintage" wood floor that always reminds me of Sofia.

It's not really the right size for shoes. Too small.

"Jazz?" Joaquin calls.

I toss him my keys. "Go start the car. I'll be right there. You can be DJ."

"Yes!" He runs off.

I pick up the box and examine the label.

Unlike the ones Patel sent me, it has a legit return address to the Amazon Fulfillment Center. I breathe a sigh of relief. I'm never going to look at an Amazon box the same way again.

Still, I wonder what it is. I grab my box cutter out of my purse and cut through the tape. I open the box.

It's full of purple flowers.

On top of the flowers is a note written in cursive on flowered notepaper.

I wouldn't touch these if I were you, it says.

I'm so confused.

The box starts buzzing.

I cry out and drop it. The flowers tumble onto the floor. I kick at the box with the toe of my boot.

A black flip phone falls out. Its little screen is lit up green. *New Text Message.*

My heart is going to pound completely out of my chest.

I have no intention of getting my fingerprints on any of

this. I grab a nearby sock from one of Joaquin's piles of clothes and use the sock to open the flip phone.

The message says, You're welcome.

Welcome for what?

In my back pocket, my iPhone vibrates. I pull it out. It's a 213 number. I slide the button to answer.

"Hello?"

"Jasmine? It's Detective Gonzalez down at Central Police Station. Do you remember me?"

"Of course."

"Jasmine, I have some bad news for you. Are you sitting down?"

"Yes. What is it?"

"Carol Coleman is dead. She was found in her home last night."

My heart beats. One, two, three.

"Dead?" I echo at last.

"Yes."

"How? What happened?"

"We're not sure yet. Were you at home last night after court?"

My head swims. "I took Joaquin out to dinner after court, with our lawyer. We got home around ten."

"That's fine, then. I'll still need you to come in and answer some questions. I'll need to speak with your lawyer, as well."

From the floor, the flip phone buzzes with another text message. I poke it with the sock until I can see it.

You owe me.

★ ★ ★ ★ ★

AUTHOR'S NOTES

AT ITS HEART, this book is a love letter to the working-class Los Angeles that doesn't always make it into books and movies. Watching TV, you'd swear LA is one huge amalgam of Sunset Strip, Rodeo Drive and Muscle Beach, but the LA I know and love is so much more than that. I hope I did it justice.

None of the Blackbirds' stories of victimization are fictional, although they have been fictionalized to protect all identifying details. I chose to include true stories because I didn't want anyone to be able to claim I was exaggerating the scope and severity of this problem the Blackbird Kill Club was formed to combat. This is the world we live in—I had so many stories to choose from that I used only a fraction of the victim accounts I collected.

A reader may observe the many homeless individuals in this book. Between fifty to sixty thousand Angelenos are currently homeless, 75 percent of them unsheltered (LA Mission and NPR). An even greater number of Angelenos live on the precipice of homelessness, where one life event might tip them over the edge. The Downtown Women's Center (downtownwomenscenter.org) has been working for forty years toward providing permanent housing and services for women struggling with homelessness and is a great place to send donations and volunteerism.

Thank you for spending time with Jazz. She is a fictional character, but she has become very real to me. Sometimes, I swear I can hear her cracking a joke in the back of my head, and I can't help but smile.

ACKNOWLEDGMENTS

WRITING BOOKS IS a highly collaborative process, and I've been fortunate to work with a group of talented writers and colleagues who continue to provide support and to challenge me throughout the demanding writing process. My agent, Lauren Spieller, helped me hone this idea, which was at first scattered and disorganized, and turn it into something book-shaped. Two different, talented editors, Michelle Meade and April Osborn, gave me invaluable feedback, helping me detangle all these story lines. They worked tirelessly to help me create something readers would connect with. Without these three ruthlessly intelligent, artful and infinitely wise women, this book would not exist in its current incarnation. Thank you for giving me the chance to tell this story.

I'd also like to thank my writer buddies and critique partners, Tracie Martin, Mary Widdicks, Kit Rosewater, Meghan O'Flynn, Layne Fargo and those readers who read early drafts and provided feedback. Lastly, I need to express my utmost gratitude to Luis J. Rodriguez for allowing me to include a line from his beautiful "Love Poem to Los Angeles" as the epigraph for this book. I was honored and privileged to do so, and I hope readers in LA will visit his nonprofit bookstore, Tía Chucha's Centro Cultural and Bookstore.